The Big Fumble

ALSO BY GJ BABB

Lara Bliss Loves Rose Madder Genuine
ISBN 9781838590147

Nude Not Naked
ISBN 9781838594053

Of Art And Eros
ISBN 9781800464377

THE
BIG
FUMBLE

GJ BABB

Copyright © 2022 GJ Babb

The moral right of the author has been asserted.

Apart from any fair dealing for the purposes of research or private study, or criticism or review, as permitted under the Copyright, Designs and Patents Act 1988, this publication may only be reproduced, stored or transmitted, in any form or by any means, with the prior permission in writing of the publishers, or in the case of reprographic reproduction in accordance with the terms of licences issued by the Copyright Licensing Agency. Enquiries concerning reproduction outside those terms should be sent to the publishers.

This is a work of fiction. Names, characters, businesses, places, events and incidents are either the products of the author's imagination or used in a fictitious manner. Any resemblance to actual persons, living or dead, or actual events is purely coincidental.

Matador
Unit E2 Airfield Business Park,
Harrison Road, Market Harborough,
Leicestershire. LE16 7UL
Tel: 0116 2792299
Email: books@troubador.co.uk
Web: www.troubador.co.uk/matador
Twitter: @matadorbooks

ISBN 978 1803132 341

British Library Cataloguing in Publication Data.
A catalogue record for this book is available from the British Library.

Printed and bound in Great Britain by 4edge Limited
Typeset in 10pt Sabon MT by Troubador Publishing Ltd, Leicester, UK

Matador is an imprint of Troubador Publishing Ltd

gjbabb.com

*'One cannot discount the unpleasant things of
this world merely by looking the other way.'*
– Saki

ONE

The whirligig of awards ceremonies, openings, charity bashes and schmoozefests never ceased. Money *certainly* changed hands, influence was bought and sold... *notionally*. Sponsors licked their lips and wondered what they were paying for. They had to trust that their association with their chosen cause ensured gold-plated publicity, but they saw the human intermediaries they dealt with as capricious harpies and hopeless *parvenus*. Big business was charitable; charities were big business. It was the world where Piers Hazlett swam, like an ugly bottom feeder. He was forever merchandising culture; he could as easily have been trading souls.

Hazlett's rise demonstrated a commendable application. As a member of the faculty at University Thames Estuary he had developed the knack of writing primers about the dense and voguish theorists who populated the margins of the arts. These books developed a certain cache as being authoritative about the fields of art these theorists supposedly illuminated with their innovative and masterly (nearly all were men) discourses. Their pioneering thoughts stuck to him and, in time, attracted the attention of companies producing arts documentaries for broadcasters wanting to fill their quota of content for broadsheet-reading viewers. His ten-part series, *The Gordian Knot: How We Think The Unthinkable In Art* was thought both judicious and revelatory. He showed aptitude as a presenter, guiding his viewers through the jungles of modernity with flair, aided by an engaging style and a famously boyish smile. In the flush of his success, he resigned his lectureship.

As was to be expected, his views did not go uncontested. Stern Marxists, in particular, complained that his account of modernism naturalised the dominant ideological givens, something he attached himself to the Rising Left to counter. As he should have expected, competition to devise and host such series was intense. His attempt to add the nineteenth century to his sphere of competence met ridicule from a number of incumbents. A raffish newcomer with credentials that allowed him to claim that he spoke from outside the Western hegemonic discourse, and who had a more whiz-bang way of putting things, was soon treading on his toes. His second series got stuck in development, a fate that befalls many a worthy project. He accepted a role as an occasional arts correspondent for a news channel, wrote reviews for the arts supplements of the weekend newspapers and made several one-off documentaries about movie world luminaries. He embraced celebrity, employed a part-time researcher, endorsed several worthy causes and worked hard to maintain a lustrous shell of academic credibility. In scholarly circles he was about as likely as Hamlet partying in Magaluf.

Rewards came, but perhaps not quite as stellar as he had originally envisaged. The words 'author and broadcaster' were often appended to his name. Those more careless with words used the term 'pundit' of him. In his heart he saw himself as a social activist of the intellectual Left, an idea – nay, in his eyes, *a concept* – he cloaked in various guises: 'cultural ambassador' and 'social influencer' being but two. He felt himself close to the moral high ground, a sort of verdant upper reach of Mount Parnassus populated by people very much like himself.

Today, Hazlett was on his way to interview the filmmaker, Cornelius Pye, who, between directorial assignments, had come briefly to rest in London. Pye, commonly referred to as Connie by his confidants, lived a life of intense, tumultuous creativity. Burnout was what everyone but his wife foretold. It had been like that for a decade or more during which he had directed and part-produced a cavalcade of the superior crowd pleasers that Americans loved to indulge as British culture: quaint, darling, with a twist like an olive in a dry Martini. His latest, *Confess, Undercover Girl!* was soon to be premiered in Leicester Square where, from his plinth, Shakespeare would have a commanding view of the red-carpet ceremonials. It was in connection with the movie's launch that Pye was enduring a media day at the Dorchester.

Hazlett had been granted a generous two-hour slot to set up and film a conversation with Pye. His producer at the documentary production company, brainchild of an American political dynasty, had provided him with a two-camera film crew and he expected him to 'strangle the cat', as his producer called the process of extracting from Pye controversial, riveting disclosures about his approach to movie-making.

Confess, Undercover Girl! was already released in America and Pye was fresh from enduring a week on American talk shows where he had perfected his lines in support of the movie. Hazlett had seen the interviews, had registered the amusing anecdotes becoming routine patter. To prevent his interview from being a re-hashing of these familiar tales, Hazlett would need to dig deeper with a sharper spade. His list of questions designed to induce such candour had been painstakingly compiled with the help of his researcher, Ms Tina Yew.

At the Dorchester, Pye's assistants, watched over by a public relations officer provided by the movie's distribution company, were marshalling the press through the suite. The man himself was somewhere out of sight in the innermost sanctum. The press were taken in to see him through one door and ushered out of another. It was a well-oiled routine. Hazlett, being an emissary of trans-Atlantic aristocracy, had been awarded the privilege of a room in which to set up. At the appointed time, Pye would come to him.

The set-up was ready. Hazlett paced the room, Ms Tina Yew walking in lock-step with him. She, Ms Tina, had just been to scout out what was going on. She had talked to the most recent of Pye's interviewers and had alarming news to impart. The interviewer before him had emerged ashen-faced from her slot with Pye. She had apparently quoted from an extensive derogatory assessment of Pye's movies, excerpts of which were doing the rounds on social media.

'He's had a blah-blah moment.'

Hazlett blenched. Every interviewer feared the blah-blah moment, the moment when the interviewee lost the will to abide by the rules of niceness, worn to a frazzle by the soul-destroying scrutiny of the public relations grind. Likely to precipitate such a moment was the mention, indelicately introduced, of some adverse opinion, supposedly already 'out there'. Cut to the quick, psyche battered beyond all tolerating, digestion a ruination, the interviewee would suddenly break and turn his skills of belittlement – often considerable – against his tormentor. Pye was known to be tolerant and easy-going. Not for him the highly-strung outburst, but even the patience of the most saintly can be worn infra-thin by a media day. Things were going downhill, averred the interviewer.

The afternoon wore on; still no Pye. Ms Tina went to investigate. Things were going from bad to calamitous. The interviews were falling way behind. Pye's assistants were apologetic in a grim-faced way that said the man himself was not happy. By five o'clock it was clear that the schedule had gone completely to pot and it was no real surprise when the apologetic public relations officer from the production company announced that, 'unfortunately, Mr Pye cannot do the interview today. It will have to be rescheduled. I'm terribly sorry, but we've underestimated how long it would take to work through today's schedule and Mr Pye's suffering from jet-lag.'

The expense and waste of time were enough to make any normal person fly into a rage, but Hazlett knew better. He needed the interview and he would have to accept what fate decreed. He adjusted his trousers and tightened his belt a notch. His producer would be disappointed, of course, but the promise of another date to interview Pye at length was probably enough to save his bacon. His calm acceptance was a reflection of his diplomatic skills. After all, was he not courtier to the merry madness of modernity?

TWO

At six-thirty, press interviews over, Cornelius Pye descended to the lobby. For a while, in a sort of daze, he stood, watching the bustle on the steps of the Dorchester. He was a neat, tanned, smooth-looking man in his early fifties. What he lacked in stature – he was lean and five foot eight – he made up for in vitality; the sort of vitality that made all those around him seem half-dead with fatigue. Something of Fred Astaire's filmic demeanour might be attributed to him: affable, lithe, a prodigy when called upon to perform, impossible to ruffle. He had his fingers in so many pies it was said that his surname was assumed. Not true. He was born a Pye, an old English name supposedly derive from the magpie: talkative, even thievish, a rascal. He was reputed to be a descendant of a Robert Pye who fought in the English Civil War, but a Robert Pye fought on both sides, so whether his ancestral attachments were to King or Commonwealth was moot.

His productions were run like most people run their household. He could co-opt the brightest, because the brightest wanted to work for him, and he was clever enough to know the brightest when he saw them. For now, he could shake off the day's unpleasantness and turn his mind to future plans. He was always one step ahead of anyone who worked for him whose job it was to look ahead. This was the reason he was waiting for Poppy Trench rather than going directly to meet his wife for dinner at the River Café.

Poppy had freelanced for Pye as a production assistant during the filming of *Confess, Undercover Girl!* At the moment she was employed arranging travel for a rock band contracted for a stadium tour promoted by an impresario who had paid not the slightest heed to the geographical given of the North American land mass: forty different venues in twenty-three states in fifty-nine days. Lucrative employment for her, but what she really wanted to do was go back to working for Pye. Equally, Pye wanted her. He greeted her warmly and they walked companionably towards the bar. She told him about the zigzagging trek she was organising across the States. He told *her* he was annoyed with himself for having lost his temper during the press interviews.

'I was asked to comment on the view, circulating on social media, that my films are "candyfloss cinema, devoid of scruple, reflexive nakedness or moralistic intent", or some such. I'm cross I made it plain I give a damn,' he concluded ruefully. 'It turned the day rather sour.'

'I could do a search and find the source, if you like?'

Pye shook his head. 'No, I don't... I gave up reading the critics years ago. You know how it is: I don't get to make anything unless the finances make sense. It's my producers I have to keep happy, not critics.'

When they reached the bar, Poppy couldn't think what she wanted to drink so Pye ordered her a Negroni. He enjoyed the look on her face when it arrived, lurid red and garnished with a miniature edible bouquet. When they were settled at a corner table, Pye explained what was on his mind.

Candide In Tinseltown: How Candide finds romance and saves the world in six episodes!

It was the title of a screenplay by Stanley Goldman. Stanley Goldman had a proven record of being box office gold. It was said of Goldman that if you had the budget to fulfil the demands of his screenplays, you stood a good chance of winning Oscars. Goldman was particular, and had grown more so over the years of his success. So concerned was he to protect *Candide In Tinseltown,* the screenplay had been restricted to one copy shown, in turn, to carefully selected production companies. In essence, it was a re-working of Voltaire's *Candide* shoehorned into a romcom chase. It was considered almost perversely clever by those who had read it, but it was the kind of clever that top-rated acting talent adored. When it was discussed over cocktails, in the dining rooms of discrete hotels, on yachts berthed off Barbados or

Mykonos, those who had read it spoke reverently of its wonderful wit and clever storytelling. Those who hadn't seen it were dazzled by the conflicting accounts of why it was Goldman's crowning achievement.

When *Candide In Tinseltown* was first in circulation a certain well-known director was desperate to film it. Fortuitously, he had the means to take up an immediate option. The cost was never disclosed but commonly believed to be colossal. In the event, the movie the well-known director was currently working on over-ran by six months due to crew causalities and an earthquake. Consequentially, he was forced to extend the option for a second year.

During that second year, Goldman met an untimely end. The well-known director, fresh from the long haul of filming in impossible jungle locations, had no idea where last he had seen his copy of the screenplay. However many times he implored his assistants to try again, they could not find it. Naturally, he went back to Goldman's PA and his wife – his third – Suzie Millichip. Neither had a copy, so they said, and when a search was made of the various computers Goldman owned at the time of his death, not a single reference to *Candide In Tinseltown* could be found.

Lawyers got involved, of course, but then, by a remarkable twist of fate, almost a year after Goldman's death, the well-known film director was, like Goldman, the only fatality in a car crash. Thereupon, the screenplay took on the fabled aura of a great, lost money-spinner. And the belief that someone was purposefully withholding it became rife on social media.

Nobody disputed that Cornelius Pye was the next in line to film *Candide In Tinseltown*. He'd read the screenplay when it was doing the rounds, one weekend in Norfolk. He'd rung Goldman when he got back to London on Monday afternoon. While they were talking, a courier arrived to pick up the screenplay. Pye, who knew about it being the only copy, had intended to hold onto it until he could talk money with his backers but his PA didn't know that and, with blameless honesty, she'd handed it over to the courier.

Although Goldman liked Pye, and thought he would make a great job of filming it, the offer from the well-known film director was just too good and he signed away the option the next day. When he saw Pye's next movie, he regretted it – they were fellow travellers when it came to filmmaking – but by then it was much too late and both had other things on their minds.

After the well-known film director's death, Pye made enquiries. Did somebody have the screenplay and, if so, what could possibly be the motive for withholding a property that was, if anything, likely to lose currency over time? The more Pye enquired, the more he began to think there was no such mysterious party, and certainly it had not, as the chat rooms insisted, been put up as a stake in a poker game and lost to a Hong Kong business man, reputed to be something big in electronics, digital platforms or take-away food delivery, depending on which gossip you listened to. Pye concluded that most likely the well-known director had left it somewhere exotic and filthy, and it had been thrown away.

But Pye was not the kind of man to let go of something close to his heart. For him, the loss was akin to the wilful destruction of a masterpiece. He still harboured the hope that somewhere there was a file on a computer or backup device, and it was only a matter of time before it turned up. He let Goldman's lawyers know he was willing to buy it should it be found. They were happy to grant him first refusal; they had much bigger issues on their hands – Goldman's widow for one – and the actuaries had determined that a lost screenplay was an asset of questionable value.

Although Goldman's agent had carefully controlled the distribution of the screenplay, a single-page plot teaser had been widely distributed. The teaser set the scene, gave a brief account of the first act, thereupon leaving the reader in a state of intrigued surmise as to how the second would develop, where the switch came in the third, fourth or fifth, and how all was resolved in the sixth. Pye still had his copy.

It was generally agreed that a treatment some thirty pages long had also been in circulation at the time, a detailed telling of the story. Pye had only recently heard of this, and had been lucky enough to obtain a fragment of it – the first few pages – from a bankrupt production company. Pye hadn't found anybody who had read it at the time Goldman's screenplay was circulating. Most believed it to be based on the screenplay but written by another hand. The value of Pye's fragment was that it described in some detail the film's prologue, which preceded the opening credits and launched the story.

In addition to these two texts, Pye had secured from a costume designer, briefly attached to the project, notes she had made while reading the screenplay. The notes provided a tantalising glimpse of the dialogue, the lightness of tone that the plot depended on, and what those who had read it considered its perfect moments of transition from disaster movie to misanthropic drama to rom-com.

Encouraged by these fragments, Pye began to think about the possibility of reconstructing the script by assembling the sum of the recollections of everyone who had read it. Better still, by assembling material from those, like the costume designer, who had, for whatever reason, made notes, copied sections, or made some other form of record of what they had read.

Although Pye was enamoured of the idea of bringing Goldman's screenplay back to life, he did not lose sight of the fact that the task might be impossible; that his idea was nothing more than a vain attempt to honour Goldman's talent and memory. That maybe so, but in Poppy Trench he had someone who would bring an unreasonable degree of stubborn intelligence to the task. And he still did not discount the possibility that if someone was withholding the screenplay, whatever the motive, news of such a reconstruction might well encourage that someone to come forward for fear that what he, or she, was withholding might become valueless.

At the end of the *Candide In Tinseltown* teaser was this note: 'running time: 115 minutes'. As a rule of thumb, screenplays equate to about one minute's screen time per page, so Pye had had one hundred and fifteen sheets of A4 paper ring-bound into a booklet. Printed on the front cover was *Candide In Tinseltown*.

'Poppy,' he said as he slapped the blank down on the table between them, 'how about seeing what you can do about filling this?'

Pye was putting this question to Poppy for a very good reason: he knew she had worked on the retrieval of the final draft of the last play of Gerard Cormorant, who had tried to immolate himself and his play in a fit of terminal despondency. He had succeeded in his own case, but, thanks to Poppy's forensic ways with singed fragments of torn paper, the play had been reborn and, two years later, had won a Tony Award in the Best Play category.

Poppy might have had a reputation as a formidable and determined young woman, but, faced by Pye's blank manuscript, she had a moment of trepidation. 'I don't...' Her voice trailed off as, not for the first time, she thought about the difficulties of reconstructing one hundred and fifteen minutes of lost screenplay. 'How long do I have?'

Pye looked inscrutable. He had no idea and it wasn't like him to give somebody he was hiring a minute more than was necessary. 'How long d'you think?'

Poppy took a sip from her Negroni and raised her eyes to the ceiling. She held out her hands to him, about a foot apart. 'This long?'

'That's a good start,' he decided, nodding approvingly. 'I'd say a little bit less, really. Wouldn't you?'

THREE

Across town, as yet only tenuously connected to any of the aforementioned by a narrative thread, sat Professor Clifford Conquest, vice-chancellor of University London Central. His anguish was a midnight of the soul not uncommon in middle-aged men of an aspiring and intelligent outlook.

Not only am I an imposter, his brain cranked out, *wherever I go I spawn Frankenstein monsters.*

This brooding figure, grim and set of jaw, sprawled in a leather and steel chair of American design, was at the end of his first day in his new office. He had moved there from Keynes House, the university's former administrative centre. Keynes House was about to be demolished, apart from its grade two Victorian façade. Behind the façade, construction would soon begin on the university's great new investment, a digital hub. Conquest regarded the development as a reflection of himself.

An ornate, sturdy façade, redolent of imperishable historical redundancies, behind which a gleaming testament to the future will soon be brought into being!

In an act of self-effacement, with political aims in mind, he had temporarily removed himself to accommodation lacking status. It was an office, plain, unadorned, planned on utilitarian lines, one of a number occupying the first floor of an extremely drab sixties building. The move had been accompanied by his reorganisation of the university's core administrative functions. The reorganisation, carried out over the months of the summer recess, had created the *Vice-Chancellor's Strategic Secretariat*, an administrative entity combining the business of his own office with that of the dean of academic affairs, Professor Murray Woolworth. Much to Conquest's satisfaction it had consolidated his control over academic matters. Woolworth occupied a similar office to his own at the far end of the floor. Between them the smaller offices were occupied by Vernon Pinhorn, the secretariat's administrative officer, a sort of *eminence gris,* always in the background shuffling papers, their respective PAs, Eunice Truepenny and Marcia Abdul, and a junior administrative assistant who spent most of her time keeping the records straight.

The fitments of Conquest's office were a study in flimsy; a panel door of the type kept rigid by a honeycomb of cardboard was the only thing isolating him from the activity of those other offices. It had a window, large, of the kind sometimes termed 'picture', with a view of sorts, and that was it. To make room for himself and his staff, the entire Department of Human Resources had been relocated to the old boiler house building. However much of a comedown his new office was for Conquest, it was far better than the hotch-potch of rooms to which HR had been consigned. A short-term shortage of accommodation for administrative functions had been cited as the reasons for the move. More to the point, HR's fate reflected its standing in Conquest's esteem.

If there's one branch of my administration able, and likely, to frustrate my ability to turn wish into fulfilment, it's HR! Guardian of workers' rights, yes! Protector of shirkers and time-servers, no!

Despite the gloomy mien of the old boiler house building, from whence coal fired boilers had once warmed much of the original campus, HR's exile failed to lift Conquest's spirits. The relocation had been made possible by the university becoming solely powered – in keeping with its enlightened credentials – by wind. Since that was the case, he reflected, indulging a little in malice, the amount vented by its own activities should have been quite sufficient. That expensive topping-up from external sources was required could only be grounds for raised eyebrows.

In some ways, Conquest's dark mood was incomprehensible. Having completed a full year as vice-chancellor, he had every reason to feel pleased with himself. Despite the odd rocky moment – which he blamed on reactionary forces trying to sabotage his reforms – things had gone well for him. Not least, judicious management had largely put right the dire financial situation that he had found on his arrival. There was a distinct feeling everywhere that the university was on the up. He had established control of the university's academic processes, something now given concrete form by his creation of the Vice-Chancellor's Strategic Secretariat. His firm but fair management style had begun to bear fruit, and even his sternest critics found it difficult to argue with the targets of his occasional wrath.

If the academic departments no longer troubled him, the same could not be said of the vast, endlessly self-generating part of the university that never had any contact with students. 'Central Services' embraced all those activities that were supposed to lend support to the university's primary aim of teaching. In Conquest's opinion they did not. He regarded them as an archipelago of fiefdoms of doubtful value to anything remotely approaching pedagogy. Here, his new broom had not yet swept away the old regime's legacy. Here there were too many post-holders flapping about in their own mediocrity, talking virtuous humbug.

In order to address these ills, he had, during the relative quiet of the summer, using his creation of the Vice-Chancellor's Strategic Secretariat as a model, been labouring on a Great Work. The result of this effort was pinned to the wall: a wiring diagram of a new management structure for the *whole* university. It had gradually been taking shape over the months, a paragon of order, of robustness, stretching to well over thirty senior management roles, all laid out with newly configured responsibilities and report lines. Only today had he, for the first time, pinned it up so he could admire it from a distance. After some minutes he rose from his seat to trace a finger over the descending lines of command. It was like a river system intruding into every backwater of the institution, with him ensconced at its riverhead. To be sure, he was not yet convinced of every detail. He needed to be confident that whatever calamity might threaten the university, the structure would flex and never descend into everyone-for-themselves chaos. Once that was assured it would be, in its own, very special way, the nearest thing to beauty he could imagine.

The titling of management roles to ensure they were truly comprehensive and descriptive was one of the details that still troubled him. He sought *terminological exactitude*. For instance, to his own title of vice-chancellor he had toyed with the idea of adding 'chief executive' and 'president'. The three designations were popular elsewhere in Higher Education and, it seemed to him, reflected the true extent and nature of his role. Reaching a decision caused him no little anguish, and the anguish did not lessen as he descended down the chain of command.

That there were details still to be finalised did not greatly concern him since the university's senate would, in the first instance, need to approve in principle such a comprehensive reorganisation. Once that had happened, it was inevitable that the university at large would become aware of his intentions. Then he expected ructions. Of this he could be certain since an intended by-product of his labours was that it would allow him to circumvent those wedded to the old, inefficient ways; to subtly demote those he considered a hindrance to the efficient working of the university and the implementation of his plans. Some post holders would discover their jobs had vanished. All-in-all, he could foresee a rush to the Department of Human Resources, where, still lingering in the air, there would be the faint smell of coal dust. Yet neither the Great Work of his wiring diagram nor his sportive mischief with HR gave him any pleasure. Something was at work in his psyche he could not yet fully discern. It was, he thought, as if his pleasure in a masterstroke of reorganisation was overshadowed by a deep anguish that in the strained parlance of the day was deemed *existential*, and as those who have experienced existential anythings know, it was an experience that fiends plunging hot pokers into their entrails cannot equal.

Not only am I an impostor, wherever I go I spawn Frankenstein monsters.

FOUR

Poppy Lavender Trench was, above all, resourceful. High spirits and feckless parents saw to that. They, the parents, had majored in inconsistency of thought, wilful lack of logic and bad timing: during the 2008 financial crisis they sold their major asset, a house in Golders Green, and decamped to a part of Wales in permanent financial crisis. In short, they were an object lesson for any young person with an iota of sense. Fortunately, Poppy was one such. As Dickens would no doubt have had it: she had tumbled up somehow, spiky attitude and all. By eighteen, she was back in Golders Green, part-time studying, part-time everything, with inexhaustible vigour. Acute good sense meant she quickly became indispensable to a succession of media types, mostly frantic men, all of whom she most vividly proved her indispensability to by moving on to something better. In fact, she soon became a snob and someone who, when it came to employment, could afford to be very snobby. This is how, at the tender age of twenty-two, she became solely responsible for the reclamation of *Candide In Tinseltown*, delighted once more to be working for a filmmaker who knew real stars and was courted by people of cultural significance.

The thing to do first, she decided, was familiarise herself with the limited documentation Pye had supplied, particularly the opening pages by an unknown hand of the *Candide In Tinseltown* treatment. Well, actually it wasn't a treatment, she decided, more of a story outline.

Unlike the Candide in Voltaire's *Candide,* Goldman's Candide was female, a starry-eyed innocent with little formal education but practical skills aplenty. The sort that always seemed to land on her feet, when all around her were losing their heads. Poppy divined this from the first paragraph of the fragment, more or less word for word. The next sentence set the action in motion.

A long-distance journey by rail ends in disaster in an inaccessible location in the high Rockies. An avalanche of snow sweeps the locomotive into a ravine. A succession of further disasters follow: two more avalanches send the first of the passenger carriages after the locomotive, marauding bears come scavenging, a galley fire in the restaurant car sparks a panic, all in the teeth of a blizzard.

The manner of the action is designed to suggest the passengers are a microcosm of the human race on a planet spinning out of control. Through it walks Candide, seeking her lost puppy, seeing only hope and splendour where others find catastrophe. Each succeeding danger that besets the stranded passengers she escapes by a hairsbreadth, apparently impervious to danger.

According to the designer's notes this part of the film was intended to be fast moving, the very best CGI by the very best animators and experts of action sequence direction. 'Voice-over narrative interspersed with chin-up dialogue', was the extent of the notes on the spoken word.

Poppy looked at the one hundred and fifteen pages of empty manuscript and wondered how many of those pages this sequence filled. She had no idea what its duration might be; some movies would make it a whirlwind, two-minute montage, in other hands it could have been an entire plot.

Whatever the tempo, this opening sequence came to a conclusion with Candide finding her puppy in the arms of movie mogul, Percy Van Holt.

Percy Van Holt is a wisecracking depressive with a mordent and little-boy-lost view of the world.

The designer's notes read:

Van Holt, a large, loose-limbed man, with a clipped moustache like Ward Bond in Wagon Train, *a military bearing, and a rather military way of running things.*

Poppy was not sure what to make of that. She read on.

A lull in the storm. A rescue team arrives. Some of the surviving passengers are evacuated to a nearby snow-bound, out-of-season hotel, struggling the last part of their journey in the teeth of the blizzard. On the way, Van Holt confides to Candide that he has taken the train to the West Coast because he has a fear of flying. Blithely, not knowing who Van Holt is, Candide tells him that she is travelling to Hollywood to break into the movies.

Once at the hotel, during a lull in the storm, a helicopter arrives to take the stranded passengers out of the mountains. Van Holt declines to leave by air. With the weather worsening again, the crew are anxious to leave. As Candide prepares to climb into the helicopter, her puppy slips from her arms and runs back to Van Holt. She chases after it as the helicopter rises in a whirlwind of spindrift.

The only part of the hotel that is heated is the ballroom where the caretaker, an out-of-work, insomniac musician, plays the hotel's Steinway to amuse himself. Van Holt has made up a bed for Candide on the bar counter. He smokes, lost in thought sitting in an armchair; she falls asleep to the sound of the caretaker playing Unchained Melody.

Shades of *The Shining* read the designer's notes.

The moment suggests the direction of the action is well and truly set. A close-up of the untroubled face of the sleeping Candide fills the frame, but suddenly the camera flies upwards as though through the ballroom's skylight to reveal – as the camera rises higher and higher – the hotel below and a wild, snowy mountain wilderness illuminated by moonlight. The title credit rolls: Candide In Tinseltown.

As the credits dissolve into hot sunshine, we see a bronze plaque on a white stucco wall dappled with the shadows of overhanging vegetation. It reads 'Styrene-Vortex Building, 972 Wessex Boulevard'. As the camera pulls back, we see the plaque is surrounded by bougainvillea flowers. The camera glides up and over the wall to reveal the Styrene-Vortex Building. It has good parking, a real vortex water feature by the front entrance and flowering shrubs. The upper floor, cantilevered out over the lower to provide shaded external walkways, is occupied by the Van Holt Production Company Incorporated. The company's business is the development of All In The Head, *Percy Van Holt's twenty-first movie.*

The camera continues to rise until it reaches the upper floor when it angles in horizontally over the balcony, plunging into the building through open French windows. We are in an open-plan office with many doors; a scene of frenetic activity. The camera tracks towards Percy Van Holt who is seated behind a massive desk. He is giving quick-fire instructions to his team of PAs, all beautiful starlets. As soon as one leaves by one door, having been given her orders, another enters by a different door to report back on what she has been asked to do. Through yet another door a uniformed pageboy wheels in a coffee-making float. The pageboy is of the noxious Mickey Rooney type, the sort with the gall to say, 'Hey doll, you should try me for size. I'd be a tight fit,' to slender starlets twice his height.

'Shift your chassis, sweetness! Comin' through.'

At the further end of the room, round a large table, several assistants to the PAs are industriously collating piles of photocopies into sets of documents. Telephones ring. Through a fourth door a delivery man wheels in a hand trolley piled high with scripts, only to be told by another PA to, 'take them to production,' and is ushered out again. In the midst of this bedlam, Van Holt is trying to give instructions to the newest of his assistants about how he likes his coffee. The coffee-making float is alongside his desk and she is struggling to get to grips with the steam valves, her back to the camera.

'I know it's not a photocopier,' Van Holt advises her, 'but really it's all the same.'

As the assistant struggles with the complexities of the machine – it emits clouds of steam – the tracking shot continues, swinging through almost three-sixty degrees, to reveal the assistant is Candide.

FIVE

In extremis, Vice-Chancellor Conquest had devised a driver's manual of his mental faculties. The details were arcane and convoluted. Suffice it to say, at precisely twenty-eight minutes past ten he was forced to put aside his despair at ever reaching the *Summit Finishing Post* and the desired *Mountain-top Praxis* – the only state in which he believed it was possible to plot the upward trajectory of his career – for more immediate, *flesh-and-blood* concerns. Crocodiles had eaten a second-year political science student. Sandra Torpington of the public relations office had called Eunice Truepenny, his newish PA, asking her to warn him. Details were scant, but apparently the student had decided to take an early morning stroll and, as is all too easy in the untrammelled wilds of Africa, had found himself deposed from top predator spot by crocodiles who had indulged in a feeding-frenzy. Now there was a concern the press might indulge in something similar.

'Tell Sandra to hold off until we know more. Only then, Eunice, will we respond publicly. Next of kin… deepest commiserations… exceptional talent… much loved by fellow students and staff… great loss to his future profession. Make sure we cover all the bases. Oh, and Eunice. What was his name?'

'Matthew Stagg.'

'Right, good, I want his head of department here. We'll issue a press release when we're clear about the facts. Get family details and the address of his parents. I want a response to this that shows we're properly concerned… and, also, *caring*. It might be an idea to get his tutor in. If presentable, we might get him, or her, whichever, to make a statement on behalf of the university if, you know, the TV people come sniffing around. More of a peer-to-peer thing. We need to show he's not just a name printed on a dossier.

I don't want a misstep on this, so I'll need to see Sandra in person before we go public. Oh, and Professor Hingley, chair of senate should be informed. I have a meeting with him later in the week but he should be informed today.'

Eunice had kept up a rhythmic nodding accompaniment while he had rattled off these instructions, and now he'd finished there was a look about her of coquettish indecision. Conquest frowned. He thought, and not for the first time, she looked, in rather a repellent way, like an advertisement for wholesome living. It was as though there were something mechanical about her that he had failed to set into motion.

Is her driver's manual total gibberish? he wondered.

'Was there something else, Eunice?' he asked.

She sprang to life at his words, and whirled out of the room in a sudden paroxysm of motion.

The thought of crocodiles and sudden death of an entirely unaccountable and unexpected kind was indeed sobering. Conquest might not know this Matthew Stagg who had come to such an end, but he felt in an abstract way the terrible coldness of life and existence that could result in such a fatal outcome, so fatuously meaningless, so utterly undoing of plan, aim or common sense. How could he achieve the exalted state of *Mountain-top Praxis* when tumbled down by crocodiles?

Not only am I an impostor, wherever I go I spawn Frankenstein monsters.

Later in the afternoon, Eunice Truepenny came in to tell him that according to the administrator in Political Science, the head of department, Professor Greenwash, was not available. He was on research leave... in Tuscany.

SIX

The best way to begin, Poppy decided, was to go and talk to Goldman's widow; pick her brains. She looked for a name. There wasn't one in the notes Pye had given her so, next morning, she went to consult his PA.

'That's a well-trodden path,' was the PA's only comment as she eyed Poppy with rather a supercilious eye.

Suzie Millichip was his name.

'Yes,' the PA assured her, 'he's a man. He's transitioning.'

In Hampstead, Poppy was met at the door by an androgynous figure dressed in slacks and what could have been a blouse, white, with ruffs. 'Yes, we're Suzie Millichip,' he said with the swift, darting movements of the highly-strung.

They went into a chintzy lounge.

'We can't get over it,' said Suzie Millichip in response to Poppy's commiserations. 'We've got the shakes all the time.' He held out his hand as if to demonstrate.

'It doesn't *seem* to be shaking,' Poppy observed.

'We know; it's inside we're shaking. We can't rid ourselves of the thought of what if we'd been with him, driving instead of him.'

'Where was he going?'

'We don't know. We don't think he was going anywhere. He loved to drive.'

'Then he wouldn't have wanted you to drive, even if you'd been there.'

'We know. Actually, we don't drive anyway.'

'Ah!'

'Yes, a pity, but true.'

'Is Suzie your old name or your new name?'

'We can't be bothered with little things like names when we're faced with a total tragedy, can we?'

'No, I suppose not.'

'We should call ourselves X. *X marks the spot*: that's what we should have on our grave.'

Poppy was at a loss what to say to that. She looked about her, thinking she should be complimentary. 'I like the house. It's very cosy.'

'Yes, the wallpaper's very pretty. We're very good at choosing wallpaper.'

'Did you help your husband with his writing?'

'No, how could we? Writing was his mistress. He knew we wanted him to give her up but he was driven by passion. It was a visceral thing, you see, like sausages. He tried to be a good Jew, but he liked sausage. The same with writing. He always fell in love with his characters. Then he fell out of love with them! Such a narcissist! Have you noticed how many of his heroines have near-death experiences? Of course, he couldn't kill off everyone in the last reel, but he'd try. That's the reason for his success. In the early days homicidal mayhem was his thing, but there were always bulletproof vests, expendable extras taking the shots, fatwa junkie gay guys turning their guns on themselves. *So predictable!*' Suzie tapped his forehead with two fingers and gave Poppy a penetrating look. 'To us that man was an open book!'

Poppy was bewildered by Suzie Millichip's attitude to his husband's demise, although she had to admit there was something penetrating in his critique of his narrative structure. Suzie seemed to think it was writing that had killed him. It was the casual nature with which he said it that was disconcerting.

'Could I ask you where you keep his archive? I assume he left a lot of stuff: proofs, notes, drafts and such like.'

'No.'

'Sorry, *no*? None at all?'

'No, we've disposed of everything, or rather, donated it.'

'*Oh!* Where to, may I ask?'

'Our *alma mater*, University London Central.'

Poppy blinked with suppressed surprise. She knew Goldman was well thought of by *cineastes*, in fact, irrevocably embedded in the last thirty years of cinema history. She couldn't believe his archive wasn't going to somewhere more prestigious. It seemed Suzie Millichip had wanted to rid himself of the remnants of his husband's life as expeditiously as possible.

'They have a film school, of sorts, and, more to the point,' he added defiantly, 'we were a student there in the nineties. It's an act of endowment.'

Poppy picked up her things and left.

SEVEN

Piers Hazlett was faintly surprised when he bumped into Professor 'Perk' Hingley, chair of University London Central's senate, at a charity gala for disabled pianists at the South Korean embassy. He considered human rights and tinkling ivories an unlikely mix.

Hazlett had been introduced to Perk by an old friend and colleague, Alistair Vox, who had once been a junior member of staff under Perk at the University of Greater Gatwick. Perk was an expert on human rights law, something he advised on, taught and practised. He was much prized at his home university. He was also a visiting professor at universities in several Western-leaning democracies, advisor to venerable think tanks and other public institutions, including the London Assembly, and sat on many important executive committees seeking to regulate the international order. His contribution to his subject was not in enlivening debate on grievous differences in interpretation, but in fostering a benign, libertarian-leaning consensus that human rights were *a good thing*. The words *moderating influence* were used about his endeavours. He was tall and angular with glasses always perched on the southern hemisphere of his nose. He had a habit of cocking his head as he listened; an effect that suggested an infinity of wisdom was being brought to bear on what was being said. He was, above all else, a progressive with a belief in caution; a man put on the road to righteousness by an indifference to luxuries, although insensibly, funded by several public purses, he had acquired the lifestyle of a gentleman of leisure.

Even his detractors admitted that Perk was a kind, well-meaning man who knew a great deal and was more than willing to share it. Undoing his many virtues, was his misconception of himself as an agent of social change, yet it was this misunderstanding that had led him to become an enthusiast for the Rising Left. That he and Hazlett shared a political allegiance, which had a secretive, almost Masonic quality about it, might well be grounds for comradeship but at that particular moment all Hazlett wanted was to mingle and flirt with the gaggle of young production assistants he'd seen when he first arrived. What he definitely didn't want to do was talk about University London Central, or its vice-chancellor, but he knew Perk was aware he'd had a get-to-know-you lunch with Professor Conquest at the Athenaeum the previous week.

'So! And what d'you make of our vice-chancellor?'

Piers Hazlett gave the question something that had the semblance of grave consideration. 'At the end of the day he ticks a lot of boxes, but he's a middle-of-the-road technocrat for whom expediency is everything,' he said, rather enjoying his phrase-making. 'Going forward, he'll sweat the assets, but he's inclined to push the envelope, which might be a prob. We on the same page?'

Perk bobbed his chin with the gravity of one who agreed, and was encouraged to share deep thoughts. 'He can be a bit of a bull in a china shop. His manner can incite the thought that one is being bullied.' He said this tentatively, as befitted a man entertaining a dangerous reflection.

At that moment there was a disturbance in the crowd thronging the reception. The crowd divided and the saturnine figure of Alistair Vox appeared, heading purposefully towards them. Since his days under Perk at the University of Greater Gatwick, Vox had risen to become a leading polemist of the Rising Left and chief strategist at the Institute of Progressive Fiscal, Educational and Social Policy – more usually known as InProFESPol. It was at Vox's urging that Perk had appointed Hazlett to University London Central's senate. He had been at pains to argue that Hazlett was not only a *bona fide* celebrity with pulling power but would also stand firm against the vulgarians of the Right, and their allies, on senate.

'Ah-ha!' said Vox, as he reached them. 'Hello Perk, I was told you were plotting with our cultural mouthpiece!' He emitted a laugh: a cruel, high-pitched sound that grated.

Hazlett signalled a greeting to Vox but was not to be diverted from his theme. 'When we had lunch, he was making vague but ambitious noises about re-jigging the university. He wants to address institutional inefficiencies, administrative laxity, staff not pulling their weight... that sort of thing. Even tuition fees!'

'Really? But the government is quite firm on the cap on tuition fees!'

'No, a *reduction*!'

'Is this Conquest of whom we speak?' enquired Vox with a look that said he feared they were discussing a recalcitrant mule.

Perk's brow furrowed. '*A reduction of tuition fees!* That's impossible; enough to give any self-respecting director of finance a fit!'

'He has some idea about replacing tuition fees with other sources of income, bringing in commercial forces and so on.'

'Laudable aim or dangerous precedent?' mused Perk. 'There's no doubting his first year has gone well but I'm a little concerned about where he might take us. He wants to do good, I suppose.' It was a begrudging conclusion. 'What's your feeling, Alistair? I suppose there's a political dimension to all this.'

Vox put his hand to his lips as though pondering whether or not to broach something he was privy to. Eventually he spoke as though the brimstone of conspiracy was in the air, but hesitantly, as if making an allowance for the fact that his audience lacked access to his level of political intelligence. 'Commercial forces...? Attacking administrative laxity...? I don't know...! It's our duty to ensure universities remain bastions of Left-leaning right-thinking. Could it be another outbreak of this private culture groundswell?'

There it was! The manner of Vox's mention of private culture implied they lacked *entrée* to the inner circles of the Rising Left where people trafficked in the newest concepts in political thinking.

'Private culture!' Perk said this musingly, as if it was something lurid in Vox's view of the world that he distrusted. 'Doubtful currency, that term,' he said finally.

Vox was increasingly conspiratorial. 'Not a bit of it! Don't be surprised if you find serious minds adopting it.' He had dropped his voice as one does who discusses great secrets of state. 'Believe me, there's something in the wind, under the radar. The grey beards of the Camlington Faction are taking it very seriously. Apparently, it's a shires thing. Original outbreaks were thought to be spontaneous; now they're not so sure.'

'Ah, a *shires* thing!' Hazlett nodding sagely. 'Anything more than backwoodsman Tories, then?'

'Yes, it's reached circles where *they* don't hold much sway. In fact, it's not a Right/Left thing, it's more internecine than that; more top-hole, so...'

'More like a barons' revolt!' suggested Perk.

Vox turned cautious. 'It's still not clear; too early to tell.'

Perk realised that Vox had no idea what the barons' revolt had been about, or even what it had been.

'We'll be issuing a position paper on this in due course. At the moment it's an emerging sub-set of the false consciousness induced by the economic base, probably the periodic outbreak of something atavistic. As far as Gregory and I are concerned critiquing it persuasively requires a new political vocabulary. Watch this space; we endorse poetic violence, not the institutional variety!'

With that he raised his hand in a silent salute and made a beeline for a group of influence peddlers he had just seen across the other side of the reception.

'You know, Piers,' said Perk meditatively, 'we wanted you appointed to senate to head off Conquest's predilection for Blairite leftovers?'

Hazlett's face lit up with his famously boyish grin. '*Ah!*' he exclaimed with relish, 'Blairite cronies with influence!'

'Exactly! Sir Norman Fleet's a good example. He's big business writ large! And he's been pestering to get Lord N'Garbi on senate. There's not a vacancy at the moment, but Sir Norman's very persistent.'

'This is what influence-mongering does,' chuckled Hazlett knowingly. 'We're going to have to keep an eye on Sir Norman! Lord N'Garbi was thought to be Labour through and through, but he's toying with the cross-benches. And Conquest is much too much of an enthusiast for enduring values and all that.'

Talking of enduring values, Piers,' said Perk, 'you haven't forgotten about Graduation Day next Wednesday, have you? It's politic we show ourselves to the meat-and-two-veg crowd in gowns and mortarboards.'

'Ah yes, we can't be seen to be disregarding the ceremonial while we're kicking out the old guard.' Hazlett had taken out his mobile and was consulting his diary. 'Oh God, I'm chocker next week!'

'You're a confidant of the chancellor, are you not?'

'Indeed! She and I chat about royal precedents from time to time. She's a great believer in the eternal return!'

'I'm sure she would be most grateful, were you present.'

'Yes, don't worry.' Hazlett patted Perk rather condescendingly on the upper arm. 'Expect me, togged up to the nines!'

As he said this, a loudly-dressed, broad-shouldered man holding a glass of wine like a shield emerged from the crowd. It was immediately obvious to Perk that he intended to take command of Hazlett.

'Piers, old boy, there's someone from programming over there anxious to have a word. Might I steal you away?' He glanced winningly, but incuriously, at Perk.

'Fevered time!' said Hazlett to Perk. It wasn't a comment on the subject of their conversation but a signal he was in the thick of things. He made to follow the interloper, who had already moved on. 'I'll keep you informed, when I hear anything.' At the last moment he turned back, a sudden thought having occurred to him. 'Perk, you might see what Conquest has to say about this private culture thing. See if he rises to the bait. Forewarned is forearmed.'

'Ah! Let me think about it. I am due to see him to discuss the agenda for senate's next meeting!'

'Good! Coming for you, he won't be on his guard. There are forces at work, Perk, murky forces, and when an attack on the state's interests comes, it comes from somewhere unexpected.'

A twitch of pained scepticism crossed Perk's face. 'Are we expecting *an attack*?'

'Always, Perk, it's the state's state of being!'

Perk made a feeble attempt at a final witticism. 'We may need a priest at hand, then?'

'Or a rabbi,' said Hazlett, in all apparent seriousness.

EIGHT

Seated at his desk, Professor Conquest was contemplating the wiring diagram of his new management structure. There was a knock on the door and Eunice, his PA entered, teetering on high heels with a cup of tea in her hand.

'Ah, Eunice!' said Conquest, rousing himself from his reverie.

'No, don't move,' she chided him as she brought the tea to him at his desk. 'You've no reason to move.'

This is a habit she's developing, Conquest thought. *There's something slightly over-protective in the way she behaves towards me. It's soothing, but could become stifling.*

She stood, expectant, making it clear in an apologetic way that she had news to impart. Conquest looked back quizzically, encouraging her to speak. Here was another thing he had begun to notice about Eunice: unless he went through the pantomime of urging her to speak, she gave the impression of being his to command, but otherwise utterly devoid of volition.

'Professor Hingley, chair of senate, is here,' she said, once prompted. 'I've given him a cup of tea. He's waiting in my office.'

Ah, yes, I'm expecting him.' Conquest nodded. 'Give me five minutes, will you, and then wheel him in.'

Senate oversaw the big policy issues that ensured the stability of University London Central and guarded its standing amongst the Higher Education fraternity. Conquest met regularly with its chair to discuss the great issues of state that had a bearing on Higher Education, and to agree the agenda for senate's next meeting. Concerning the next meeting, Conquest was in a quandary. He rose to his feet and placed himself squarely before his wiring diagram. He deliberated for some seconds and then, in a sudden burst of activity, unpinned the diagram, rolled it up and dropped it in the umbrella stand. Not a moment too soon, for almost immediately Perk knocked and entered.

'Hello, Perk. Hope I didn't keep you waiting?'

'Ah, Cliff, well met!' Perk looked about him with a slightly dazed expression. 'Aren't we in what was Human Resources? I seem to think this was Howard Huddle's office.'

'Ah, of course, you know Howard!'

Indeed, I do! We managed the departure of the previous management, they being woefully... *Well, you know all about that!* Howard was immensely helpful in advising those required to move on. There could be no doubt the head of Human Resources had supported them in their fight for the most beneficial of terms.'

'Ah, yes! You must tell me the details sometime,' said Conquest facetiously.

'Well, as you know only too well, there were confidentiality agreements on all sides and I'm not at liberty to −'

'So there were! Sorry, I had forgotten.'

There was a moment of awkwardness, Conquest having been rebuffed several times when enquiring after the details of the scandal that had brought him to University London Central.

Perk cleared his throat and changed the subject. 'Sorry to hear about the crocodile thing. I suppose we should be thankful the press doesn't seem to be making much of a thing of it.'

'Perk, it happened in the depths of the summer vacation,' Conquest protested, sensitive to any suggestion the university was implicated in the demise of Matthew Stagg. 'His untimely end is in no way a reflection on us.'

'No, no, I know. It's just that it was tragic. A young man full of promise, I'm sure.'

'Indeed.' Conquest waved Perk to take a seat on the sofa, newly arrived, that faced his steel and leather chair of American design. 'I think I can say it's being dealt with on all fronts.'

'Good. Then let it detain us no further. How are things with the digital hub? I see demolition is about to begin. Everything on course for a new academic year?'

'Yes, a bit of temporary squeezing up, but otherwise all fine.'

'And what business do we have for senate?'

'Let's look; I've drawn up a draft agenda.'

Perk had played a significant role in Conquest's appointment as vice-chancellor, but thereafter their paths had diverged. Perk thought Conquest an impetuous thruster, Conquest, Perk a great vacillator. Considerably more irony attached to the former than the latter considering University London Central's dire plight at the time of Conquest's appointment, *and* that he had been brought in to wield the big stick following a clear-out of the university's principal officers. What Conquest saw in Perk was a studious boy easily terrorised who had become a man with a great well of sympathy for the underdog, but timid to a fault. In the round, his attributes readily brought him to the mind of anyone wanting to moderate the excesses of a room full of opinionated committee members. Here was a man, thought Conquest, who had, in his time, chaired more committees than had overseen the decline and fall of the Roman Empire.

As usual, senate's business for this, the first meeting of the academic year, was thin. Following the summer break there was never anything of real substance for the agenda. The best the members of senate could hope for was up-dates on finances, capital projects and consideration of the latest policy *diktats* from the Minister for Higher Education. Humdrum stuff.

Perk was half asleep by the time Conquest had taken him through the draft. Conquest took a certain malicious pleasure in promoting Perk's drowsiness and now, the task completed, he hoped to send the sleepyhead on his way. Roused, Perk had other ideas.

'I hear you've been having radical thoughts,' he said.

'Oh? Tell me more!'

'Piers Hazlett seems impressed, anyway.'

'Ah, yes, *my lunch with Piers*! I wanted to give him a sense of where I was coming from. We agree this university still needs to improve, do we not?'

'Improvement is something we should all be striving for, Cliff.'

'But you think we're a middling university doing middling good work, and that's good enough, don't you, Perk?'

'I wouldn't say that,' said Perk, caught off guard by such an unguarded reference to his reputation for timidity.

'Don't you think our motto rather weak? *To Do What We Can*. Who thought that up? That's surely a sign of limited ambition.'

'I think it's thought to be effective without being bombastic,' said Perk faintly.

'Well,' Conquest pulled himself upright, 'there are people in post in this university depriving the students of their due.'

'*Surely not!*'

'Stretches of rank incompetence.'

'Pockets... maybe!' said Perk with great reluctance.

'Swathes. It would be a great step forward if we could find a way to make the non-teaching parts of the university accountable to the students.'

Perk's gaze wandered to the view through the picture window, disconcerted by the direction their discussion had taken. A stiff wind was blowing from the southwest and the line of trees across the way was swaying in a syncopated rhythm; a rhythm that reminded Perk of something vaguely disgusting like a disembodied peristalsis. The thought jolted him back to his predicament, the predicament of a holder of lines, a resistor of hasty, untried innovation by the rippers-up and tearers-down of institutional settlements. As chair of senate, he was, he reflected, the custodian of University London Central's values. 'I am the custodian of the university's values, long term,' he said out loud. 'Can't compromise that.'

'Wouldn't dream of asking you to.'

There was politics and there was *politics*, Perk thought, and he was alarmed at what lay behind Conquest's drive to upset the *status quo*. 'I imagine,' he continued, wringing his hands as he tried to find the vaguest possible way to introduce into their conversation what Piers Hazlett had advised him to have out with Conquest, 'we wouldn't want to be identified with new tendencies arising on the Right, would we? I hear some in Higher Education circles are flirting with all manner of heresies. I understand you have an agenda. *Fine!* All well and good! But we don't want to find ourselves identified with anything too radical, do we? Especially if it emerges from thinking on the Right? Take private culture, for instance. We can't condone that, can we?'

'*Private culture?*' Conquest was mystified.

'I gather there's some rather questionable initiative afoot; on the Right, you know. It seems it's an attempt to delegitimise the common culture. Cultural UDI, if you know what I mean.'

Conquest had no idea what Perk meant; thought it was probably something he'd picked up at some European conference. 'Look,' he said with some asperity, 'some ideologues of the Left always think everyone else is on the Right. If we want to get back in power we need to move with the times. The *Centre Left* is where we who have the care of Higher Education *in our hands* have to stand! The Centre Left has to hold the middle ground... so to speak... in Britain as elsewhere. It's the only intelligent response to the larger social dynamics! Private culture sounds like a misnomer dreamt up at one of those dreary conferences the *arrivistes* of the Rising Left have been organising. They can't abide practical initiative because they're all for purity and controlling elites.'

While he was speaking, Conquest had been trying to decide whether or not he was going to show Perk the wiring diagram of his management reorganisation. As he studied Perk's face the conviction took hold that his instinct to hide it had been right. Its time was not yet. He smiled disarmingly. His mind made up, he was ready to move on. 'Well, a matter for another day, I think. Let's discuss Graduation Day.'

Graduation Day, the annual awarding of degrees to the students completing their courses, was the following week. Perk, as chair of senate, would formally welcome the Royal Personage, the university's chancellor, who would be presenting those graduating with their degree certificates. The presence of the Royal Personage confirmed the university's reinvigoration under Conquest. The members of senate would form the bulk of the platform party supporting her.

'You're up to speed on Graduation Day, are you not? Did the events officer give you a call?'

'Ah, yes, Derek Puttle! I gather you've given him free rein to organise me.'

'Yes, I have.' Conquest had given Derek Puttle the powers to do whatever was necessary to organise the ceremony, and particularly to ensure that when the platform party processed in and out of the Great Hall, it didn't become the struggle of refugees it was, by nature, inclined to resemble. 'Last year, if you remember, he saved Graduation Day from utter chaos. This year, with him properly in charge, I think you'll find things much improved.'

'Well, he's been on to me. I gather he's insisting on full regalia for everyone on the platform. He's a bit of a stuffed shirt, but I suppose we must have the pretence of ancient ritual.'

'It would be nice, Perk,' said Conquest, with a slight air of reproof, 'if, in the England we *should be* building, ancient ritual and new thinking went hand-in-hand! That's what I want this university to stand for! We rely on you; last year's speech was memorable.'

Soon Perk departed. Conquest slumped in the steel and leather chair of American design. He tried to be sorrowful about the crocodile incident, but it was an annoyance called Piers Hazlett that occupied his mind. Perk had insisted on his appointment to senate and, as he had departed, he had, not for the first time, spoken warmly of him.

'It's a matter of the political balance on senate, Cliff,' was how Perk had put it. 'He's very in with the coming crowd on the Left. And his charity work has been marvellously strategic.'

Conquest was of the opinion that Hazlett's appointment had upset the balance that ensured his was the decisive voice in senate's decision-making. Had a representative of the Left been required for the purpose of political balance, his preference would have been for an ineffectual intellectual of the Daft Left.

The fact is, I was cajoled into agreeing to the pip-squeak quack Hazlett's appointment when my susceptibility to being persuaded of something not to my liking was at its greatest. Besides being an adherent of the Rising Left, Piers Hazlett is a ghastly species of TV celebrity, and the times are when universities seemed to live and die by their ability to attract the right sort of celebrity. In my view, Hazlett is not the right sort. He's the noxious, opinionated sort. But he's used his celebrity to raise money for the re-purposing of ecclesiastical buildings, which makes him also the right sort!

Conquest had done his best to hide his aversion to Hazlett's appointment. Forced, at the last, to make welcoming overtures to him, he had taken him to lunch and found the man even more unbearable than he had expected. Being a pragmatic agnostic of the Middle Left, Conquest loathed the Rising Left. To his mind, the adherents of the Rising Left espoused an ideological purity that was only possible because they had never done anything except chatter like monkeys in a banyan tree. He, on the other hand, had devoted his working life to the enhancement of institutions emblematic of an enlightened state. Regrettably, the *arrivistes* of the Rising Left were adept at palace intrigue. It was whispered widely that they were pursuing power and certainly they were gathering intellectual authority within the party. It was even rumoured that the fingerprints of the Camlington faction were all over the draft manifesto! Positioning oneself for the opportunities of the next Labour government was something Conquest eternally struggled with, and he feared the Rising Left was out to eclipse the Middle Left. Was he not ambitious? And weren't those of the Middle Left, like him, those with experience of power, those carrying responsibility for institutions, the realists in a room full of blinkered idealists, the ones to bring back authority, credibility, *realpolitik* to the citadel that was Labour?

Conquest vowed that the time when Perk had a hand in the membership of senate was over. What Conquest really wanted was to see Perk gone, and Piers Hazlett too.

Not only am I an impostor, wherever I go I spawn Frankenstein monsters!

NINE

Poppy had gone back, part-time, to organising the travel arrangements for the rock band and its retinue while she waited for Pye to secure access to what she hoped would be a treasure trove of material, now in the care of University London Central, related to Goldman's *Candide In Tinseltown*. She didn't give up entirely while waiting for clearance; she went to interview Goldman's agent. His name was Saul Pickles. He was a large – nay, fat – gentleman with red braces and the congested look of a man who had eaten too many literary lunches, and drunk too many straight-up, literary vodka Martinis. Nevertheless, literature, even at the practical, market-led level at which he was engaged, gave him a sophisticated and expansive view of the world, and of people. Thus he was pleasant, obliging and thoroughly entertained by the idea of Poppy's task.

'Recreate Goldman's lost *magnum opus*, eh? That'll be quite a task: there were more twists per page than you'll find on a plate of fusilli.' He smacked his lips appreciatively and gave her a twinkle.

'Is it true,' wondered Poppy, thrilled that Pickles' office found her in proximity to literary lions, 'that one of your clients is Arthur Frost?'

'Indeed, it is my eternal pleasure to represent that gentleman. Why do you ask?'

'I just love his books. I've got everything he's ever written. I was wondering... Could you get me his autograph?'

'Ah, you're an autograph hunter, are you? Well, I believe my secretary might have some signed photographs in the drawer of her desk. But what about this screenplay?'

She pulled a self-deprecating face. 'There's not much hope, is there? I don't know that I was very wise to take on the task. I've a promising fragment that describes the beginning but apart from going through his archive I'm not sure where else to look. The magic surely must be in the way he interweaves the story and the dialogue, mustn't it? It's his wit, isn't it? I can't see how anybody can remember anything like that in anything except the vaguest terms. What about you? Surely you must have read it?'

'Yes, I read it, of course I did. It was amongst his finest, there is no doubt.'

'Is there anything specific you can tell me about the plot or – I don't know – the mood of the writing?'

'Let's see, what do I remember...? I remember this: Candide, our heroine, is guileless, the butt of other people's jokes, but somehow she blunts all the malicious nonsense aimed at her. She turns it into something worthy, or ridiculous or self-defeating. It's done with subtlety, I suppose you might say. I mean, the Armstrong character, her nemesis to start with, tries to trick her into doing ridiculous things for him, but she always gets the better of him, without trying. It gradually becomes something he's aware of, and he has to accept his defeat, and that's the start of the begrudging regard he develops for her. It's then that he really sees her for the first time.'

Poppy nodded thoughtfully, and shuffled through her notes, underlining a character note she'd already made about Lionel Armstrong. 'I've started well enough, but I still think I've got an impossible task.'

Pickles chortled to himself. 'Well, if you came anywhere near rewriting it from scratch, I'd surely take you on. Shall I tell you what I remember about Candide arriving in Hollywood, and how she first meets Armstrong?'

'Yes, of course. You must.'

'Candide's drama teacher has told her she has a marvellous talent. Do you know what the talent is? To see the world as the best of all possible worlds. Her face is radiant with that thought. It's a radiance that quite changes the people she meets. It's not the beauty, it's the radiance that's so alluring. It changes people's feelings about themselves and the world around them. Call it purblind optimism, if you like.'

'And the point is that this is Hollywood, where scumbags rule. Is that right?'

'Let's say you have a feeling that her trusting nature is bound to lead her into escapades where danger is very real, where she appears to be very vulnerable –'

'– to kidnap, rape, mutilation and death.'

'Okay, but let's not get ahead of ourselves! You've got the idea but nothing about this story is straightforward; it always plays with ambivalence. Candide meets Van Holt, the movie director, by chance, in a train wreck. He offers her work and thinks no more about it. He's surrounded by beautiful assistants. Candide's days are a round of attending screen tests and working for Van Holt Productions Incorporated, where she starts at the bottom by making coffee.'

'Of course. That's how Hollywood success stories always start.'

'In her first week at the company, she's put to work in a windowless cubbyhole with only a photocopier for company. It's an example of what Mr Van Holt likes to call *in-house training*. When, on the Monday morning of her second week, Candide arrives at work still smiling, she's considered fully qualified. She's sent to the airport to meet the English actor, Lionel Armstrong, the male romantic lead of *All In The Head,* the movie Van Holt is readying for shooting. She accompanies him to the guesthouse on the Mayerbecker estate that Van Holt has rented for him. Later she meets a man at Van Holt's office; let's say his name is Dwayne. Dwayne gives her a package and asks her to deliver it to Armstrong. She's driven there in Van Holt's limousine. We have a nice scene with the driver, Clyde Dallas. He's a wisecracking blarney type with his chauffeur's hat tipped to the side of his head and a dead cigar butt rammed in the corner of his mouth.'

'Oh yeah, I know the type: hard-bitten but homely in an Irish bar sort of way, full of homespun wisdom.'

'He offers her five tips for leading the good life in Hollywood. The last is: *Go Home!*'

'What about the other four?'

'Go home.'

'What, all five are *go home?*'

'Yes. As she's leaving the car, he points out that the package she's carrying is leaking – a white powder – just as a police car comes alongside.' Pickles paused, a wistful expression on his chunky features.

'What happens then?'

'Oh, same as always: he saves her. You see, he's kind of falling in love with her. You know, in his own way, sort of protective. Looking out for her. Fatherly, I guess.'

'So how is –?'

At that moment Pickles' mobile emitted a warning sound and he reached for it. He fiddled with it for some moments, making a series of grunts and noises of disapprobation. He ended by giving a prolonged tutting noise. 'The oaf!' he said, distractedly.

Meanwhile Poppy was underlining a character note she'd already made about Clyde Dallas. 'I still think I've got an impossible task,' she said.

Pickles laughed vaguely, his mind clearly on matters related to the message he had just received. 'Don't despair, Mavis Goodenough read it and she has a photographic memory. She can recite train timetables with uncanny accuracy.' He got up and made a wandering circuit of his office.

'*Photographic…?* You mean she might remember *the whole thing?*'

'Mavis was the best continuity girl in the business. She could remember every shot in every scene of every film she'd ever worked on. She had a gift for detail that meant she could marry up two shots from the same scene filmed months apart. Knots on neckties, quiffs, lipstick colour… She could keep drinks in glasses reducing at the right speed over multiple takes, so that when the scene was put together you could tell the characters were drinking at an appropriate rate without ever seeing any of them put glass to lips. In the world of continuity girls that is the gold standard. She had an eagle eye in spades, so to speak.'

Poppy looked troubled. 'But if she's so good, why haven't *you* got her to write out what she remembers? It should be more or less perfect if her memory really is that good.'

Mr Pickles looked confidential. 'Not politic, movie world politics.'

'So, what happened?'

'Mavis could remember so much she was drowning in memories. Her continuity notes became encyclopaedic. The detail increased and increased until she couldn't disengage from her memories to deal with the present, or plan for the future. The upshot was she had to stop working. It turned out she had a condition: hyperthymesia. It's said her husband made her memorise the cards in a single-deck game of blackjack. The other players didn't care for that. It wasn't sporting, was it?'

'What happened?'

'They broke his back and made it look like he'd fallen off a trampoline.'

Poppy blew out a lung full of air through pursed lips. That was the sort of detail she didn't like to hear about someone she was hoping to seek a favour from.

'Since she succumbed, she's been living with her mother. She has a reputation for running when her mother isn't looking. And when she runs, she runs to Jaywick because that's where her worthless, son-of-a-bitch man, Billy Manson, lives.

'So, she might tell me. Is that what you're saying?'

'She might.' He gave her a speculative look, up and down. 'I couldn't say. She might very well. If I remember rightly, she too is a fan of Arthur Frost. *Look*, you've something in common already!'

Just then all hell broke loose. The telephone began to ring, Pickles' PA marched in gesturing with his appointments diary to remind him events awaited him. It was all the time he had for Poppy. She picked up her things and left.

TEN

The sky was full of bustling grey clouds blowing in from the southwest. As Conquest watched a band of darkness swept towards him with increasing velocity, eating up the buildings in his field of view until the sombre shadow arrived overhead, and every detail, once sharply delineated by sunlight, was thrown into dull uniformity.

Like my mind, he thought.

The longer Conquest oversaw the processes by which the university was readied for the new academic year, the more his feelings of dissatisfaction with himself intensified. Across from him the Great Work, his wiring diagram of the new management structure, was again pinned up. He had been on the point of sharing it with Perk Hingley, but some instinct had made him hold off. He finished his tea, rose to his feet and approached the diagram as though stalking it. He examined it with the despair a false dawn brings to an insomniac. Why had he hidden it at the last minute? Following with his eyes the descending lines of responsibility, something close to divine discontent gripped him. The fact was, a new management structure was barely more than tinkering. *Radical* was his watchword and this effort of institutional reconfiguration fell very short indeed! Now he understood what his concealment portended: he needed to be much bolder, and a reorganisation of administrative posts was but a part of a much greater revolution. And yet he feared that senate would stall and water down anything that threatened the *status quo*!

Since sending the text of his Kennedy brothers' book, *Siblings: Success And Strife,* to his academic publishers, he had been casting around for a new subject and found his mind blank. With the clarity of a sudden shaft of sunlight on a stormy day, he saw now that what he should do was bring together in a coherent, publishable form all his ideas about university education. It was precisely what Higher Education needed: a serious critical study of a system stuck with practices and processes that were a century and more out of date. Now *more than ever* it was a system that called for a revolution to meet the needs of a modern, progressive Britain! There was a dark, satanic part of him that would like to unleash a Maoist revolution; to have those he was thinking of gracing with grand, new titles planting potatoes on Rahmallah Green...

But no that will never do! That would be going backwards, not forwards! Nothing is more important than to harness the energy of the proletariat, but students don't make a very satisfactory proletariat. They tend towards oafish ill-discipline and inappropriate enthusiasms. Nevertheless, I, Clifford Conquest, will write my revolution's Little Red Book!

He heaved himself out of the steel and leather chair of American design and took himself over to his desk. On the first page of a new A4 notepad he wrote the following: *A Plan For The New University: a Vision for Higher Education fit for Today and Tomorrow.* As a title it was, he had to admit, somewhat cumbersome. Better to be comprehensive he thought and, after all, it was still provisional. More to the point, it sounded rich with promise; he was sure that when he mentioned it to the right sort of people they would be impressed.

This book won't sell a tenth of the copies of my Kennedy brothers' book, but it'll give me professional kudos, enhance my standing as a leader re-thinking the great wealth-creating machine that is The University. My book will be only part of something greater, magnificent, game-changing: the boldest reconfiguring of The University in a century. I will proselytise! I will catch the eye of those in power! And I'll kick some misshapen, blue-bottomed fundaments along the way, if I can! And yet...

He rose to his feet and did a circuit of the room as if he'd had a sudden crisis of confidence, and confidence was a physical thing he had misplaced.

Yet how am I to proceed? Not only am I an impostor, wherever I go I spawn Frankenstein monsters.

ELEVEN

Poppy Trench was not one to lounge about checking her social media. She became increasingly impatient as Pye's office waited for University London Central to grant her permission to access the Goldman papers in its library. In the end she didn't wait; she went anyway. Inevitably she found herself entangled in bureaucracy. The head librarian let it be known through the person of an assistant librarian that Poppy, being neither staff nor alumni, was not eligible for a pass to enter the library. Poppy was polite but obdurate. Protracted negotiations finally produced a one-off day pass and she proceeded to the enquiries desk where a second assistant librarian told her the Goldman archive was not available to readers. By this time, Poppy had a distinct feeling that the attitude to the Goldman bequest of those she was negotiating with was thoroughly negative. Finally, as a further mealy-mouthed concession, she was forwarded to the assistant librarian responsible for special collections. The special collections librarian, who was an enthusiast for collecting stuff, but, it turned out, only part–time, was actually welcoming and bid her come beyond her reception desk into special collections itself, which was housed in the oldest part of the library.

Poppy explained to her that, having spoken by phone to a Mr Lester, whom she believed to be the archivist cataloguing the Goldman papers, she had decided to come and take a look at the extent and character of the bequest.

She was directed to a wide, cave-like corridor lined with shelving. The floor was mostly taken up with archive boxes, piled three and four high. It was dark and dowdy and if this was special collections, she thought, it looked less like part of a university library and more like a bogged down Fraud Squad enquiry.

'Hello,' said a studious looking young man in shirtsleeves occupying an alcove half way along the corridor. He rose from behind the schoolroom desk he was sitting at and offered his hand in greeting.

'Hello, I'm Poppy.'

'Oh! You're Poppy, are you!'

She gave him a curt smile. 'Are you Graham Lester?'

'I am.' He gestured to the four points of the compass. 'Here it is: the Goldman archive!'

Poppy looked about her in something close to despair. 'This is pretty unfortunate, isn't it?'

Lester nodded, slightly crestfallen. 'Actually, I'm not really an archivist; I'm a research student. I thought I could help out. Pocket money, you know.'

Poppy nodded, too diplomatic to be blunt about the state of the bequest.

Seeing the expression on her face he nodded in the direction of the special collections librarian. 'If we had our way there'd be a Goldman study centre. It's more or less impossible to consult his papers at the moment, as you can see.'

'But what are you doing?' Poppy wondered, somewhat bewildered. 'Are you cataloguing or what?'

'I've been wading through these boxes,' he said, waving vaguely. 'There's thousands of pages... Nobody knows quite what's what. Mrs Goldman was very helpful, although helpless too.' He smiled winningly. 'Actually, I've been told to get everything out of the boxes. They're a fire hazard and Health & Safety wants them moved.' He pointed to the far end of the corridor where there was a fire door labelled to affirm it was only to be opened in case of emergencies. Again, he looked apologetic.

Poppy hadn't arrived with a clear idea of what Goldman's archive would be like. Now she could see that searching it methodically would be a daunting task.

'Seen anything of a screenplay called *Candide In Tinseltown*?'

He laughed and shook his head. 'We were told about this. Somebody from the solicitors handling the estate searched through everything before it was delivered here. Made a hell of a mess of any order there might have been.'

Poppy produced the opening pages of the treatment of *Candide In Tinseltown* that Cornelius Pye had given her.

'This is the first few pages of the story outline. In all it was probably about thirty pages, which tells you how much of the whole film these two pages represent: it's pretty compressed so maybe eight to twelve minutes.'

Lester studied it and almost immediately his expression told her there was something wrong. 'This can't be right! I *have* seen this, but it's not the thing you're looking for; it reads like the beginning of *Expressway To Fear*. Yes, I'm pretty sure I saw this yesterday.'

Poppy looked at him, hardly daring to hope. 'That's odd.' She pondered his news. 'Maybe he changed the title. Is Candide the name of the chief character?'

'I don't know. Let's see if we can find it.'

He sized up the shelving, trying to remember where he had stowed the documents of which he was thinking. 'I had thought it might be possible to wade through all this stuff systematically, you know,' he said, turning to check Poppy was still listening. 'But there's far too much. It seems sometimes he'd do maybe a dozen different versions of the same story. I hate to think what his lifetime word count was.'

While speaking he had climbed up on a chair and now he ran his hand along a row of box files on the uppermost shelf. 'I seem to remember it was in one of these.' As he steadied himself, several sheaves of paper stacked on top of the files cascaded to the floor.

Poppy smiled indulgently. What he lacked in expertise he certainly made up for in enthusiasm. He, as well as the Goldman papers, was something she would have to take in hand.

He found the box file he wanted and handed it down. She took it to his desk and opened it. It contained several spiral-bound documents. All were entitled *Expressway To Fear*. She checked the opening pages of one of them.

'You're right. It is in some ways similar, except the lead character's name's Rebecca! But how can that be? Is Goldman trying to make life difficult for me?'

'I don't know,' he said. 'Maybe he was always cannibalising his own story ideas. Isn't that what writers do: string together clichés in the hope the story isn't one big fat cliché?'

Poppy gave him a look. 'Well, maybe so.' She checked her list of Goldman's screenplay credits. There was no *Expressway To Fear* but there was a *Night Train To Terror*, made much earlier in his career. What's in that?' She pointed to the next box file, which looked similar to the one she had already had.

It was heavy. Gingerly he pulled it out with both hands. 'This?'

'Yes, that.'

He opened it and tried to fan through its contents. 'Looks like more copies of *Expressway To Fear*.'

'Are they all the same?'

He passed several to Poppy. It didn't take her long to see that she had several different versions of the train disaster.

'These are bits of shooting scripts, not treatments. Maybe he took the opening sequence of *Expressway To Fear* he liked best and made it the start of *Candide In Tinseltown*!'

'Could be.' In his loose-limbed way, Lester struggled to keep the still half-full box file from slipping from his grasp, gratified that the focus of his work, if not his work itself, was being taken seriously. 'Does that help?'

'It certainly could!' She stopped him. 'But look, you can't keep emptying these boxes without some sort of system. Otherwise, all these papers are going to be in an even worst state than they are now.'

'Then you'd better come and help me!' he said.

Poppy congratulated herself she had found something that could be very close to the shooting script of the opening sequences of *Candide In Tinseltown*. True, she could see at a glance that once Rebecca and D'arce – Candide and Van Holt – were at the hotel the story took a different turn from that of *Candide In Tinseltown*, but here was something she could work with. Maybe, after all, her task would prove less difficult than she had been anticipating. She looked about her at the corridor full of document boxes, at the vast quantities of files and papers, and found it easy to believe that somewhere there must be much more related, in one way or the other, to *Candide In Tinseltown*.

The effort of going methodically through all the material would, she could see, require several weeks, maybe more. She would go back and report to Pye, but not before she had made a copy of one of the drafts of *Expressway To Fear*. As she was leaving, she took Graham Lester aside.

'Look,' she said, 'it's no good just transferring the stuff in these boxes to the shelves unless we organise it so we know what we've got and where it is. Promise you won't do any more until I can sort out my permission to be here. Help me do this properly and I'll make sure you get *paid* properly. How about that?'

And so they struck a deal... and while she was waiting for her permission to come through there was Mavis Goodenough to track down.

TWELVE

The one thing Clifford Conquest liked about his temporary office was the picture window. It stretched for nearly half the length of the room and from floor to very close to the ceiling. He decided to move his desk so when seated at it he could see the entire view head-on. True, there wasn't much to see, just the backs of some businesses adjacent to the campus with a straggle of sycamores growing along the boundary and, in the distance, taller and taller buildings receding to the west. But his office was on the first floor so at least his view was elevated above the stretch of low-maintenance landscaping that ran to the boundary fence. It spoke to him of expansive possibilities... of flight.

When Eunice entered, she was slightly disorientated to find the desk, and hence Conquest, were not where she was expecting. Changing direction to collect his teacup she nearly twisted her ankle. She always came in to collect his empty teacup; it was a ritual Conquest had begun to notice. He had timed her and suspected that she gave him twelve minutes to drink his tea. She had a file with her and with great deliberation, as though laying a tribute on the altar of a minor god, she placed it on his desk, not immediately in front of him, but in a corner where it didn't interfere with the documents he was currently consulting.

'It's your mail,' she said.

'Anything of note?'

She reached out for the cup and saucer, pressing with her upper thighs against the edge of the desk as she did so. Her two-piece suits always looked incredibly figure-hugging, thought Conquest, not in the least aroused. And her shoes were extraordinarily high-heeled, and the heels narrowed to a point in the manner of cranium-piercing bludgeons.

'Invitations mostly. There was another letter from some company wanting access to the library, something to do with the Goldman bequest.'

'*Goldman bequest?*' Conquest had never heard of such a thing. '*Another* letter?'

'I forwarded the first to Sandra Torpington in public relations.'

'I see. When?'

'Oh, last week, I think. They've written again. They haven't had a reply to the first one… or some such.'

'Goldman, you said?'

'Yes, a writer, apparently. Sandra Torpington knows all about it. I believe his widow was a student here and she's given his papers to the university. An act of gratitude, I suppose.' A little tinkle of sardonic laughter escaped her lips.

'Really?' Conquest looked at her suspiciously, thinking her attitude lackadaisical and her laughter unbecoming. He prided himself on his instinct for something that was not quite right and this was definitely of that ilk. 'I'd better look,' he said gruffly. He reached out for the file. 'Get Sandra over here. I'll speak to her myself.' He flicked through the file looking for the second letter, but couldn't find it. 'Could we perhaps find the letter?' he asked wearily.

'Oh, sorry! Yes, I've already redirected it to Sandra.'

He gritted his teeth. 'Can you get it back?'

'Of course, it's still in my out tray.' She looked at him coyly, almost as though she expected him to say something complimentary.

'Well,' he said, wondering what else she was redirecting away from him, 'could you go and fetch it for me, please?'

'Was the tea to your liking?' she wondered, still lingering.

'Yes, lovely. Thank you. Could you…?' He flicked his hand more vigorously. 'Call public relations!'

Bearing his teacup, she turned and left his office at a clipped pace. He watched her go, his mind momentarily a fog of contradictory emotions. She was protective of his interests, that he understood and thought excellent, but was she already assuming too much responsibility in deciding what was, and was not, brought to his notice? He seemed to think that somewhere in their encounter he had experienced a swaddling sensation, but a glance towards the picture window reminded him of the positives of being free to concentrate on the bigger picture.

While he waited for her to return with the second letter he stood up and went over to scrutinise the wiring diagram. He did so to remind himself that public relations was re-named *Marketing and Communications* in his new management structure. It would be one of the business units under the direction of the *Chief Operating Officer and General Counsel*. Therein lay a problem! To his mind, the in-post potential appointees ranged from weak to abysmal. There was a conundrum and a half! He returned to his desk.

He had no idea what Eunice had said to Sandra Torpington, but he was surprised by the speed with which she appeared at the door of his office.

'Vice-Chancellor,' she said in a rush, 'I did consult our top film expert.'

Conquest gazed at her, thinking she already assumed she was guilty of some misdemeanour. He immediately wondered what little wheezes they had going in public relations. 'Come, sit down.' He made a guiding motion to the chair in front of his desk. 'I just need you to brief me, that's all. Tell me about this bequest.'

'The library has a special collections section, mainly first editions and specialist periodicals only available to readers under supervision. Well, it's a locked cabinet with glass doors, actually. Mrs Goldman approached us about making a bequest of her husband's papers. The special collections assistant was very enthusiastic, but when they arrived, they were much more than anyone was expecting. The feeling is they were rather dumped on us; I think the wife wanted them out of the house.'

'I see, but this is *Stanley* Goldman, is it not?'

'Yes, Stanley Goldman.'

'Have you looked him up, because I just have?' He turned the laptop on his desk so she could see the screen. 'It seems he's quite a significant figure.'

'I did speak to the director of film studies.'

'Who's that, exactly?'

'Professor McWhelk.'

'I see. Film studies being a section of the Department of Media and Communications – Bert Pocock's lot – I take it?'

'Professor McWhelk said it wasn't our kind of thing and I should forget it. Too late, as it turned out. Then the head librarian told me to discourage requests for access because it's just a lot of uncatalogued papers. I had been meaning to let Mr Pye know.'

Conquest stroked his upper lip thoughtfully. 'Mr Pye being the person requesting access?'

'Yes.'

'Good, Sandra! Unlike Professor McWhelk, I think you were quite right to accept Mrs Goldman's gift on behalf of the university. But I think I should have been informed, and in a timely manner! And I also think it would have been proper if I had thanked her personally for her generosity.'

'But you did, Vice-Chancellor. Eunice sent a letter over for us.'

The calmness of Conquest's responses was becoming more and more strained. 'Strange, I can't recall doing that, but never mind! Thank you for coming across so promptly, Sandra. I appreciate your input.' He rose to show her out. When she had reached the head of the stairs, Conquest signalled for Eunice to join him. By the time she entered his office he was again sitting at his desk.

'Eunice, am I losing my mind? I can't remember ever seeing a letter to Mrs Goldman thanking her for her bequest.'

'I provided Sandra with a *pro-forma*.'

'A *pro-forma*? What's that?'

'A letter with a facsimile of your signature.'

'A facsimile? That sounds like a species of forgery.'

'I use it to lighten your workload of inconsequential correspondence.'

'*So…!* And how is that achieved?'

'I have a jpeg of your signature in red, blue or black, and I insert it in the appropriate place on letters coming from you. It's immensely life-like, so you can't tell the difference between it and the real thing.' She smiled at him as if she expected to be commended for her ingenuity.

Conquest slowly put his hand to his forehead as though succumbing to a migraine. 'Eunice,' he decided, with great deliberation, 'we'll talk about this later. Perhaps you could be so good as to find out if Professor McWhelk is here. I'd like to speak to him as a matter of some urgency. But first, tell me, who is this Mr Pye wanting access to the Goldman papers, and why?'

Blithely she handed over the second letter she had rescued from her out tray. He unfolded it and saw the heading: *Cornelius Pye & Associates Incorporated*. He quickly scanned the letter and registered that Pye was writing again because he believed there might be material of considerable interest amongst the Goldman papers and could his researcher be provided with access 'to conduct research to verifying the extent of drafts relating to the screenplay *Candide In Tinseltown*'.

'This,' observed Conquest, 'is a perfectly valid request for assistance from an external entity, is it not?'

'At the moment the head librarian feels the Goldman bequest is in no condition for access to be granted.'

'And Cornelius Pye? Does that name ring a bell?' He opened a new tab on Google and typed in *Cornelius Pye*. He studied what came up, noting that one hundred and sixty-nine million results had been found in 0.56 of a second. 'How come public relations didn't register this name?'

'Well, I suppose it's still the summer vacation.'

'Eunice, we were about to put our collective foot in it! Would you speak to the head librarian and ensure that Mr Pye's researcher is offered every assistance? And let Mr Pye's office know immediately!'

Eunice still stood there, stock still, although she positively radiated the impression she was his to command. He wasn't at all sure what it meant. Was she, he wondered, willing him to think more closely about what he was doing? Whatever it was that caused her to stand there, he did, suddenly, have another thought.

'It's a bit late in the day but would you also see to it that Mr Pye is invited to Graduation Day? It might be taken as a tacit apology and an attempt to repair the damage. And find Professor McWhelk. I want to see him and his head of department, Bert

Pocock, as soon as possible.' He tapped the desk several times with his index finger. 'Here. *I want them here, now!*'

Conquest seethed for some while, but soon enough found himself immersed in the many other matters that called for his attention. It wasn't until much later that he found time to work on his book. He had only sketched out a couple of paragraphs before he found himself pacing in front of the picture window. He looked back at his desk. His computer, displaying his text, glowed repulsively. A book was all very well, but only...

Only if I turn University London Central into a test bed for my educational ideas. Only then will I rise above the herd of vice-chancellors, some one hundred and twenty of them, threatening to steal my light. The fact is that a year into this job I'm restless. I want a better me, a me that stands higher in the circles of the great and the good. I wanted prestige and the ability to play on a larger stage where my leadership skills will be truly extended. If I am to experience moments of guilt, I don't want them to be the footling, commonplace guilts of broken promises, of peremptory dismissals and betrayals. If I'm to best my fellow men with honour I –

He started from his reverie at the sight of Eunice standing at the door. She was wearing her coat. Conquest looked at his watch and was surprised to see it was going home time.

'Finally, I've heard back from Media and Communications,' she said, hand on hip in a way that indicated she was disgusted by the length of time she had been kept waiting. 'Their administrator says Bert Pocock and Professor Whelk are both on research leave.'

Conquest, apparently still three-quarters consumed by his reverie, nodded acknowledgement of her news.

'Goodnight, then,' said Eunice, pulling to the door. As door and doorframe were about to meet, one single word came from within, expelled with the force of an imprecation: '*Tuscany!*'

Eunice threw open the door. '*Vice-Chancellor!*' she cried, fearing her boss had had some kind of seizure.

Conquest was still on his feet, standing in front of the picture window. 'Have I *met* this Professor McWhelk?' he demanded.

'*I don't know*,' she said wildly. 'I expect you have, *yes!*'

'That's funny,' he responded with ferocious zeal, 'because I can't recall his face, and I've no idea what he does!'

'Well, there's nobody in Media and Communications except the administrator.'

'No, so it seems!' he said bitterly. 'One more thing before you leave: would you contact Professor Cronker? He should have oversight of Professor McWhelk's activities for the Research Excellence Exercise. Can you tell him I'm interested in Professor McWhelk's research and I'm wondering if he has evidence of any of his outcomes?'

THIRTEEN

Poppy arrived in Jaywick by bus at three-thirty in the afternoon. It had been raining recently, but now the clouds were rattling away to the southwest before a brisk breeze blowing off the North Sea. There was, she thought, a note of raffish gaiety about the place. Everything in sight looked as though it had been bought on eBay. She walked through the maze of shacks, semi-assembled beach huts and mobile encumbrances looking for Spanish Spice. When she found it, she noticed there was a ramp to the front door. She thought of Billy Manson's broken back.

Mavis Goodenough was a quick, small woman with an unfocused quality about her eyes that suggested a sensibility dulled by pharmaceuticals. The living room was a sea of clutter, but curiously well-organised, as if she had the time to fret over something she was unable to do anything about. She was alone and more than willing to talk about *Candide In Tinseltown*.

'I don't remember much of it verbatim any more. I have the medication to thank for that. All that's left of some of it is a kind of picture. Should I begin where Mr Pickles left off?'

Poppy nodded appreciatively.

Mavis spoke as if reciting, her eyes closed, a mug of tea at hand.

We jump to a couple of weeks after Candide starts working for Van Holt. An establishing shot: the three-mile mark of Wessex Boulevard, where the gradient eases off. The neighbourhood has a laidback character. Long shot: the Styrene-Vortex Building. Cut to a close-up: Coral Strick, Van Holt's Principal PA, announcing that Mr Armstrong has called. 'He wants Candide to get him some seven-eleven.'

'What the hell is seven-eleven?' demands Van Holt, drumming

his desktop with his fingers. 'You sure he didn't say go to the 7-Eleven?'

'No, he said he wanted seven-eleven.'

'And he said Candide?'

'Yes.' She pouts.

'Find her. Maybe she knows what seven-eleven is.'

Coral goes to the rest room where she finds Cindy, her assistant.

'Have you seen Candide? No? Well, leave that coffee and go and find her. Lionel Armstrong wants seven-eleven and she knows what it is.'

A little later in the morning, Clyde Dallas, Mr Van Holt's driver, is cruising Wessex Boulevard between Upper Street West and Lowdown Avenue when he spots Candide on the sidewalk. He pulls over and leans out of the window.

'Hey, ma'am, don't I know you?'

'Oh!' She approaches the car. 'It's Clyde, isn't it? You took me to Mr Armstrong's house.'

'Sure! I seem to remember you were being taken advantage of.'

She laughs. 'No, that's not right, Mr Armstrong's a gentleman. And very important to Van Holt Productions.'

'What are you doing down here, if you don't mind me asking? There's a lot of miscreants hang out on this block, hell bent on destruction ... you know? It ain't safe for someone as eye-catching as you, ma'am.'

'Oh, sir...that's not nice! Mr Armstrong asked I should buy him some seven-eleven.'

'Huh? That don't sound right! No 7-Eleven store I ever heard of sells seven-eleven!'

A delighted smile lights up her face. 'They've got no idea at the office!' she exclaims. 'Mr Armstrong has some eccentric ways about him and no one dares ask him what seven-eleven is. When he arrived from Europe, we stopped on the way from the airport and he had a pistachio Slurpee at a 7-Eleven store, so I guess he's developed a taste for them. I mean, Slurpees are real good if you want a pick-me-up, and he's been working hard on his lines, so I guess he's in need.'

'I don't recollect Slurpees coming in pistachio, ma'am. Maybe raspberry... or what about wild cherry?'

'Well, the flavour's not so important right now. I have to get Slurpees all the way up into the hills without them turning warm. I've bought myself this cold bag and I'll go up there with every flavour I can get.'

'Don't seem right, expecting you to do something like that.'

'I don't mind; it's my job, and I'm so pleased to be working for Mr Armstrong... and for Mr Van Holt, naturally. It's a pleasure to work for talented people doing important things, don't you think? Everything takes on a sense of meaning it doesn't normally have. It's like running the country, or saving people in a worst-case scenario.'

Clyde pushes back his hat, a little dazzled by her enthusiasm. 'Well, I wouldn't know, ma'am. I expect you're right about things sometimes seeming important, sometimes not. It's a matter of perspective, I suppose.'

She seizes on that. 'Yes, that's it: perspective! My perspective is that it's a cheerful task for a cheerful day, that it is!'

'Okay, well, I guess I'd better be taking you up there. I don't care for this Mr Armstrong. I've a suspicion somebody had you delivering illegal substances to him, and that's not the sort of thing that ought to be allowed.'

'Oh no, at Van Holt Productions we don't allow any such thing! And hardly alcoholic beverages neither.'

'If that's your take on things, I wouldn't know,' he decides, baffled by her unquenchable cheerfulness.

There was a low rumble followed by the bang of the front door. An ill-favoured man with an over-developed upper torso and arms appeared at the entrance; Billy Manson had driven his mobility scooter up the ramp and into the house. He looked suspiciously at Poppy from beneath lowered brow.

When fully appraised of why Poppy was there, he was brief and to the point. 'What Mavis knows has value; what she knows about that screenplay is valuable. Tell Cornelius Pye *that*! I don't like snoopers; nobody does around here. We're the independent nation of Jaywick.'

Poppy picked up her things and left.

FOURTEEN

It was the Monday of a new week and the campus had thrown off its drowsy summertime mien as the preparations got underway for Graduation Day. It was late afternoon and Conquest had just returned from Ramallah Green where a marquee had been newly pitched to house the after-ceremony refreshments. Derek Puttle, the events officer, had accompanied him on his inspection. Puttle had been granted tyrannical licence to organise the Graduation Day ceremonials. Miriam Micklethwaite, the university secretary, had overseen the previous year's. Conquest – barely arrived in his post and his guard down for once – had accepted the proceedings as the previous regime ordained them. As a consequence, he had found himself playing a prominent role in a scrappy embarrassment, only partially rescued when Puttle had stepped in. He considered it a great good fortune that the Royal Personage, the university's chancellor, had not been officiating. This year she would be, and he was determined the ceremonials would be performed with more dignity and less sloppy individualism. Miriam Micklethwaite's accident-prone organisational skills had been shown up several times since then. It gave Conquest a frisson of pleasure to think of how, in its latest iteration of his administrative reorganisation, he could grace her with the title of *Chief Operating Officer & General Counsel,* or make her post vanish.

Is Micklethwaite worthy of such a title? Is it possible she could fulfil the duties of a title that sounds so exalted? Cometh the appellation, cometh the woman? No!

Conquest was adamant; the title was much too grand for someone of Miriam Micklethwaite's capabilities. But Derek Puttle was a different matter, a man with the humourless force of character to ensure his vice-chancellor's instructions were carried out to the letter. Conquest was certain that on the morrow, Puttle would not tolerate the slightest deviation from the orders of the day. Now, relaxing in his office with a cup of tea, Conquest wondered vaguely whether Puttle, someone with a mere handful of GCSEs and a background in scouting, could be appointed to the post of *Chief Operating Officer & General Counsel* and decided... probably not.

Eunice was at the door. 'Professor Cronker to see you.'

Professor Alan Cronker was the dean of the Faculty of Material Sciences and Engineering, and the university's Director of Research. He was a severe, unforgiving man hewn from the granite of his native Scotland; a child of the Scottish Enlightenment whose research, of exemplary international impact, was something important to do with water.

'Ah, Cliff,' said Cronker as he entered Conquest's office, sniffing the air as if for unexploded bombs.

'Alan, good of you to come!'

'Glad to see you in your new office, Vice-Chancellor. I hope that one day soon we might have the pleasure of your company in the science administration block.'

'Indeed, Alan!' responded Conquest heartily. 'Though I thought your building was called Faraday House?'

'Aye, there a plaque at the entrance says that's so, but we call it the Science Administration Block. It's long gone under that name, and the tradition dies hard.'

'Isn't that likely to be a source of confusion for your students?'

'It's inches and centimetres; we seem to get along perfectly well using both.'

'Well, well, I suppose it's good to test the flexibility of their minds! How's the research going, Alan?'

'Fine. There's a lot of water in Scotland, Cliff. I'm trying to get it to run up hill to you nobs in Southern England.'

'Good for you!' Conquest ignored this as the usual SNP dig. It was part of their relationship that Professor Cronker brought a slightly combative approach to their meetings, an approach that was based on his knowledge of his faculty's strategic importance to the university, and his own worth as an academic administrator and researcher. His consequential attitude was that the vice-chancellor should treat him as an equal, just as England should Scotland.

'It's not like you to be interested in the research of an individual member of staff,' said Cronker, who was forewarned as to why Conquest wanted to see him. 'You cannot micro-manage your way out of an indifferent research return.'

This, a dig at the less than stellar research in some departments other than his own, was delivered as though a homily from the pulpit. Professor Cronker was better apprised than anyone else of the quality of the university's research effort since he had oversight of the research returns of all academic staff. Well, not all, just those deemed to be research-active for the purposes of the current Research Excellence Exercise. In his care in Faraday House was a repository for the physical evidence of their research, mostly books, or papers in learned journals, but also a bizarre collection of oddities from the less conventional fields of research. As the university's research supremo, Cronker took a broad-minded view of these vagaries, although he was a stern judge when it came to reviewing what he considered to be the serious research fields of the sciences and medicine. Both men were only too aware that the research standing of the Faculty of Material Sciences and Engineering far outstripped that of most of the rest of the university.

'Well, Alan, I must use the tools the Lord sends me to manage members of staff, particularly those whose research brings them meagre returns.'

'Aye, well, I can see you might well have a question or two for Professor McWhelk then, but I wouldn't want our talk to result in any form of disciplinary action. That's not what research assessments are about.'

'Alan, Alan, Alan, you're here to express your opinion of Professor McWhelk's research... from the position of a disinterested and learned authority, *of course*! It's information-sharing with no consequences as far as I'm concerned.'

'I find that very hard to believe, Cliff. Can I ask why you've the sudden interest in McWhelk's research?'

'He's been put in the position of advising the university on a sensitive matter to do with film studies, and I need to understand where he's coming from.' Conquest pulled a face of bland innocence and set about out-waiting Cronker.

Eventually, as it extended to the point of awkwardness, Cronker broke the silence. 'Well, Cliff, the man's an advocate of something called *cinema concrete*, which is scarcely my field of research. As you probably know, I'm interested in fluid dynamics. Always have been.'

Conquest raised a soothing hand. 'I assure you, Alan, I'm here to learn. Can we be clear about what Professor McWhelk *does*? I mean, are we talking about a practitioner of *cinema concrete*, or is he a theorist?'

Professor Cronker had a number of journals with him, the top one of which he now held out. Even at a distance, Conquest could see the cover was emblazoned with *cinema concrete*. He took it and saw it was volume twenty-one.

'It's the *cinema concrete* house journal. Apparently, it appears twice a year.'

Conquest was puzzled. He studied the cover. He read, *International Journal of Cinema Concrete*. Beneath, in slightly smaller type it said, *Proceedings of the Fifth International Convention of Cinema Concrete Practitioners*. It was printed on something like dun-coloured sugar paper. Production values were so low they could only be so purposefully. Glancing inside, he saw there was an editorial written by the international president-elect, Professor Malcolm McWhelk. He was not sure what to make of what he was seeing. 'And this is his research?'

'Well, Cliff, that's all he's submitted up to now.'

'Yes, interesting!' Conquest said, very smoothly, passing the journal back to Cronker. 'I think I should speak to Professor McWhelk personally, don't you? Best to observe the protocols.' He smiled his most benign smile. 'What I love about my job, Alan, is it gives me occasion to discover the most arcane hinterlands of our fantastically rich research culture.'

'Is that it then?' said Cronker gruffly, dissatisfied that their discussion of McWhelk's research seemed to have already concluded.

'You've given me a glimpse of the lie of the land, Alan. Do you think there might be something a little more indicative of the quality of his research he hasn't yet submitted to you?'

'I couldn't say, Cliff.'

'Well, perhaps we might enquire.' Conquest stood, signalling the end of their meeting. 'Thank you for coming over.'

Reluctantly, Cronker heaved himself to his feet. 'I'll be getting back, then. There's plenty to be done.'

As he made his way towards the door he noticed, pinned to the wall, the wiring diagram of Conquest's reconfiguration of the university's management functions. It stopped him dead in his tracks. 'Is that *us*?' he said, regarding the thing with suspicion.

Conquest laughed as though he had been caught out in a modest deception. '*Quite right!* Between you and I, it is us.'

Cronker approached the wiring diagram with caution. Had political science student Matthew Stagg been similarly circumspect when approaching the crocodiles, he would doubtless have survived the encounter.

Conquest joined him in front of the diagram. 'Have you not noticed there's sometimes a degree of uncertainty in this university about who's responsible for what to whom?'

'Aye, well, clarity is always an aid to efficiency, Cliff,' observed Professor Cronker, continuing to study the diagram. 'Looks quite a revolution! I take it you've thought long and hard about this?'

'Well, it's not really as radical as it looks,' said Conquest, warmed by how apprehensive it was making Cronker. 'It's mostly a clarification of how things are now, with clearer lines of command, clearer delineation of roles and an up-dating of core administrative activities to reflect an institution on the move!'

'I see. No consequence for current post-holders, then?'

'At the moment it's a speculation, Alan, that's all. I certainly don't see any change in your role; you're much too valuable. Perhaps I should put it away.' That said, Conquest took the diagram down, rolled it up and returned it to the umbrella stand.

When Professor Cronker reached his office in Faraday House he was quite out of breath. He picked up the phone to speak to his assistant who was responsible for collecting and cataloguing the university's research outcomes.

'Simon,' he said, somewhat conspiratorially, 'see if you can contact Professor McWhelk and ask him whether he has more research outcomes than those already submitted. I seem to remember he finds the university's interest in his research a bit of an intrusion so he may not have been particularly forthcoming. Tell him it's possible he might be picked out for a random citation check to assess the impact of his research interests. It's just precautionary, so we know how to respond to any such request... Thank you Simon... Yes, as soon as possible. Time is of the essence.'

This done, Professor Cronker felt able to relax. He didn't know McWhelk well, but he was not a man to let a fellow east coast Scot be made an example of. Particularly, made an example of by someone whose grandfather had been a Hungarian with an unpronounceable name who, in the fifties, had been forced to flee his native land and soon after arriving, penniless, in England, had taken the name Conquest. To a Scot forced to ply his trade in London, Scottish Nationalism meant nothing if it didn't mean looking after the interests of one's own.

FIFTEEN

On her return from her day trip to Jaywick, Poppy Trench was informed by Cornelius Pye's PA that University London Central had officially granted her access to its library. In preparation, she spent the weekend transcribing her notes of everything Saul Pickles and Mavis Goodenough had told her about *Candide In Tinseltown*. She then appended them to the opening sequence of *Expressway To Fear* she had photocopied on her first visit to the library. The result was twenty pages of screenplay. She had to admit the several links she was required to add for continuity's sake were quite speculative. Nevertheless, as a first attempt, she was heartened by the result.

Poppy's reception at the library that Monday morning was markedly different from the one she had experienced on her first visit; she was ushered through to special collections in no time at all. She found herself alone in the corridor, where, to her relief, things were still pretty much as she had left them. There was even a note from Graham Lester saying he would be in to help later in the day.

Now her presence was official, she was determined to impose her own sense of order on the archive. What she wouldn't countenance was a continuation of the willy-nilly manner in which Graham Lester had been transferring the material from the archival boxes to the shelving that lined the corridor.

For the first hour, Poppy did little more than dip here and there into the archive boxes as she began to find her way around. It quickly became obvious that the greater part of the archive was a vast hoard of notes and fragmentary drafts. Some of these were semi-organised in folders or box files. Others were simply a few sheets of paper stapled together, yet others a paragraph or even a few words on the picturesque notepaper of an expensive hotel. For the most part, the whole was a study in incoherence, lacking any index or other form of guide. She concurred with Graham Lester's estimation that the little order there had been when the archive was in Goldman's possession had been significantly undone by the efforts of the probate lawyers to find the screenplay of *Candide In Tinseltown*.

By mid-morning Poppy was ready for a break. She went to the students' canteen and bought a cup of coffee.

When she returned, she began her first attempt at a systematic search. In preparation for her task, she had viewed most of Goldman's movies and acquired a comprehensive list of his known screenplays.

It was a long, frustrating day.

As she dug into the material, she began to see she could only make sense of what she was finding if she assumed Goldman always had several movies in development at the same time, and was adept at switching dialogue or narrative episodes from one setting to another. He was perfectly happy to start a story idea going and take it in several different directions. If all came to a dead end, they were not abandoned but became a source for chunks of storytelling that cropped up elsewhere, lightly transformed. He also had a habit of changing the title, and the names of the chief protagonists, in closely related versions of the same story.

If all this was a prescription for befuddlement, Poppy did also find a long roll of paper on which Goldman had listed the scenes and dialogue he was assembling to complete one of his finished screenplays. She hoped somewhere there might be a similar list for *Candide In Tinseltown*.

Having consulted various biographical sources, she was certain Goldman had started to write *Candide In Tinseltown* not more than five years ago and had completed it a year later. Sometimes he annotated his work with the date, something that would be useful in distinguishing material belonging to *Candide In Tinseltown* from scenes or dialogue intended for screenplays that post-dated *Candide* but remained unfinished at the time of his death.

It was mid-afternoon before she left to buy a sandwich. She ate it while twice walking the perimeter of the campus to clear her head. When she got back, Graham Lester had turned up and was eager to help.

'What are you researching?' she wanted to know once they had established a working procedure. 'I suppose if you're a research student you must be researching *something*, right?'

'Oh, yes, I'm writing a thesis on new directions in *cinema concrete* in Latin America.'

'Ok! What's *cinema concrete*? Something new?'

'I guess so. I suppose you could say it's the antidote to the kind of stuff Goldman wrote.'

Poppy felt protective of Goldman, and although she wasn't a student, she had studied him in depth. 'He's proper cinema: dense plotting, always visual, witty dialogue, great storylines.'

'Yeah, I guess so.' He said it as though he was indulging her.

SIXTEEN

The dawn broke bright on the day of the graduation ceremony, the university's formal farewell to its graduating students. It was the end of summer event that put to rest the old academic year and signalled a new one was about to begin. Gowns and mortarboards had been rented; across the Home Counties suits and floral hats were being laid out on newly stretched duvets.

Conquest's hope and expectation was that at least today, for one day in the year, University London Central would succumb to the semblance of ancient ritual. Soon after ten o'clock, in full vice-chancellor regalia and accompanied by Eunice, he made his way to Ramallah Green. Now the day had arrived he felt an acute sense of foreboding. It had seemed reasonable to expect that gown and mortarboard would protect him from the voices whispering he was a fraud, but since donning his regalia he had felt like a laughingstock. He feared something disgraceful was bound to occur and only Derek Puttle, the events officer, stood between him and catastrophe. The sun shone and the giant marquee pitched on the green made a festive backdrop to proceedings. Already gathered there were those required formally to welcome the Royal Personage, the university's chancellor.

Look at them, thought Conquest, *the assorted worthies and numbskulls who supposedly propped up the university's credibility by lending their names to its senate!*

Derek Puttle, who had been on duty since nine o'clock, was a much more encouraging sight. Resplendent in morning coat, he looked the very image of a functionary. 'Morning, Vice-Chancellor,' he said, dipping his head in the semblance of a bow.

'Morning, Derek, everybody behaving?'

'I do believe so, sir!'

Conquest found it reassuring that Puttle had assumed the role of beadle with such frightful solemnity.

One thing you can always rely on with Derek is a kind of pukka rigidity!

'Are we ready?' he wondered hopefully.

Puttle nodded. As he did so, behind his back, Conquest saw the royal flotilla sailing into view. Puttle had just enough time to herd the last begowned straggler into his place before the cars drew up at the edge of the green. Perk Hingley was at the head of the line, positioned to effect introductions, feverishly clutching a prompt in his hand. Conquest looked down the line.

Here, in all its glory, is my senate, a self-satisfied group of people receptive to nothing that might threaten their own lumpen ideas of the status quo*!*

Just then, from the opposite direction, Piers Hazlett came rushing up, looking decidedly untidy until he gathered his gown around him to conceal the sponge bag trousers of his much-creased linen suit. Conquest's gloom deepened.

Typical media type. String instead of braces; flies at half-mast. Probably hasn't bathed since yesterday!

When Conquest was introduced to the Royal Personage, she said, 'I was sorry to hear about your terrible incident with the crocodiles', as if the crocodiles had been negligently let loose on the campus. Otherwise, the welcome seemed to go smoothly enough, although it grated with Conquest to see that Hazlett was the only person in the line to have any sort of meaningful exchange with her.

The Royal Personage was then shepherded to the foyer of the Media and Communications Building where she looked, with apparent interest, at an exhibition of environmental design expressly put on for her. Then, without much delay, she allowed herself to be shunted towards the senior common room in the Pearson Building, which had been turned into a sort of green room for the occasion to allow the members of the ceremonial procession to drink sherry and wait for the moment of their entrance into the Great Hall. Drinks were lined up on silver salvers and an impromptu cloakroom had been set up in a corner so those that wished could leave behind bags and other encumbrances.

The room was filling up, the hubbub loud. At the door, Puttle was assiduously ticking off the arrivals on his VIP list. As Conquest entered, he left his post to brief him. In normal circumstances, Conquest found his attempts at briefing annoyingly footling, but since today he considered him an absolute bulwark, he mimed close attention and tuned out. Most of what Puttle said might well have been footling – it drifted in and out effortlessly enough – but Conquest suddenly realised that *sotto voce* he was delivering a warning: '…hasn't got a tie'. Puttle cocked his head in the direction of an exceedingly meek-looking little man standing by himself by the magazine rack. He had an ill-advised moustache cultivated with resolute horizontality across an otherwise unmemorable face.

Puttle looked at Conquest with meaningful intensity, making it clear he was speaking of the recipient of this year's honorary doctorate, the theatre director, Angus Farthing.

While blanking Puttle, Conquest had been gazing at that very man whilst attempting to prime his convivial self with a glass of the caterer's sherry. He now reacted with energy. 'Inform Eunice,' he said. 'She has a spare for exactly this contingency!'

Perk Hingley had nominated Angus Farthing for an honorary doctorate at about the same time he had over-ridden Conquest to appoint Piers Hazlett to fill the seat on senate vacated by a retiring City of London alderman. It was in what Conquest had dubbed *Perk's over-weaning period*. It was a moment of vulnerability when Conquest considered he had been taken advantage of. His irritation at Perk's insistence that honouring Angus Farthing would 'mark us out as doing the right thing', had been greatly intensified when Hazlett had enthusiastically endorsed the idea at their meeting over lunch.

'The man has a beautiful way with the Greats,' Hazlett had opined. 'He finds contemporary relevance everywhere! The politics of his drama is the ideological bedrock of his realism.'

The latter sentiment so infuriated Conquest he took to declaiming versions of it as he lay in bed, waiting for sleep:

The drama of his politics is the bedrock of his ideological realism.

Or: *The ideological realism of politics is the bedrock of his drama.*

And: *The ideological bedrock of his politics is his drama's realism.*

Once Farthing had agreed to accept the honorary degree, Conquest had met him briefly at the Groucho Club. Subsequently, Conquest had learnt that he had made a bit of a fuss in the press about turning down a CBE, or some such. Ostensibly, it was in protest over some obscure slight to the East Fenlands Trust by the Inland Water Board, but it was mooted that what really lay behind his refusal was republican sympathies. If that were the case, it was only a matter of time, Conquest feared, before the irascible Royal Personage found out. He thought it quite possible she already had. If so, she was capable of awarding Farthing his doctorate with some kind of subtle but unmissable demonstration of bad grace. The bad grace would also be tantamount to a public rebuke for University London Central.

Conquest was even more alarmed to discover that Farthing wrote an occasional satirical column for one of the Sunday papers, the one Conquest considered to be staffed by the Tippex wielders of the Rising Left. The last thing Conquest wanted was for him and his university to be lampooned by some Rising Left theatrical firebrand, although what he observed across the senior common room was scarcely firebrand material. Time, he decided, to weave his vice-chancellor's magic. He gave Puttle a few words of encouragement and abandoned his empty glass on the plinth of an assemblage donated to the university by an undistinguished, although thoroughly likeable, former head of fine art.

Cursing mutely, muttering blandly, nodding greetings to everyone as he passed, Conquest worked his way through the crowd until he reached Farthing. He gripped his limp hand. 'Ah, Angus,' he said breezily, 'Glad to see you've made it! Ha, ha!' and pumped his hand prodigiously.

The little man looked grateful at finding a friendly face. 'Gah! I do hope I'm not expected to say anything,' he said diffidently. 'My wife, you know, was very pressing.'

'Well, I'm sure she was right to do so! It's an honour we're delighted to bestow… and it will go down in the annals. Is she with you, by the way?'

'Well, no, she's taken her mother straight into the hall.'

'Good! Excellent!' Conquest moved a little closer and dropped his voice. 'The only thing is, Angus, we have to put you in a tie… so to speak. With the Chancellor, you see, we have to be particular. You know how it is with the Royals: a bit… *hidebound!*'

Farthing examined Conquest's tie with interest. 'Haven't worn one of those in yonks,' he said cheerfully. 'Last one was a kipper.'

Conquest suspected satirical thoughts were being had. 'We keep a selection for just such occasions. I expect Eunice will find you something dashing.'

At that moment, Eunice bustled up, a limp dark blue specimen in her hand. She smiled at Farthing, a smile quite unlike the smiles she bestowed on Conquest. It was grim, coercive, suggesting Farthing should think himself lucky to be the beneficiary of a charitable act.

Conquest detected dismay in Farthing's face. '*Yep! Not quite* what I had in mind either,' he said and, determined to head off any objections Farthing might have, added '*Splendid!*' as if Eunice had, nevertheless, conjured up something more than sufficient to the occasion.

'I thought these dos were a great deal less formal these days.'

'Good Lord, *no*! The parents, you know, expect a show for their money. We try to be obliging: marquee on the green with plated sandwiches. I did draw the line at a disco.'

'The disco being inside or outside the line?' said Farthing.

Farthing intended this as a jocular repost to what he took to be a jocular remark; Conquest sensed further satirical intent. Eunice proffered the tie. Reluctantly, Farthing took the thing and held it up to his throat to give them both an impression of the finished effect.

'Excellent!' Conquest raised his arm and threw back the hem of his gown to reveal his watch. 'Time's getting on. I'll leave you in Eunice's capable hands. She'll make sure it's straight. I must spread myself thin with our guests.' He smiled winningly and moved on.

Despite the throng, there was one area of the room where the population density was notably low, the reason being the presence there of the Royal Personage, who emanated a highly effective exclusion zone. She was deep in conversation with the Lord Lieutenant of Kent. The Lord Lieutenant, thought Conquest, might as well have had a 'Do not disturb' sign hanging off his ample behind. Yet, as he looked, Piers Hazlett insinuated his way into their conversation.

Hazlett is the sort that turns up at Sandringham wearing a yellow Cashmere sweater!

The sight of Sarah Micklethwaite, the university's secretary, signalling to him from across the room, diverted Conquest's attention. Before he could make a move in her direction, he fell foul of Nancy Spurling, newspaper columnist and member of senate. The adherents of the Rising Left on senate considered her the most prominent of the vulgarians of the Right. Her Tory heartland views on every conceivable subject were anathema to them.

'How come you're making that little twerp Farthing a doctor of philosophy?' she demanded indignantly.

Conquest gestured with meaningful vagueness. 'Proposed by chair of senate. Radical voice in theatreland.'

She laughed raucously. 'Oh yes, the deep state, macrobiotics and hair shirts for all.'

'You cannot dispute his success with the classics,' replied Conquest. 'He's a master at bringing moribund texts back to life.'

'The subtle art of ventilating a corpse! *And* he's a low blow to the art of writing an opinion column.' The writing of opinion columns was something Nancy Spurling felt deeply about since it was an art she had practised for many years from fairly far right on the spectrum of political opinions. 'I shall be shaking his hand ironically.'

'Good. Quite right. Excuse me, Nancy, but there's something brewing I must attend to.' He slipped on past.

Beyond her, Perk Hingley was deep in conversation with Olaf Gundersson, a member of senate dubbed *Arts Council Olaf* in quarters where the Arts Council's funding policies were greeted with suspicion.

As Conquest passed, Perk detained him by the arm. 'Ah, Cliff!' he exclaimed, 'may I have a word?' Apologetically, he turned back to Arts Council Olaf. 'I fully understand what you're saying about the importance of dance collectives, but will you excuse me a moment?' He indicated Conquest with his chin as if he were something choice on a deli counter. 'I won't be long.'

His hand still on Conquest's elbow, Perk guided him away with an urgency that seemed to betoken bad news. 'I'm glad to catch you; busy time, I know. You're not intending to bring any last-minute business to next week's meeting of senate, are you?'

'No, I'm not. Why do you ask?'

'It seems there's an air of expectation.'

'Expecting what?'

'The impression's abroad that you've something radical in mind.'

'No, nonsense, Perk. As you know, I'm having thoughts – that's my job – but the digital hub is handful enough at the moment.'

'Ah, yes, but the digital hub is hardware. I'm concerned you don't spring institutional software on senate without forewarning me.'

Hardware? Software? Conquest was brought up short by Perk's choice of words. Did he think it was modern to talk in such terms?

'I'm not sure where this is coming from, Perk, but before bringing anything to senate I'd certainly want to discuss it with you. Whatever I decide to do, I'll be wanting your support, of course!'

'Ah, Cliff,' boomed a voice in the nape of Conquest's neck, 'Nancy tells me we're again blessing Her Majesty's loyal opposition with this year's honorary doctorate.' It was Sir Norman Fleet, possibly the only person in the room to have no scruple about breaking into what was obviously a private conversation. 'I've always thought theatreland is much the best place for the Rising Left to exercise its wellie.'

Not only was Sir Norman not averse to butting in, he also had a habit of greeting Perk with a reference – supposedly comedic – to human rights.

'Ah, Hingley, dear chap! Still fighting the dark forces disapproving of foreign crims in stolen BMWs?'

'Ah, Sir Norman!'

Perk had to bear the ribbing with good grace. Sir Norman had, in days of yore, donated handsomely, if somewhat strategically, to New Labour, but old allegiances were said to have worn thin with him. Whatever his politics, his social mores seemed suspiciously Tory, and he was still well connected in the corridors of power. Even those, like Perk, who considered Sir Norman to be a confederate of the vulgarians of the Right, had to admit he had his uses; most recently in helping the university secure the funding for the digital hub. Sir Norman was also the chair of Wainwright, Carter & Expandite, the company that had subsequently secured the design and build contract. Perk believed, somewhere in his innermost being, that one day soon it would be discovered the bid had been fraudulent and Sir Norman had used the contract as an opportunity to funnel money out of the university.

Conquest caught sight of Miriam Micklethwaite, still signalling for him to join her. Her persistence was worrying.

'Ah, Sir Norman, I find myself beset, I'm afraid,' said Conquest hastily. 'Might we speak later?'

'Don't think you can escape!'

'Indeed, I don't!' Conquest turned to Perk. 'Let's get the ceremonials over. I promise we'll discuss senate later.'

In her role of university secretary, Miriam Micklethwaite was responsible for the services that supposedly supported the smooth functioning of the academic life of the university, a task she was peculiarly inept at. She offered opinions on every conceivable aspect of the university management, usually with the prefix, 'from a legal standpoint, it looks ill-advised', something she felt qualified to do because her duties required her to be in frequent contact with the university's solicitors. She was plump, but not the least bit cuddly. Conquest found her voice reminiscent of the scurrying monotone of a particularly sanctimonious pulpit penguin. She was fixed in his mind as Her Exalted Inefficiency.

'I've heard from the parents.'

'Ah!' Conquest felt a touch self-congratulatory at the deft way he had handled the crocodile tragedy. 'I trust the condolences expressed on behalf of the university were appreciated.'

'To no avail, I'm afraid, Vice-Chancellor,' said Miriam in a voice in which warmth and fellow feeling were conspicuously absent. 'It seems the parents – or, more precisely, the solicitor acting on their behalf – wish to know why there was insufficient supervision to prevent the crocodiles eating their son.' She gazed at the floor sombrely for several seconds. 'If I recall correctly, the words "gross negligence" were used.'

Conquest was taken aback, but quickly rallied. 'Really? How about "dereliction of duty"? That mentioned anywhere?'

'I believe not.'

'No? *Quite right!* How can they claim...?' Wordless, he scanned the room for some moments, unobtrusively grinding his teeth. 'This *unfortunate* event occurred during the summer vacation, thousands of miles away! It didn't happen on our watch; I understood he was on a safari holiday!'

Miriam Micklethwaite looked skywards, a picture of forbearance. 'It seems there's an email, a memo. They construe this memo as constituting a course requirement issued on the authority of the department.'

'I see,' Conquest said, his nerves suddenly shredded. 'This memo came from whom? The head of this boy Hind's department?'

'Stagg.'

'Sorry?'

'Matthew Stagg, not Hind. It was authored by one Frodo Figg, reader in Third World studies.'

'*Frodo Figg!* For Heaven's sake, what kind of background produces a name like that? It sounds Norwegian!'

'I believe, sir, Frodo is the name of one of the principal characters of Mr Tolkien's famous trilogy, *Lord of the Rings.*'

Conquest shook his head as if warding off her words. His parents hadn't been the sort to introduce their off-spring to fantasy novels peopled by wizards, hobbits and elves, nor, when a rising academic, had he had the time to attend screenings of popular cinema. 'And do you have a copy of this supposed memo?'

Silently, Miriam Micklethwaite offered him a sheet of A4. He read as follows:

Dear Seminar group C, I understand you will be joining me

next year for the 'Post-Colonial Africa: The Politics of Liberation & Repression' module. As I know many of you have benefited from a thoroughly privileged First World upbringing, your outlook on the subject would benefit immensely from some first-hand experience of the continent. And I am not talking about the easy option of a safari holiday, although frankly even that would be a great deal better than whiling away the summer on the usual vacation indulgences. Ask yourself this: are you a fellow traveller of First World repression or are you willing to use your voice to confront the current world order? Yours, Frodo Figg.

'*What is* all this underlining?' exclaimed Conquest as if it were the use of underlining that most affronted him. 'It scarcely strikes the dispassionate, clinical note expected of an academic, does it? Don't we have conventions about addressing students by email?'

'I could not recommend this kind of communication on any account.'

'No, quite right.'

'The Stagg family solicitor argues, Vice-Chancellor, that Figg's email can be construed as meaning that experiencing Africa in some manner or other was a prerequisite of the module.'

'Yes, but does this form of words mean Figg is recommending safari holidays?' It was clear to Conquest that whether he was, or wasn't, had some bearing on the parents' complaint.

Miriam Micklethwaite's lips twisted suggestively, but otherwise it was a question she seemed unwilling to answer. 'They argue that the university had a responsibility to supervise the student experience. Clearly, a risk assessment had not been made of the circumstances Stagg met.'

Conquest was silent on such a preposterous requirement. 'On whose authority was this email sent?'

'I understand Figg sent it on his own initiative, not sanctioned by the department.'

'I should hope not! This Figg must have been out of his mind to write this.'

'Quite. The family's view is that the university is responsible for Mr Figg's actions, he being a full-time member of the academic establishment.'

'That's as maybe. I shall deal with this matter personally, *and* with the issue of whether this memo can be interpreted as Figg recommending safari holidays! Leave it with me.'

He dismissed her. Here was something, he decided, that would, in the first instance, require some sort of formal apology to Stagg's parents, possibly an emissary delivering something extravagantly grovelling, abject and servile. Instead of brooding on Figg's purblind stupidity, he found himself brooding on Miriam Micklethwaite, the post of *University Secretary and General Counsel* and his new management scheme. Certainly, she was not the emissary to send! The big hand of the senior common room clock was nearly vertical. He eased his way between the knots of gossiping dignitaries, nodding to left and right, noting for future scrutiny those that stopped talking, their faces guilty, as he passed.

On the stroke of eleven o'clock the procession would wend its way to the Great Hall where the recipients of this year's degrees would be waiting with their families. Little did the families, presently filling the auditorium, abuzz with anticipation, realise that the awards ceremony was an excruciating farrago that went on for hours and hours while Professor Woolworth, a medieval scholar who had, in his role of dean of academic affairs, become keeper and interpreter of the innumerable clauses of the university's statutes, stumbled through the job of announcing the names of the graduating students as each, in turn, came up to shake the hand of the Royal Personage. 'Mr Khosrowshahi, Ms Khmelnytskys, Mr Kveseladze, Ms Kwiatkowski…'

'Derek!' Conquest cried as he approached Puttle, 'time to move off. Would you call the great unwashed to order?'

'*Vice-Chancellor?*' exclaimed Puttle, mystified by Conquest's reference to the great unwashed.

'Round them up, eh, Derek? The Great Hall is, I fancy, overflowing.'

Conquest watched as Puttle took control of Perk and ushered him towards the Royal Personage with much obsequious nonsense. In response to Puttle's ministrations, the vexatious atoms of the platform party began to coalesce into an orderly gaggle. The Royal Personage had been wheeled about and was now, as befitting her role as chancellor, at the head of the procession, chatting amiably with Perk Hingley in *his* role as chair of senate.

Conquest moved to his place immediately behind them. He glanced to his left to check he was twinned with playwright Farthing, recipient of the honorary doctorate. Farthing's hired gown, he noticed, was trimmed with what looked suspiciously like cat.

'The day will come,' said Conquest fatuously, 'when gowns are trimmed with Velcro.'

'Sorry,' said Farthing out of the corner of his mouth, determined to be companionable, 'did you say *Velcro*?'

'Oh, no,' apologised Conquest, 'Apologies, I was thinking of the fluffy part of Velcro.'

An awkward silence ensued, Farthing being unsure what to make of Conquest's remark.

'In an age of exam mark inflation, you have to bear it in mind we'll be awarding some third-class degrees today,' said Conquest, trying a new tack.

'Yes, I suppose that's rather hard on some.'

Conquest gave a harsh laugh. 'Have you *any idea* how hard it is to be awarded a third?'

The procession lurched into motion. It wound its way down the stairs and into the Founders' Lobby, which led to the Great Hall. Conquest looked back and saw that, thanks to Puttle's respectful but resolute chivvying, what had, upstairs, resembled a disorderly queue had actually fallen into something like a proper double column. Puttle was even now overtaking the procession on one flank so he could lead it into the Great Hall. To Conquest's amazement, he saw that Puttle was wielding a ceremonial mace. How he had acquired such a thing he had no idea.

'I saw your Hamlet,' Conquest said to Farthing, struggling for a compliment. 'I thought your leading man was rather well chosen.'

'Ah, yes, Lionel Armstrong. He's gone into films; snapped up! Quite a loss to the stage, I'm afraid.'

'Yes, he had presence; something of a firebrand. I imagine you found him difficult to handle.'

'No more than usual. Artistic people always respond to calm reason, I find.'

'Oh! *Do they?*' Conquest was incredulous. 'You should come and try directing my lot!' He laughed bitterly, so bitterly, Farthing began to think he was in the company of a man who had, to use the vernacular, *lost it*. He was not too disconcerted by the idea; his tutor at Cambridge had been similarly inclined. He looked down at his tie. He had thought it was a sober dark blue, but now the light was brighter – the procession was approaching the entrance to the Great Hall – he saw that it was patterned with circles, each made up of many concentric rings. He further observed that his every movement activated an optical illusion whereby all the rings seemed to be in motion like the whirling blades of a fan, alternately clockwise and anticlockwise. Fascinated, he lifted the tie to the horizontal to get a better look. At this moment the Royal Personage and Perk were negotiating the single, shallow step up into the Great Hall. When it came to Farthing's turn, mesmerised by the kinetic effect of his tie, he stubbed his toe against the step, while the rest of him continued forwards. Chairs squealed as several members of the audience just inside the entrance tried to shuffle out of the way as he was sent sprawling. There were a few seconds of fluster and consternation. Conquest gaped. At the moment of maximum disorder, a security guard with skin of a lustrous indigo stepped forward. His uniform was of the order of perfection normally reserved to the offices of Saville Row tailors. Farthing, somewhat shaken, was lifted bodily from the ground and set gently on his feet.

'I say, that was nasty. Are you alright?' said Conquest, taking a grip on Farthing's arm to steady him.

Farthing nodded mutely but couldn't put his full weight on his left ankle.

His commission fulfilled, the security guard stepped back to his Puttle-appointed place by the entrance.

Conquest glanced back at the procession, which gave him the impression of piling-up like a slow-motion road crash. To the front, the Royal Personage was eyeing proceedings with the look of guarded indifference to which that family was prone. He could see he had no recourse but to assist Farthing down the central aisle and up the steps to the platform. This he accomplished under the watchful eye of the Royal Personage with a slowness that was mortifying. She seemed to have been in her seat for an age by the time he lowered Farthing into his place in the second row, directly behind the lectern, where thankfully he was almost entirely concealed from the audience.

SEVENTEEN

On behalf of the university, Perk welcomed the Royal Personage with the respectful indifference Conquest considered typical of the Rising Left. It was then his turn to give a brief report on the year just finished. He addressed all the salient points expected of a vice-chancellor successfully completing a first year of office. It went well, so the nod from Professor Woolworth told him. With that his role in proceedings was done. Adrenaline expended, it was now that he began to feel the true hopelessness of his situation. He felt his throat constricting. He examined the faces of the audience and tried to give each one a brief biography.

Diversity, ah diversity! he thought without much conviction. 'Ms Plimp. Ms Plump, Mr Porklington...' he heard Professor Woolworth intoning. He felt the impossible weight of the institution crushing him. How was he ever to make University London Central a shining, new Jerusalem?

Eventually, the dire proceedings were brought to a close. Conquest was almost overwhelmed with relief. As the platform party processed out of the Great Hall and into the lobby it began to break up into gossiping knots of people. The crocodile incident was festering in Conquest's mind. He wondered about this Figg who had piled blight on blight. What sort of hopeless, unprofessional academic type was he? Somehow the image of a teenage nitwit carrying books in a satchel presented itself.

Derek Puttle was signalling to him wildly. The Royal Personage had another appointment and would not be staying to join the other guests in the marquee. A small delegation, including himself, conducted her out of the building and to the far end of Rahmallah Green where the royal flotilla was drawn up expectantly. The goodbyes were clipped and seemly.

As the vehicles disappeared from view, Piers Hazlett, looking cheerfully relieved, clapped him on the shoulder. 'That went as well as could be expected,' he said, giving Conquest one of his famously boyish smiles.

Conquest wondered what Hazlett had expected and what had, and had not, gone as well as that. Hazlett had been towards the back of the procession and in all probability been too busy gossiping to notice the hold-up while he had helped Farthing hobble to the platform. He felt a strong desire to be scathing. Instead, he said, 'Must go and hobnob.'

The green was now crowded with parents and students, the latter high-spiritedly photographing one another in their gowns and mortarboards. The parents, in their finery, were heading for the open-access end of the marquee. As he left Hazlett behind, Conquest found himself wondering about the etymology of hobnob. He was irritated the word had come to mind.

Repellent commonplace! It speaks of mediocrity, my own mediocrity!

It calmed him to think of what forms of extreme rendition he might visit on Hazlett; forms that even a human rights expert like Perk would have difficulty identifying as torture. He marooned him in a grey suburb surrounded by grey, uninteresting people for the rest of existence; he trapped him on a cruise ship where he ate an eternity of breakfasts with the worst sort of chatterbox; entombed him in a labyrinthine library worthy of Borges stocked with nothing but the reminiscences of sports personalities. In a moment of monstrous vindictiveness, he conceived of the reminiscences as several generations out of date.

Conquest admired the floral decorations as he entered the VIPs' end of a marquee. They looked suitably decorative and rather expensive. Professor Woolworth hoved into view.

'Excellent summary, Vice-Chancellor,' he said with a deference that suggested the grandeur of the occasion had bestowed new status on Conquest.

As a consequence of the combining of their two offices to create the Vice-Chancellor's Strategic Secretariat, Conquest had added to Woolworth's existing role of dean of academic affairs the title of deputy vice-chancellor. If the new title implied anything it was not new status for Woolworth but Conquest's increased control over academic matters at his expense. Conquest reflected gloomily that were the new scheme of management he had been working on over the summer brought into being, Woolworth's title would again be inflated to *Provost and Pro-Vice-Chancellor (Quality Assurance & Advancement)*. Where he was, in the VIP enclosure, refreshments were abundant, but beyond the roped-off cordon, in the greater part of the marquee, he could see that parents were fighting over the plated sandwiches. Since Woolworth was arguably the university's longest-serving member of staff, he was consulted on all matters concerning its traditions. Conquest indicated the melee. 'What's that about?'

'Ah, yes! The parents are supposed to reserve sandwiches in advance. Some don't and they think the sandwiches are for anybody. It usually ends up with the odd bust-up every year.'

'Can't we do something about it?'

'Oh, security will take care of it.'

'No, I mean plan the sandwiches differently, so it doesn't happen?'

'Oh, yes, I suppose so. It's a detail, isn't it? It only happens once a year so people don't remember until it happens again.'

Conquest thought this a maddening response, but he remained silent, watching as the security guard who had put Farthing back on his feet now put the plated sandwich area back to rights. It struck him, not for the first time, that nobody in the whole university looked as professorial in a mouldy, bookwormy way as did Woolworth. Here was the perfect emissary to make peace with the Staggs and apologise for the crocodiles eating their son.

'Murray, would you do me the favour of taking coffee with me first thing tomorrow? There's a little task I'd like you to undertake for the university.'

Woolworth bobbed his head obligingly. 'Certainly, Cliff. No problem at all now I'm so conveniently close.'

Grimacing inwardly, Conquest moved on. The next half hour was an endless round of face-to-face inconsequentials. Topical small talk was what was called for, but he felt an overwhelming desire to apologise; an unaccountable need for absolution. The coleslaw sandwiches gave him a credible pretext. Coleslaw in sandwiches stood in for all manner of things wrong with the world and, more particularly, for those things he needed to apologise for: his misanthropy, his inadequacies, the betrayals he's committed on his rise. His use of 'hobnob' troubled him greatly; it was a touchstone for his tremendous sense of lack.

I am an impostor and everywhere I go I spawn Frankenstein monsters.

'Sorry about these sandwiches. I never did understand why someone thought coleslaw was a suitable filling for a sandwich.'

'I do apologise if you've happened on one of the coleslaw sandwiches. I don't know what the caterers were thinking of.'

'Coleslaw isn't, I feel, really at home in a sandwich. I do apologise.'

'I'm afraid we all deserve better than coleslaw sandwiches.'

The topic of coleslaw and sandwiches had the bonus of allowing him to sail through every encounter, requiring no other conversational gambit. His interlocutors were charmed that someone as grand as the vice-chancellor had his finger on such a small detail. His admission that coleslaw sandwiches were really not good enough for the VIP end of the Graduation Day marquee reassured them of his jealous regard for the university's standing in the ranks of the institutions of Higher Education.

After half an hour, he sensed he might step out for a breath of fresh air without it being remarked upon. The marquee had several exits. It was a lovely day and lengths of the sidewalls had been rolled up. He took a few measured steps across Rahmallah Green, as though having something important in mind that might give him cause to rush away. Not far away, looking towards him, although the rest of her body was in profile, was an exceptionally handsome woman dressed in a cascade of pale, summery colours. She had about her the cosseted look of a rare and beautiful thing. She gazed at him steadily, her lips slightly up-turned in the birth of a smile.

'I've lost my husband,' she said it as though the man in question was a hopeless case, always lost, never hers to command.

Her voice wasn't husky, but it had about it something of old oak, patchouli, sandalwood and expensive gin. She now approached. It was as if she had identified him as a co-conspirator.

'You're thinking of escape, aren't you?' She gave him a mischievous smile. 'It must be an awful bore for you when you have so much to do; all this ceremonial.' She spoke with a certain familiarity, as if she knew not only who he was, but also what he felt. It had the instant effect of putting him at his ease.

'Actually, I quite enjoy the ceremonial,' he responded. 'It's as if all the vagabond loose ends are in their place for once, somehow.'

She nodded understandingly. 'But enough is enough, is it not?'

He found it infinitely soothing that she comprehended his desire to get away. She made it seem so reasonable when he knew most in the marquee expected him to remain there, eager to play host, until the last stragglers had had their fill. There was something so charming, so utterly winning in her smile that he felt her capable of lifting the blackest of moods, and his, he recognised, had been black dog black.

'Well, *I'm* happy to be here,' she confessed, 'I enjoy the atmosphere of universities. I find they exude a kind of charge, like pheromones; all that intellectual spunk, I suppose.' The last she said as one might splash a little iced rose water in another's face.

'Yes, a university's generative ability is never in question, but sometimes a little over-eager,' he said gamely, trying to match her provocation, knowing he'd been set a test. 'I'm sorry, we haven't met, have we?' he added, vexed he didn't know who she was.

'Oh, I'm Fawn Williams,' she said. 'Everyone thinks I've said Vaughan Williams, which would be ridiculous, would it not?' She cast her eyes around the green and saw, at a distance, two men, deep in conversation, had wandered into their line of sight. 'Ah, there he is! Why don't you come and meet him?'

Conquest saw that the man in question, her husband, was talking to Angus Farthing, newly invested by the Royal Personage with an honorary doctorate of philosophy and, even more recently, supplied with a crutch. She coaxed Conquest into motion with a deft little gesture, hardly noticeable, somehow rather endearing as though she wanted him terribly to meet her husband. Beguiled, he walked with her; the spell she cast, if anything, intensifying.

They were heading for a smooth-looking middle-aged man; maybe a little older than Clifford but in prime condition. He was also a little shorter than his wife, but Clifford could see that he was the possessor of the sort of vitality that made him seem larger than he really was. Like his wife, he exuded an easy-going charm.

The husband made a little obeisance. 'It's never too late for our friend here to get a little learning,' he said, patting Farthing on the arm. 'Cornelius Pye. Call me Connie,' he added, holding out his hand to Conquest in the manner of a man who was used to shaking hands to the effect of 'my word is my bond'.

Conquest was taken by surprise, but rallied in a moment. In the press of events, he had forgotten about his invitation. 'Good Lord, of course! I'm so glad you were able to make it.'

'Well, Angus and I go back a long way. Only right you should honour him. I see you've met Fawn.'

'Yes, your wife has been conspiring with me,' replied Clifford. 'I was about to offer her a tour.'

'Ah, yes, a tour! Your university is quite the coming place, I understand. I suppose Angus here is going to infect your drama department with his radicality.'

'I do hope so!' agreed Conquest affably.

'He'll be demanding more Ibsen and Chekov,' Fawn warned with mock solemnity.

Farthing demurred, apparently believing the quip called for a rebuttal of some seriousness. 'It doesn't matter what the text is, it's interpretation that says it all,' he observed.

'Ah! There speaks the director,' decided Pye, shaking his head with the same mock solemnity that his wife had just used.

The way they teased Farthing, thought Conquest, spoke of a certain professional intimacy, and the way Farthing submitted to it with owlish good-humour was rather endearing, something until now his appreciation of him had singularly lacked.

'I'm sorry we were so slow to respond to your request for your researcher to study the Goldman papers. I hope that's cleared up now.'

Pye smiled. 'I believe so. Poppy, you know, is quite exceptional. I expect she'll drive your people mad with her demands.'

'Would you care to see some of our facilities?' Conquest wondered. 'I could spare some time.'

'Perhaps Connie would like *to use* the facilities,' said Farthing, moved to play the jester.

'No, no, we'd love to,' said Fawn, touching Conquest's sleeve in a moment of intimacy, 'but we've agreed to take Angus off for some late lunch.'

'Ah, yes, I must apologise for the coleslaw. I can't imagine –'

'Heavens, we were spoilt for choice!' Fawn assured him, reaching out again, this time to touch the back of his hand. 'These men are always talking business and they have to do it over red meat! I try to civilise them, but it's nigh on impossible.' She laughed, apparently delighted by the absurdity of her task.

'It's true,' agreed Pye. 'Not content with stealing my wife for his latest production, Farthing wants to pick my brains. Another time I'd love to see what you're doing here. It's good to visit a university that's not part of the old order.'

As they talked, they were making their way towards the far end of the green, to the point where the Royal Personage had embarked in Her Rolls-Royce. A Rolls-Royce was again parked there, no less regal but somewhat newer, its livery the gorgeous sapphire blue beloved of desert princelings. It glistened in the sunlight as though on the point of melting. The uniformed driver opened the rear door as they approached. Fawn was perfectly aware that Conquest was dazzled by its opulence.

'Luxury,' she confided, 'is not a matter of vulgar display or material excess, is it? I think of it as an investment, not in terms of money or quantity, but in beauty. For me it's heritage; a few exquisite possessions is all one needs, don't you think?'

Conquest gaped, nodded, unable to muster a cogent response. Pye, he realised, was holding out his hand to say goodbye. Before he could reciprocate, Fawn had looped her hand inside his left forearm to bring him round to face her. 'Promise you'll let us see the students' union when we come back. I'd love to see your students entertaining one another.'

Pye again sought Conquest's hand and shook it with the delicate grip of an expensive surgeon. 'Ah, yes!' he said, 'Fawn thinks youth will inherit the Earth. She's right, of course. But not yet awhile, not while it's still our plaything.'

'I was wondering,' said Conquest hesitantly, 'whether you might be willing to help us with our film studies provision.'

Pye looked at him with sharpened interest. For a moment he pursed his lips doubtfully. 'I'm always willing to help push the door open a little wider for the young. Perhaps you could write to me. Anything I feel able to do, I'd be glad to lend a hand.'

Fawn had already disappeared into the rear of the car. Now Pye followed. There was the faintest of muffled thumps as the chauffeur closed the door.

Conquest was wondering whether a contract of sorts had been sealed. Then something wonderful happened: Pye lowered the window. 'Rather short notice, I'm afraid, but come to the premiere of my latest thing. I'll have my office send a ticket and pass. There's a party afterwards. We can talk about your film school then.' He sat back and the window closed.

Now it was Angus Farthing's turn to bid Conquest farewell. 'Thanks for lending me the crutch. Useful things, crutches!' He presented it to him before limping around the rear of the car to get in beside the chauffeur.

'*Your mother-in-law!*' cried Conquest, thinking he'd forgotten her, and his wife.

Farthing shrugged and gave Conquest a sly look as though he'd seen him skewered by some seductive harpy and left to dry to a husk.

EIGHTEEN

Conquest watched as the Rolls-Royce swanked its way off the campus. Standing there, alone, dazzled, he felt suddenly bereft. Such charm, such gaiety! Sophisticates – that was what was missing in his life; the debonair *gaie savoir*!

As he made his way towards the marquee, Piers Hazlett came rushing out.

'Was Connie Pye *here*?' he cried like a lost soul. When he saw Conquest's expression, he knew the rumour was true. '*I missed him!*' He suppressed a groan of frustration. His whole body sagged and suddenly he looked utterly dishevelled. He had been waiting almost a week to hear from Pye's office about the rescheduling of his interview, and now he had missed an opportunity to buttonhole the man himself!

'What's the premiere?' Conquest wondered.

Hazlett's face turned from crushed to aghast. 'He invited *you*?'

'He did. Am I honoured?' asked Conquest in all innocence.

'*You are!* He only invites film people. They're coming from all over to be here!'

'Ah, well!'

Hazlett was discomposed. '*Why was he here? Ah*, because of Angus Farthing! That's the reason, isn't it?' He wasn't really consulting Conquest and didn't wait to hear his view on the matter. 'I'm desperate to reschedule an interview, and missed my chance! The fact is,' he confided, 'I'm told the son of the lead guitarist of King Wideboy graduated today and is here with his parents. I've been trying to find *them*! They're straining for cultural significance, you know.'

'King Wideboy…' said Conquest, pointing dreamily '…At the other end of the marquee.'

Hazlett made off in a sweat.

The first person Conquest ran into once he was back inside the VIP cordon was Derek Puttle. He felt a warm sense of gratitude towards him. Something, momentous, he was beginning to realise, had just occurred.

'Derek, that couple...?'

'The ones in the Roller?'

'Yes, the blue... The woman was Fawn Williams.'

'Oh, didn't you know? She's a film star. She's married to the filmmaker, Cornelius Pye.'

'Yes, he did say his name.'

Puttle still thought Conquest hadn't heard of him, 'He's famous, you know.'

Conquest nodded his acknowledgement, but didn't offer any comment. He was thinking of the lustrous sense of preciousness the couple had given off. They were feted, respected, objects of fascination for the Great Generality. He was as sensitive as the next man to the heady mix of glamour and wealth, and he was doubly impressed because *they had come*! They had out-shone Angus Farthing; they were of the stuff his university needed to be associated with. They shed an unearthly brilliance, and something of them had rubbed off on him! Here was the future, not Piers Hazlett and the Rising Left. Suddenly he realised he was leaning on the crutch. He straightened up and gifted the thing to Puttle.

'All things considered it went exceedingly well, Derek, thanks to you! But next year I'm extending your remit to cover the parents' end of the marquee. We can't have them fighting over the plated sandwiches.'

Deeper into the marquee he went. The crowds had hardly thinned at all and everyone had been drinking the caterer's wine for a good hour. On all sides there was the sound of raised voices. He caught sight of Perk helping himself from a table still laden with refreshments.

'Perk!' he called.

Perk's mouth was full and he had a sandwich of some description in his hand. Conquest felt emboldened. 'What we were discussing earlier,' he began without preamble. 'You're right: at some point – not necessarily now – I would like senate's backing to go public with a few ideas about the shape of the New University.'

Perk swallowed his mouthful of sandwich. 'I've been meaning to suggest one or two things myself, Cliff. We must attend to the basics.' He said this with great solemnity. 'Evolution, not revolution. If you want to re-organise, what about making the collection of our statistical information a stand-alone unit, separate from Human Resources, to sharpen up accountability? We all like to see the numbers; it's a matter of keeping a check on our behaviour. Instinctive behaviour will always betray us. Let's work on the granulation of our data. We need to attend to quotas without being seen to attend to them. I mean – to use a non-hierarchical figure of speech – we must reflect purple concerns!'

Conquest was used to obliqueness but this one baffled him. *'Purple concerns?'*

'Purple concerns *vis-à-vis* yellow concerns. They're complementaries, not binaries... In the spectrum, I mean. Binaries are all well and good but...' He made a vague gesture in the air as though binaries were a topic too large to be taken in present circumstances.

Conquest nodded at the remains of the sandwich in Perk's hand. 'You mean being even handed with vegans and carnivores... that sort of thing.'

'Ah, you may laugh, but that's exactly right. Look, the weather forecast is an excellent example: it's tempting to think more time should be spent on the detail in the southeast because that's where most people live. If, instead, weathermen – *and women* – concentrate their detail on the places where nobody lives, nobody feels left out. I just know things are being done in the right spirit when I can tell my wife what the weather is in Ormskirk.'

At this point Conquest realised that Perk was leaning solicitously in his direction at a more acute angle than normal and he wondered what he had been doing for the past hour. His encounter with Pye and Fawn Williams had lightened his mood utterly, making him feel exuberant and the world full of possibilities. Perk's influence was the absolute opposite and he recoiled. 'Look, Perk,' he said winningly, 'you and I know there's no real business for senate. The members were splendid scenery today; no need to make them come back next week. Why not postpone? Let's not allow the feeling to get abroad that senate's a rubber-stamping body.'

'I don't know, Cliff,' cautioned Perk. 'Certain things can't be trimmed. It's a slippery slope. There are certain shibboleths we must all respect.'

NINETEEN

Piers Hazlett had been busy making contacts. Derek, of King Wideboy, had assured him that he had seen the celebrity chef, Miles Longbourne, and his daughter, Satsuma, earlier in the afternoon. While scouring the VIP section of the marquee for them he observed Perk Hingley deep in conversation with Conquest. As he watched, Conquest moved away and almost immediately Professor Cronker who, as well as being the dean of the School of Science, was one of the two elected representatives of the academic staff on senate, had joined Perk. Hazlett continued to watch and a third member of senate, Alistair Vox, chief strategist and mouthpiece of the Institute of Progressive Fiscal, Educational and Social Policy, made his way towards them. Hazlett sensed a conspiracy, a feeling that was intensified when, on passing, a fourth member of senate, Fred Crannick, the local MP, was drawn into their discussion. Hazlett suspected they were complaining about Conquest. It still irked him that Conquest, and not he, had been invited to the premiere of *Confess, Undercover Girl!* He couldn't comprehend why he should have been favoured. It smacked of something he needed to know about. Something untoward was brewing, confirmed by the sight of this conspiratorial foursome. He made his way towards them.

'Ah, Piers!' cried Perk as he became aware of his approach.

'*Yon Cassius has a lean and hungry look,*' said Hazlett, giving the conspirators his famously boyish smile.

'Do we expect fireworks from the VC at senate,' demanded Vox in a stage whisper, 'or has he been frightened off?'

'Well, apparently so!' said Perk. '*Abstract generalities* just about describes Cliff's outlook at the moment. He says he wants to make the non-teaching parts of the university accountable to the students, but how I've no idea.' He rubbed his chin meditatively. 'He's mentioning student fees; it's pie in the sky as far as I'm concerned.'

Crannick cleared his throat noisily and meaningfully, and squinted to right and left as if to ensure they were not being overheard. '*Party discipline is everything!*' he announced threateningly. Crannick was an Old Labour stalwart, loyal lobby fodder for thirty years. In the higher reaches of the party, he was widely considered of no consequence.

Alistair Vox was more than ready to stir the pot. 'If he was contemplating changing the tuition fee, he *has to* bring it to senate! We must be prepared to talk out any attempt to detach the university from current funding arrangements.'

'Do we think…' wondered Perk, vaguely apprehensive for his own standing as chair of senate '…the VC might start something without consulting us? He's just floated the idea of postponing senate's next meeting.'

'I can tell you, gentlemen, that a wiring diagram has been seen,' said Professor Cronker in his dour brogue.

'A wiring diagram?' exclaimed Vox. 'Meaning what?'

'A new management structure. I saw it yesterday evening and it redefines more than thirty management roles!'

'I had a meeting with Conquest last week,' said Perk crossly, 'and he didn't mention a wiring diagram to me, or anything about a new management structure.'

'I know what I saw,' insisted Professor Cronker. 'It was pinned to the wall of his office'

Vox raised a warning finger. 'This is how private culture works. It circumvents and makes irrelevant the state organs of culture.'

Perk laughed nervously. 'I don't think we can call this university a state organ of culture.'

'Aye, and why not? It's the sort of thing the Russians would do,' said Cronker, as if that were reason enough.

'Collectivist terminology,' agreed Hazlett sagely, 'has the capacity to throw new light on old verities!'

Talk of collectivism stirred Fred Crannick. 'You're right, universities are the last bastion of a proper collectivist, state-funded public provision! It sounds as if Conquest aims to circumvent the normal checks and balances of public accountability.'

'We have to show solidarity with the collectivist impulse,' agreed Vox. 'Any hint of privatising provision would definitely be a breach!'

'He's no said anything about that,' said Cronker dismissively.

Alistair Vox's excitable state was not assuaged. 'From a wider viewpoint the private culture thing is definitely gathering momentum!'

'Well,' decided Cronker, his face set in grim determination, 'the politics here in England are none of my concern, but we don't want that sort of thing spreading to Scotland!'

'And what about the crocodile business?' said Hazlett, 'I hear the parents are making trouble. Nobody should be sent to Africa as a course requirement.'

'The Students Union's been warned about head injuries, but still we have a rugby club,' said Perk, rather warming to the theme.

'Aye, and rock climbing.'

'It's all linked to the manners of laissez-faire capitalism,' said Alistair Vox in full dialectical flow. 'We should get Arts Council Olaf over here. He talks to everyone, that's his job. Look, he's talking to that Spurling woman *right now*! He'll know how this private culture thing's spreading. The Arts Council is going to be absolutely central if we're going to turn the tide on it. I'll go and fetch him.'

Fred Crannick watched him go with a crazed gleam in his rheumy eyes '*Ah, hotheads!*' he exclaimed. 'It's bloody marvellous to see there are still a few in the party!'

'Quite right,' said Hazlett, rubbing his hands together in a business-like way. 'With people like Alistair leading the charge we'll soon have a social policy worth talking about.'

Perk felt moved to explain his outlook to Professor Cronker. 'Well, I can't say unifying theory has any business in *my* thinking. I don't believe anyone has a grand plan, do you?'

'Well, I can't speak for this side of the border, but north of it I'd say, definitely, *yes*!'

'Oh dear!' said Perk apologetically. 'Yes, I'm sorry, Alan, of course! Maybe that was a little presumptuous of me.'

'I'll no object to Unionist sympathies this side of the border,' said Professor Cronker magnanimously, 'but don't expect they'll be welcomed in Perth. I see a modicum of sense in what yon Alistair's saying, d'you not think?'

Cronker's admission of nationalist convictions had put Perk in something of a mental disarray, and he made another attempt to express his philosophical principles. 'It's the meat-and-two-veg folk that keep us safe, Alan. And humane elites, of course.'

At that moment Conquest suddenly reappeared. 'Ah, some of my most favourite senators!' he said. 'We are all but a museum of past possibilities, are we not?'

Perk was taken by surprise. He sensed Conquest's playful aspersion should be challenged, but before he could call him to account, Vox and Arts Council Olaf joined them.

'So, here come more, gathering where the pasture's greenest!' Conquest eyed Vox, his manner within a whisker of implying his displeasure that Vox had already discarded his academic gown.

'We were discussing private culture,' said Hazlett mischievously.

'Ah!' exclaimed Conquest, giving Perk a pointed glance. 'That seems to be today's mania. I'm sure there's something in it. Perhaps you'd give me a guided tour?'

'Oh, it's not a today thing,' said Hazlett, deploying that famously boyish smile. (A wolf in sheep's clothing if ever Conquest saw one). 'It's a coming thing, Cliff, and going to be an invaluable tool for critiquing institutions and their failures.'

'Marvellous!' exclaimed Conquest. 'I await its coming with baited breath! In the meantime, gentlemen, *seize the day*! I still see coleslaw sandwiches aplenty!' He gestured magnanimously to the buffet and moved on, leaving behind the perception that he was uncommonly ebullient and they had been toyed with.

Finally Perk broke the silence. 'Conquest's a little too trigger happy for my taste. I'm gratified to think there's a consensus that we keep an eye on him. I'll not agree to a postponement of next week's meeting of senate.'

'Quite right,' said Vox. 'He'll break cover soon enough.'

TWENTY

Still later, in yet another part of the marquee, semi-hidden behind a huge potted palm, another conspiracy was afoot. Nancy Spurling, considered by the Rising Left to be the doyen of the vulgarians of the Right, had buttonholed Sir Norman Fleet, the property developer. Sir Norman was thought to be her chief co-conspirator on senate. What was beyond doubt was that they were at ease with one another. Her trenchant way of dealing with the world was similar to his own. Sir Norman being Labour by instinct, it might seem odd to those unfamiliar with the picturesque by-ways of English politics that they were confederates, and plotting. Sir Norman's father had been a signalman at the great rail *Entrepôt* of Crewe, and some thought his attachment to Labour but a vestige of his upbringing as a supporter of Crewe Alexandra FC. Far from it! Others mistook his allegiance as strategic. Again, incorrect! At its core it was tribal, instinctual, ancient, allowing him to live with all manner of contradictions, such as happily conspiring with Nancy Spurling, who was in the throes of a complaint.

'This university only honours those on the Left. It's the same year in and year out. I thought Conquest took a balanced view of these things. Did you see Farthing's *Hamlet*?'

Sir Norman considered theatrical entertainment more than a stone's throw from Drury Lane little short of tourist fodder. 'No, can't abide Shakespeare togged up in modern dress. It's giving fish shoes as far as I'm concerned.'

'I found it painful. I understand he's planning to do *War and Peace* in a car park. The point is,' decided Nancy, 'Perk Hingley smuggled Hazlett onto senate when we weren't looking. Hazlett's the kind that prefers Mexican muralists to Stubbs and Gainsborough. It's the Rising Left flexing its muscles. It was bad enough having to listen to that toad Alistair Vox throwing his weight about. Did you know Vox is said to be the chief strategist of the Camlington faction?'

'Camlington faction? What's that?'

'They're the knitted-tie cabal at the heart of the Rising Left? They're formulating the latest astringent to be force-fed Labour to prepare it for power.'

Sir Norman looked baffled.

'Camlington's a compound of *Camden* and *Islington*; their politics are *witheringly* North London! As far as they're concerned, elitism's a dirty word. They've already taken possession of the Arts Council and are insisting on public funding for the arts going to all manner of shabby little projects in community halls where the money's spent on aerosols, tea bags and sugar paper. I was talking to Arts Council Olaf not long ago. He won't confirm it's a *diktat* from the top, but he doesn't deny it either. Meanwhile, the big institutions are dumbing-down so fast they've overtaken Saturday evening fare on Freeview as *loci* of asininity.'

'*Loci of what!?*' Sir Norman's cultural reference points, unlike Nancy's, were not the result of assiduously poring over the weekend's broadsheets, so he had little grasp of what she was talking about. Nevertheless, she sparked a rare moment of introspection: 'Perk Hingley has me down as the sort of chump who likes brick wallpaper.'

'The Rising Left is claiming the universities as its own. So much for them being bulwarks of free speech!'

Sir Norman was fired by talk of free speech. 'The government's supine, of course. They're only interested in the sort of trades that work on my building sites: the thirty-thousand-a-year blokes.'

'Time we held Clifford's feet to the fire. He's an ambitious chap. I'm sure you can find something to dangle.'

'Ah, well, Lord N'Garbi is at work behind the scenes. He's going to give Clifford more visibility. There's a role for him on the Shadow Secretary of State's advisory committee that will put him in exactly the right spot to influence the way the National Executive develops policy on Higher Education.' Sir Norman's thoughtful expression deepened. 'It would be helpful if we had a clearer idea what Perk and his crew are up to.'

'Didn't I see Conquest's new PA earlier? Eunice Something-or-other. She has a ringside seat. Dressed like that there's no way she's North London tottie. She must be around here somewhere.'

'Yes, she's quite a study,' mused Sir Norman.

'Where does she come from?'

'Blessed if I know. Somewhere near Gatwick? Horsham? Conquest's old PA lost the plot; kept indenting for shredding machines. She had five or six of them before anybody noticed.'

'What was she shredding?'

'Paper, mainly. I tell you, Nancy, it's a topsy-turvy world out there.'

'What about that man Puttle who marched us up and down the hill? That mace of his looked Masonic and he's over there. I say we have a word with him.'

'I don't know, Nancy,' said Sir Norman. 'Aren't we in danger of undermining the vice-chancellor if we go behind his back?'

'Don't be ridiculous. This is how journalists work all the time.'

Their attempt to extract inside information from Derek Puttle was a flop. He was not the sort for institutional intrigue. Nor would talking to Eunice have been any more helpful, had they found her, such was her loyalty to Conquest. The unlikely event of her being torn limb from limb by wild horses would not have induced her to speak of the vice-chancellor's tea drinking habits, let alone his thoughts on major issues of policy. And anyway, she had already returned to her post, as her devotion to her duties dictated. She had several letters to type before she left for home. As she typed, she glowed with the thought that she alone, of all the people that work for Conquest, had his best interests at heart. Her duty was to sustain him and prevent him from being over-whelmed by the demands of a hostile and unfeeling world!

Dear Jane Dace, she wrote, *please pass on my thanks to the Shadow Secretary of State for his invitation to advise him concerning the future of Higher Education under a future Labour government. Unfortunately, I am at the moment indisposed due to the burden of my duties, especially with the new academic year imminent. I am sure you understand that the burdens of a vice-chancellor are such that....*

TWENTY-ONE

Conquest carried off the rest of the day in the avuncular, learned and faintly distant spirit that was the very essence of vice-chancellordom. What a change of mood! How bracing had been his brush with real celebrity! When all but the last stranglers had left the marquee, he felt able himself to make an exit. Standing for a moment of reflection at the entrance to the marquee he saw Tommy Ballantyne some distance away, taking his ease in front of Emirates House, home of the newly named Department of Sustainable Energy Engineering. In contravention of the university's ordinance that designated the campus a no-smoking zone, Ballantyne was enjoying a cigarette. Conquest strolled over.

Ballantyne, the university's director of finance, had joined University London Central at the same time as Conquest. He was a big, solid man with a demeanour of an old-fashioned police inspector, although the rimless glasses also suggested a man inclined towards the importance of small details.

Ballantyne and Conquest were a team, had been for many years. Their success was built on the mutual acknowledgement that each supplied the other's wants. Ballantyne was a skilled nuts-and-bolts financial manager. In both their previous collaborations he had shown himself to be an assiduous student of spreadsheets and the deft ploys of accountants. He rooted out spendthrifts and those engaging in petty larceny in unruffled haste. He was already fully accepted as a member of the informal drinking club of the senior administrative officers of the university that met in nearby pubs, an association that would have dissolved instantly had Conquest tried to join. Membership gave Ballantyne an unparalleled chance to marvel at the foibles of those who ranked alongside him in the management of the university. Unlike Conquest, he was a man for the shadows, watching for the miscreant with a sharp eye. Conquest was perfectly sensible of the fact that none of his plans or ambitions were possible without someone working for him with the rare disposition of Ballantyne. That being the case, he loved him like a brother.

Ballantyne took a last, meditative drag on the cigarette. 'There's been fire and brimstone talked all afternoon in that tent of yours,' he said, giving the marquee a nod.

'Ah!' said Conquest.

'You've got tongues wagging.'

'Really?'

'Members of senate getting agitated; senior staff a-twitter. What's going on, Cliff? Want to tell me about it?'

Conquest's eyes were fixed on an abstract something in the far distance. 'Come back to my office, Tommy, and I'll tell you what I have in mind. Everything's suddenly fallen into place.'

TWENTY-TWO

Conquest poured Ballantyne a large malt whisky. Then he took the wiring diagram from the umbrella stand and laid it out on the floor in front of the sofa where Ballantyne was sitting. While Ballantyne studied the diagram, Conquest paced up and down the length of the picture window with the air of a man about to hold forth. After a while, Ballantyne looked up. 'Well, Cliff, what's all this?' He sat back with the whisky balanced on his lap, expectant about – and wary of – what he was about to hear.

'Tommy, we can't stand still. If we do, we die. What we're going to do is turn University London Central into a laboratory for new ideas about university education.'

Ballantyne laughed, thinking this was a fine joke, until he realised that Conquest was serious. Then he gulped and reached for his cigarettes, despite knowing he couldn't light up.

'I've known what I wanted, but been at a loss to see how to proceed. Suddenly, opportunity's smiled on us.' Conquest gestured impatiently at his wiring diagram. 'I've been toying with this for months. I can now see it's no good. It won't cut it, giving a load of hopeless freeloaders fancy new titles!'

'I notice I'm destined to become the *Chief Financial Officer*,' noted Ballantyne wryly.

'Yes, won't do, will it? We have to do something much more fundamental. There's more: only by the application of practical solutions to a public sector in need of reform will we of the Centre Left prove Labour worthy of being elected. I spend my weekends in Wolverhampton and I can tell you the North London quibblers of the Rising Left will never lead us back to power! Look, Tommy, reforming Higher Education is one of the very few ways we can show the political dreamers and theorists the way to go. As I see it, the universities are the true battleground for the Centre Left. We must take the initiative; our ideas must be entirely innovative!'

'Everyone says that,' said Ballantyne.

Conquest waved that aside. 'Let's take funding. Our aim in the medium term must be to make university education free. That will throw open the doors of University London Central to the best and brightest from across the world! London and England are insignificant in the greater scheme of things. We must find new sources of funding to replace student fee income.'

'That's a hell of a lot of money you're losing, Cliff,' responded Ballantyne. '*A hell of a lot!*' He paused, dazed. 'In fact, it's more or less the whole bloody lot!'

'If we don't set ourselves targets, we don't change, do we, Tommy? I'll set up a student fee reduction taskforce. Even better, I'll make it the opening chapter of the book I'm planning to write. We'll get our great industrialists to endow subject areas, specialisation by specialisation.'

'Cliff, there aren't any great industrialists. We've sold everything.'

'Then American and Chinese industrialists will fill the breach. We'll make this university a kind of free port for intellectual ideas. It'll be magnificent!'

Ballantyne's scepticism was untouched. 'You can't rewrite the rulebook without consulting senate! I mean, our track record's good enough but we've only been here a year. Another disruption right now with the digital hub in the offing?' He shook his head.

'No, you're quite right; I don't want to take anything to senate, they're a bloody shower. So, they think there's something in the wind and it's set them squabbling amongst themselves. Good, it'll keep them occupied!'

Ballantyne gave him a long, dubious look. Being first and foremost a chartered accountant, he was a man for rules and rectitude and, after many years working with Conquest, was wary of his wilder flights of fancy. 'Then it can't be done, Cliff. It's that simple.'

'Ah, but I'm thinking about something practical, on a small scale.' He indicated the wiring diagram with his toe. 'Not a superficial reshuffle like this! We may not have industrialists, but what we do have is a film director called Cornelius Pye! What I have in mind is a proper film school, one that's sponsored by an actual filmmaker. Pye is a world-famous, money-making machine, and I'm convinced he wants to do good works!'

'But Cliff, we don't have a film school, or anything like!' Ballantyne objected.

'Ah, but we will have. I'm going to create one!'

'And how in the name of all that's holy are you going to do *that*?'

At this point Conquest sat down opposite him in the steel and leather chair of American design, an almost mesmeric intensity to his gaze. 'We put the boundaries of our departments in question; they're like potholes on the road to true learning! Start with the dead wood! We have – *supposedly* – a film studies course in the Department of Media and Communications. It's devoted to something called *cinema concrete* and, according to registry, film studies is an option no undergraduate student has taken in the last umpteen years. They have six research students writing theses about *cinema concrete* supervised by a professor called McWhelk, and a half-time lecturer. It's being subsidised by the rest of the department!

'In the Department of English there's an undersubscribed creative writing option with a senior lecturer, Dr Alice Shellbrooke, in post. The only thing it seems she encourages is poetry, and mighty *puerile stuff* it is too! Shall I read you one of her poems?'

Ballantyne shrugged and took a sip of his whisky. Conquest went over to his desk and picked up a printout. Much to Ballantyne's surprise he launched into a full-blown recitation.

Krazy

'Mellifluous notes wing the welkin
And with fragrant fanfare,
Assail the harmoniphile.
Angel fingers atwang upon a lute of gold –
How sweet,

How sweet.
Oh, that such phonetic beauty should emit
From so invidious an instrument,
By the hand of so mean a maestro!
Ah, the delight that came to my ears…
Ah-h-h, the bitterness that twitted my eyes
Oh, the sweet sourness of it all.
So low a life,
So exalted a gift.
Ah, me!'

Ballantyne was momentarily struck dumb, as much by the vigour of Conquest's delivery as the poem's import.

Conquest sighed, exasperated. 'Do we harbour such stuff?' he exclaimed.

'Where did you get *that*?'

'Eunice extracted it from Alice Shellbrooke's website.'

'Okay, Cliff, what you have here is two academic backwaters,' decided Ballantyne with a calming motion of his hand. 'It's none of management's concern if the academic departments think they're significant. You can't stop them moving their staffing resources around as they think fit as long as they don't exceed their overall staffing allocation.'

'That's it exactly: *stagnant* backwaters!' He gesticulated at his wiring diagram. 'This Professor McWhelk is, in academic terms, senior to the head of department. He did his stint as head of department a decade ago and my guess is that since then he's been drifting!'

'Ah, yes, Malcolm McWhelk!' mused Ballantyne. 'He's been enquiring about enhanced voluntary redundancy.'

'Has he indeed! What came of it?'

'Insufficient enhancement.'

Conquest scoffed. 'Pfff, let's hope he's the man for the job! My plan is to create a film school by expanding the range of film courses – *an initiative McWhelk is perfectly capable of leading* – and buttress the offering by bringing it together with creative writing, thus providing the teaching resources necessary for directing, screenwriting and the rest! With enough institutional support, and external funding, it would be something with a real effect in the world of work, *not* theoretical posturing!' He came across to Ballantyne and again sat down opposite him. 'Cornelius Pye is the perfect prototype for what I have in mind. Right now, he wants access to our special collections for one of his researchers. He's more than willing to help. With a bit of persuasion, I think he might make a significant financial contribution.'

'Have you actually *met* him?'

'*Of course!* He was here today! He's invited me to the premiere of his latest film!' He saw that Ballantyne's resistance was lessening. 'Look, I don't need to take a small reshuffle of modules and associated teaching resources to senate. Good Lord, senate would be drowning in minutia if I did! It's a matter for academic board.'

Begrudgingly, Ballantyne decided that Conquest might have the germ of an idea worth pursuing. What's more he could see that a comparatively small-scale intervention of the kind he was proposing was unlikely to cause as much aggravation as had some of his schemes. 'So, none of this' – he waved his hand over the wiring diagram – 'is in the papers for the next meeting of senate?'

'No, the agenda's so empty I've suggested to Perk we postpone.' He slapped Ballantyne heartily on the knee. 'You know I don't reveal my hand all in one go. I'll take it to senate when I've landed something big and solid from Pye. You'll see, senate will think it's good stuff and give me *carte blanche* without really knowing what they're agreeing to. If Pye doesn't come across, no matter. I'll try something else. As soon as Professor McWhelk turns up, I'll put to him and his head of department the idea of turning his little conceit into a proper film school. Then we'll see if he's up for a challenge! It'll do him the world of good. From what I can see, he's been stuck in idle for years! If we don't lead the revolution somebody else will! The world of Higher Education is ripe for a radical make-over!'

TWENTY-THREE

Leicester Square was in a seething state of carnival excitement. The living statues had moved up from Trafalgar Square *en masse*. The red carpet had been laid on the east side of the square, leading to the cinema's black, cavernous entrance. An exuberant crush of tourists and fans was marshalled behind barriers snaking up from Charing Cross Road and into the square. Black security guards prowled the red carpet from drop-off to the cinema. They – the guards – would not have disgraced the court of the Sun King.

Having very little idea what to expect, Conquest had arrived early. At the first checkpoint he had been directed to a second at the northern end of the red carpet, where the pass and ticket delivered to him by courier that morning were checked against a list and someone was informed of his arrival by mobile. He lingered there, somewhat dazed, as the parade of celebrities made their way towards him from the drop-off. It was indeed, he thought, like watching a throwback to a more deferential age when the populous gladly turned out to greet a gilded aristocracy. A striking young woman – Conquest had no idea who she was – came up the carpet in the company of two men in eveningwear. She was the focus of both the press photographers – who slung their cameras like six-shooters – and a forest of up-held mobiles. A rolling barrage of flashes agitated the details of the scene and bleached out the first intimations of evening as she made her way towards the cinema. For Conquest, it was an induction into the flaming, Dionysian exaltation of stardom that flickered round that youthful figure, exquisitely shaped by couturier magic, elongated into a mythical formalist being. The way she responded to those pressed against the other side of the barrier was entrancing. Laughing, skimming along her side of the barrier, she accepted their adoration unafraid, without pomp, stepping back, posing for the cameras, stepping forward, always moving on between the two men in their sober eveningwear.

Then a security guard was urging Conquest to enter the cinema. A crowd was backing up behind him and reluctantly he gave up his vantage point. As he made his way across the foyer a voice cut through the hubbub.

'Professor Conquest!'

He turned to find a young woman approaching him.

'I'm Poppy Trench. I'm researching the Goldman papers for Mr Pye.'

'Ah, yes!' He shook her hand. 'How is it going?'

'Not bad, actually. I'm to look after you until we get to the reception. Come, I'll take you to your seat.'

Inside the auditorium it was hot and noisy. Poppy led him directly to their places. The voices all around him were so animated it was as though the audience had mislaid the reason for being there. It was not until the lights began to dim – so slowly it was as if nightfall was coming on – that quite suddenly it assembled itself into a single, purposeful being, intent on immersion in the spectacle about to unfold. As for *Confess, Undercover Girl!* a great deal of it engulfed Conquest in a shapeless kaleidoscope, so distracted was he by his thoughts. There were several charismatic actors, one of whom might possibly have been the young woman he had seen on the red carpet. There was also a Roman marble dug up in a vineyard, smuggled to Hong Kong, then rescued by a trio of archaeologists with some connection Conquest didn't understand to an aristocratic goof who was highly placed in a UNESCO type organisation infiltrated by Chinese spies trying to undermine the European accord on the protection of cultural artefacts. Entwined with this was a romantic sub-plot: a sly comedy played out between the three archaeologists, which was both compelling and charming. This, at least, was the way Conquest explained it to himself when he thought about it the following day.

The end credits were greeted with wild applause and for the first time he saw Pye, down at the front, being urged to his feet to accept the acclaim. Apparently, those around him were the chief protagonists in the making of the movie, for at his urging they too climbed to their feet to accept their share of the plaudits. The audience stood, the applause rising to a crescendo. Conquest found himself standing, quite caught up in the enthusiasm. It was a collective moment of joyful innocence, the kind of joyful innocence, it struck him, from which he was forever exiled. What *he* did was for the students of his university, and for them alone; for their educational betterment. It was not in the nature of things that he would ever experience such a moment of joyful accord with them.

For me it is always at a distance; a figurehead, forever struggling with those who would, in dribs and drabs, defraud them of the education they deserve.

Poppy was laughing. She, too, was on her feet. 'That was fun, wasn't it?' she said. 'Come on, let's get ahead of the crowd. There's a car waiting to take us to the reception.'

The reception in the ballroom of the Park Lane Hotel was no less tumultuous, Pye and his entourage basking in their moment of glory. The women flitted here and there like gorgeous dragonflies. Conquest expected to be overlooked, to feel as though he was an outsider, but not a bit of it. Fawn Williams sought him out almost instantly and took him in hand, chaffing him in her charming, seductive way.

'No coleslaw sandwiches,' she said at one point, in a voice that Conquest found positively alluring.

Pye, too, had time for him, speaking positively about offering him help with what he was firmly calling 'your film school'. Conquest felt he was almost drowning in kindness, doubtless aided by the copious draughts of champagne that came his way.

'A great success, great fun. I enjoyed your film tremendously.'

'So, I haven't lost my grip?' said Pye.

Conquest was caught off-balance. 'Not at all, not at all,' he replied, disconcerted that Pye could possibly have doubts – and share them with him – in the midst of such a resounding success.

'My detractors accuse me of making candyfloss cinema.'

'It's just envy, I'm sure.'

'I don't read reviews, so I couldn't really tell you what it means.' Pye smiled, suddenly a little careworn. 'That's a lesson I learnt long ago.'

'I quite understand.'

Eventually, things took a turn towards the sentimental melancholy of parting. The crowd was thinning and even those around Pye were talking about 'making a move'. Reluctantly, Conquest realised the moment of ecstatic mutuality that, even as an outsider, he had found intensely stimulating, was at an end. He announced his intention to depart and expressed his gratitude. Fawn walked with him towards the street entrance.

'You must keep Connie to his word,' she said, clutching his arm. 'You understand, he's so much to do, he over-promises.'

Conquest nodded understandingly. She had said it with such shining honesty that he felt a pang of guilt that his film school was little more than the rudiments of an idea. 'Do you think he might stretch to financial aid; something solid that will allow us to help the students; supply them with the proper resources?'

She laughed. 'Why not? It looks like this movie is going to be his greatest success. And you're a charitable organisation, are you not?'

Conquest laughed too, at the happy thought of University London Central's charitable status.

'Do you like music?' she asked, apparently innocent of the thought that the question invited but one answer. 'We're having our annual music festival at Thieves the weekend after next. Why don't you come up and join us! I expect it'll be quite exciting. Connie gets all his friends to play. Our marquee won't be as big as yours, but then there won't be quite as many of us.'

'I'm sorry,' said Conquest, 'did you say *Thieves*?"

'Yes, Thieves is our place in Norfolk. Strange name, I know. Sounds like a joke, but it's the manor house of Thieves Cross, near Sandringham. Lovely countryside. You'll enjoy yourself. It'll be a break from all your hard work.'

All too soon she had bid him goodbye and he had pushed through the doors into the street. The pavement glisten with rain. He lingered for a while. As others came out after him the ballroom's exuberant atmosphere spilt out onto the pavement for a brief moment and he was unwilling to depart for his *pied-à-terre* at Butler's Wharf.

In the ballroom, Pye was in the company of Avril Morgan, one of his producers. Morgan was a big, burly American, and a long-standing stalwart amongst the financial backers of Pye's films. He towered over Pye physically to the same degree that he was indispensable to the smooth running of Pye's productions. There was something in the way they stood together, at ease and without speaking, neither looking at the other, that typified their relationship. They watched as Fawn made her way back towards them through the thinning crowd, a beatific smile on her face.

'Who is that funny-looking guy Fawn was paying so much attention to?' asked Morgan.

Pye stroked his chin, his face expressionless. 'He runs a university. He wants me to help with his film school.'

'Ah, you mean cough up!'

'Fawn thinks it would be a good idea. Part of paying my dues.'

Morgan gave him a doubtful glance. 'Those places burn other people's cash. I've seen it back home.'

'He's been helpful over the Goldman papers. Stanley Goldman's lawyers couldn't stop his widow donating the Goldman archive to his university.'

'So I heard. Strange woman! You want me to look into him and his university? You'd have to think of it as an investment.'

Pye pondered for a moment. 'Maybe. I don't know. I'd like some advice, I suppose. The tax implications might be useful. Perhaps while you're here…'

'Leave it with me. Meanwhile, keep him at arm's length. Otherwise…' There was something of a warning in the way the big man left the sentence unfinished that spoke of his distrust of importuning strangers.

Outside the ballroom, on the rainy pavement, everyone was looking for taxis and Conquest started to walk along Piccadilly. Soon he was alone in the damp, dark night.

This is what it is to be in awe of something! he thought as he made his way eastwards, regretful that every step was exiling him from something magnificent. It made him quite emotional to think of the fraternal, unconditional love he had felt on every side. It hadn't all been directed at Pye; it had radiated outwards from everyone there to everyone else, all aglow, as it were, with their sense of a collective achievement. It was the '*I love you*' moment in an American movie without the cloying sentiment. He felt inspired to think that he could, in his own way, do something equally magnificent at University London Central. There was no thought of being an impostor, no accusation of spawning Frankenstein monsters.

TWENTY-FOUR

The transformation was complete. Conquest had abandoned the unworkable desire to alter everything.

I see now that renewing Higher Education is a grand political project and for that my book must come first. As far as my university is concerned, I can put aside the immense difficulties implied by a single moment of revolutionary transformation. Thanks to Cornelius Pye, I can see it had become an unnecessary burden. Now my aim is clear. We need to change and to make my point I'll create something small that will be an example to the whole university. Thanks to him, my overwhelming sense of predicament has eased. These two men I am ushering towards the upright chairs facing my desk are unaware of the sudden illumination that has come to me! If they were, they might think my brush with celebrity has turned my head! Ah, but I am well aware of the star struck syndrome! I prided myself that I'm above the weakness such a phrase implies. I know the phenomenon; it's a commonplace enough story, but no, I have not succumbed! I have been gloriously enabled!

The two men across the desk from Conquest were Professor McWhelk, exponent of *cinema concrete*, and Dr Albert Pocock, his head of department. Both were on research leave and had been called in especially for a meeting with their vice-chancellor. McWhelk looked surly, Pocock uneasy. Conquest's rule was *forewarned is forearmed*, but he had purposefully enquired no further about McWhelk's academic interests, or his relationship with his head of department. He wanted to assess the man in person and discover why he had recommended turning away the Goldman archive.

McWhelk was somewhat older than his head of department, but, nonetheless, he looked more youthful than he. This effect was achieved by a slender figure, a full head of hair, somewhat *bouffant*, and possibly dyed, a face almost entirely unlined, except for furrows at the corners of his mouth denoting disdain. His skin was uncannily pale, as though, far from having spent time in sunny climes, he had been stored in a cupboard all summer. His clothes achieved an appearance of à *la mode* in existentialist black: austere, utilitarian, in a way that spoke of highbrow objections to the passing whims of fashion. Not for nothing was he known by his colleagues as the Prince of Darkness.

'If we are to set up a film studies research centre it would be entirely illogical if it were not devoted to *cinema concrete*,' declared McWhelk, in response to Conquest's benign opening words of enquiry about the possibility of developing a film studies research centre around the Goldman papers. '*Cinema concrete* is what we teach. Nay, we espouse *cinema concrete*! We are one of the world's principle centres for the advancement of *cinema concrete*. That's why students come here; bourgeois cinema is of no interest to them. Goldman and fellow-travellers constitute the antithesis of *cinema concrete*!'

If I'm not mistaken, Conquest thought, *this man is an instance of the polemical guru and an attempt at intellectual drubbing is in the offing.*

'It is the frame that interests us; the optics and mechanics of delivering that frame – the logic of illusion, if you will – rather than movement *per se*,' continued McWhelk. 'That is why "movie" is a misnomer. We eschew the term "movie"; a word that *exactly* –' here he raised a forefinger in a gesture of pedagogic absolutism – '*exactly* identifies the deception that marks out bourgeois cinema's false consciousness. The ambition of *cinema concrete* is nothing less than the abolition of the codes that have made cinema what it is; its habits, discourse and institutions. We dismantle the screen as the space of illusion and conjoin the lens with the eye of the beholder, a beholder reborn as active, *critical* participant in the spectacle!' He laughed softly and triumphantly as if he had articulated a beautiful, self-evident truth.

The odour of sanctity hung heavily in the air. The tenor of what Conquest had heard was far from unprecedented in his experience. He rather admired the academic thwarting, but at every word he had resolved afresh he was having none of it!

This McWhelk is a species of senior academic whose specialism has narrowed to a final redoubt, which he guards like a wounded beast at bay. He doubtless muscled his way to seniority by proselytising about this fatuous dead-end. It's so self-evidently ridiculous, I feel almost entitled to say so out loud. Extemporise reasonableness!

'Gentlemen, have we not been presented with the germ of an idea? Is not a film studies research centre with broader aims exactly what we should have at this university? The Goldman archive has been here hardly any time at all, yet already an important film director is requesting access. That is precisely the kind of external relationship a film studies research centre would allow us to cultivate!'

'And who,' said McWhelk in challenging tones, 'is this film director, may I ask?'

'Cornelius Pye.'

'*Ah!*' He gave a sardonic snort of laughter. 'But, *you understand*, this is candyfloss cinema! It is not something any serious institution intellectually invested in global *cinema concrete* would countenance for more than a moment. He uses film stars and all manner of illusionistic nonsense to tell commercial tales devoid of scruple, reflexive nakedness or ethical intent, never mind considerations of truth to materials! Its successful suppression of other narrative forms oppresses the disenfranchised!'

Conquest coolly examined the two men sitting on the other side of his desk. He was certain McWhelk's theories would be inviolably hermetic and he had no intention of arguing with him on his home territory. The head of department was blithely disengaged, confident he was superfluous to the discussion. There was clearly history here, Conquest thought, and – *Good God!* – this man McWhelk was quite oblivious of the power dynamics at work in the meeting. He laughed with a mildness that should have warned McWhelk, as anyone with even the slightest knowledge of Conquest's reputation would have been, that he was standing somewhere high and exposed with no security barriers to protect him, and the man on the other side of the desk had no compunction about pushing him off.

'Professor McWhelk,' said Conquest, 'I do believe your enthusiasm has caught my interest; an opportunity to widen my horizons! Perhaps you would allow me to see some of your recent *cinema concrete* research outcomes. I understand you edit its journal. I'm sure it's illuminating and of great interest.'

The man blandly, self-satisfiedly nodded his agreement.

'Clearly,' added Conquest suavely, 'the theoretical complexities of the field I've wandered into are greater than I had imagined.'

Now it was Dr Pocock's turn to laugh. It was the sly laugh of someone well acquainted with backtracking before McWhelk's pulverising logic. The whiff of disaffection about it made Conquest turn his attention to him.

Bert Pocock had been raised to the headship of the Department of Media and Communications at the end of the previous academic year. In a department of busy, research-active senior staff it was sometimes the case that a fill-in candidate was elevated to the headship, only to fulfil the role as a kind of proxy for more senior colleagues. The qualifications were to be not very dynamic, reliable – hopefully – and able to steer a steady course on a bearing determined by the professors. Pocock was only a senior lecturer, which suggested to Conquest that *his* professors had identified him as just such a proxy. His ears stuck out and his pudgy face sported the steady-state look of five days' growth of beard. It turned a weak chin and jowls into a region of sand dunes unevenly covered with a grey grizzle of marram grass. As Conquest appraised the man, he marvelled that it was an effect his local ASDA in Wolverhampton sold, not one, but several electrical devices to achieve. His assessment was that Pocock was probably awkward and unworldly, a reliable teacher, possibly fated to be eternally passed over as more ambitious colleagues jostled for advancement around him. Conquest did not detect in him any great love for McWhelk, or the slightest academic loyalty to *cinema concrete*.

Doesn't McWhelk realise that if the university insists on changed priorities, his head of department will abandon him to his fate? This ideological fraud has been intimidating his colleagues for years with his cinema concrete. *I rather admire his purblind bravery; he could have caved in to my wishes, but no! The man is willing to be a martyr for* cinema concrete, *no doubt about it. Even now he does not see an executive directive is heading his way.*

'As for film studies,' Conquest began portentously, 'I'm going to ask your head of department to put a paper together for my consideration.' He turned an encouraging smile on Pocock. 'I think to enhance our film studies offering we need – as a first step, you understand – to develop a broader portfolio of film studies modules at both undergraduate and postgraduate levels. Let's be ambitious: I'm thinking of a film school! I'm certain there are prospective students out there seeking all kinds of skills, and I rather feel there's an opportunity for us to provide them. Bert, for this academic year, you need to be thinking in terms of an expanded range of film-related modules for the second semester. And for next year, I would like to see a proposal that allows your media degree to be majored in film studies... all aspects of film studies. I'm thinking you could do with some help with narrativity. We'll move resources around to make that possible.' He saw McWhelk had blenched as he laid out his proposal. 'I'm sure my plan has legs, so let's set out and see where we get to!'

Conquest beamed. McWhelk looked sullen and discomforted as the realisation took hold that he was being co-opted to supervise, perhaps even teach, courses of study to which he was intellectually opposed. Pocock, being a good institutional man and spared his colleague's ideological baggage, was a willing enough tool of Conquest's instructions. He rose to his feet with the vim of a man given an unexpected opportunity to shine, or experiencing, perhaps, a sneaking sense of glee at the discomfort Conquest's instructions would mean for his senior colleagues.

TWENTY-FIVE

Professor McWhelk was contemptuous of those whose horizon encompassed little more than the local politics of department and university, and he left the meeting with a feeling that his precious project, which he saw as a global crusade, needed support from on high to save it from institutional meddling. His recourse was to Alistair Vox, senior strategist at InProFESPol, a long time fellow-traveller whose politics were his own, and who, in turn, thought *cinema concrete* was a vital re-statement of the cinematic arts.

'Alistair,' said McWhelk in a world-weary voice, once they had exchanged greetings, 'I'm forever troubled by the ghastly politics of this bloody university. I'd love to take the *cinema concrete* project elsewhere but for the moment I have to make it work here. They're trying to get me to contribute to some God-awful ideas about film studies that Conquest is promoting. It's totally mainstream multiplex ideas for idiots. Not even a passing familiarity with a single concept later than 1950! *Really!* Could you have a word with Professor Hingley? I was at a conference with him some time back and he seemed very supportive of what we're doing with *cinema concrete*. I rather think he might stick his oar in if he was told it was under threat. He understands the cultural politics better than most.'

'*Oh God,* it's this private culture syndrome raising its foul head!' commiserated Vox. 'Leave it with me; I'll have a word.'

Thus it was that Perk Hingley came to hear of McWhelk's stand for *cinema concrete*. So moved was he, he went as far as an exchange of emails with him promising he'd do his bit to save *cinema concrete* from the impositions of mainstream cinema. Constrained from direct action by his role as chair of senate, he reached out to the cultural mandarins of internationalism. Here allies were found and, in due course, from distant parts, opinions supportive of *cinema concrete* began to filter back to the United Kingdom.

TWENTY-SIX

It was Poppy Trench's third day bringing order to the Goldman archive. A significant improvement was evident in the special collections corridor. Despite the strictures about the corridor being kept clear as an emergency exit, a table had been provided to aid in the identification and sorting of the myriad pieces of text. Most of the archive boxes had gone and the shelves were beginning to have an orderly appearance. Graham Lester, the research student Poppy had found working there when she first visited had, in effect, become her assistant. He had read the opening sections of the screenplay she had put together from the sources she had previously consulted and enthusiastically committed to dividing his time between working for her and writing up his thesis.

There was a moment, early on her second day, when Poppy had begun to think that fully cataloguing Goldman's papers was a possibility. Then she found a large envelope stuffed with Post-its. Her heart sank. She could imagine the Post-its stuck to a wall, a constantly changing bank of parts, each one with a snatch of dialogue, a plot idea or the revision of an existing one. The variables they implied appalled her and changed her mind about the scale of their endeavours.

After that setback their search was low on rewards until Graham Lester found a fragment of text that corroborated, and provided dialogue for, the episode that Mavis Goodenough had describe to Poppy on her visit to Jaywick. They tried to flesh out later scenes, but what happened next remained a mystery until, late on that third morning, Poppy came across two pages of text stapled together. This is what she read:

... shots of frenetic activity in the offices of the Van Holt Production Company. Voice-over: 'That morning the word did the

rounds: He's coming in, the enfant terrible *is coming in! Lionel Armstrong himself is about to descend from his hilltop rental!'*

The announcement causes a thrill of anticipation amongst the ranks of the PAs and their assistants, who all vow they would have dressed differently had they known, for isn't this the actor who electrified as Colman Porter, Riviera cat burglar and heartthrob, in Deepest Indigo; *and whose* Hamlet *on the New York stage had cast the prince as a despairing, existentialist shapeshifter, a performance acclaimed as the defining interpretation of the decade? When Van Holt is informed of his imminent arrival, he begrudgingly clears half an hour in this schedule, that's how important he considers Lionel Armstrong to the success of* All In The Head.

Armstrong cuts a raffish figure reclined on the couch in the private office where Van Holt meets important visitors. He comes straight to the point.

'I've come to the conclusion – this is a most peculiar state of affairs – that the house you've provided me with is haunted.'

Van Holt closes his eyes as though meditating, juggling a pencil between his fingers. At last he speaks: 'Max Brinkmeyer has had guests staying there, off and on, for fifteen years, and not one has ever mentioned ghosts.'

Armstrong looks indifferent to the experience of Max Brinkmeyer's guests. 'I see! I've hardly settled in and I'm making unreasonable demands, is that it?'

Van Holt smiles. 'No, no, Lionel, if you have reason to complain… We can't have your sleep disturbed.'

'It's not that. It doesn't clatter around or make ghostly noises.' *He pulls a face of gleeful disgust.* 'It's the poo on the sofas.' *Van Holt sits up, suddenly rigid.* 'What, on those white leather sofas?'

'It's perched there like a kind of insult, twice now in the past four days.'

Van Holt is disbelieving. 'Lionel, are you sure some animal isn't coming in off your yard? I don't know; a racoon or some such?'

'It would have to open and close the patio door. Anyway, are there any animals left in Los Angeles except humans and rats? Of the two, it doesn't look like some piddling rodent left it; it's human-sized.'

'I'm sure —'

'It's there in the morning... when Lorraine starts.'

'Well, Loraine wouldn't do something like that, surely? It must be some kind of infestation.'

'Yes, exactly, a ghost infestation!'

Van Holt snaps his pencil with constraint. 'Okay, what am I to do about it?'

'Get a ghost catcher; see if it can be trapped. There's plenty of ghosts been laid to rest in Hollywood!'

'Okay, Lionel, a ghost catcher!' says Van Holt. 'Fine! I'll see if I can find you a professional ghost catcher. Is that all right?'

'Thank you, Mr Van Holt. I appreciate your assistance. Now...' Armstrong heaves a battered, much-thumbed document filleted with numerous Post-its from a grubby rucksack '...can we move on to this new script you had delivered yesterday?'

Van Holt's face takes on a decidedly disagreeable look.

It seemed reasonable to Poppy that this might follow on from what they already had. She had nothing better, so she put aside her misgivings and added the scene.

TWENTY-SEVEN

Having sent Pocock and McWhelk away with their instructions, Conquest imagined scenes of intense activity in the Department of Media and Communications. It gave him enormous satisfaction to think that even now those instructions were being turned into the concrete outcome of a film school. And he felt certain he had done McWhelk a great favour by directing his attention away from *cinema concrete*.

By good fortune the day following the meeting was almost free of commitments. Saved from interruption, he devoted himself to his re-imagining of The University. His writing began to fly along, the words tumbling out of his mind in an energetic stream, seemingly unbidden, persuasive, coherent, magnificently insightful. Having worked at it solidly for several hours, he looked at the word count and saw he had written nearly twelve hundred words. He had by no means finished for the day, but it was mid-afternoon and his endeavours were about to be interrupted by the arrival of Professor Linda Moxey, the head of the Department of English.

It was with the grim demeanour of a jailer leading a prisoner to her execution that Eunice ushered in Professor Moxey. Conquest greeted her with cheerful enquiries into her health and whether she had managed to get away with her family. He asked Eunice to bring them tea. They chatted amiably until Eunice returned with a tray. After she had gone, he saw she had, as was her custom, provided Professor Moxey with a digestive biscuit accompanying her tea. When he looked for his tea, which she had placed out of his line of sight on his desk, he saw that, instead of a biscuit, there was a peach on a side plate next to it. As it happened, he had a slight aversion to the plush texture of peaches. For some reason it made his skin crawl. Did Eunice know this? Was that the point? For a moment he was tempted to interrupt Moxey, who was already speaking of academic matters, to enquire of Eunice the meaning of the peach. He resisted the impulse, but it was some time before he could marshal his thoughts.

'The Department of Media and Communications needs to strengthen its offering in the area of film studies,' he began, finally back on track. 'To support this initiative, I'm proposing that there's some re-allocation of resources, and that includes a senior member of staff from your department.'

'I see,' said Professor Moxey, her chin drawn back defensively.

'I want to transfer your Dr Alice Shellbrooke to put some credibility into narrativity. It seems to me that at the moment the film studies staff regard narrativity in an entirely negative way. I have every reason to think that some stringency in creative writing would not go amiss.' He held up his hand as Moxey tried to speak. 'Dr Shellbrooke may not be perfect for the role, but I seem to think she is currently under-employed. I've looked at your department's spread of research interests and I can see you're strong in literature: nineteenth and twentieth century, Chaucer and the Romantics. That's where you should concentrate your efforts as a department. Creative writing might well be happier elsewhere. Perhaps somewhere where its lessons can be put to more pragmatic ends.' Conquest produced the poem he had read aloud to Ballantyne and slid it under Moxey's nose.

Moxey looked at the poem. 'But, Vice-Chancellor, you must understand, this is a charming appropriation of –'

'No, please, don't tell me it's an appropriation, or some such literary fandangle! I know poetry, of whatever stripe, is a minority sport, and in saying that I'm being generous.'

'Her lectures are very popular.'

'But in the last three years nobody's taken her third-year option.'

'Well, there's something in that, Cliff. Her course competes with the *Twentieth Century American Novel* module, you see. It's seen as a much better career move than *Practical Poetics of the Commonplace*. But we see her as an ornament, in the true spirit of ornamentation.'

'And what's that?' said Conquest, wondering whether this was a serious attempt to resist his plan.

'Oh, not mere decoration; ornamentation as an enhancement of significant form.'

It was a cunning defence, but Conquest was determined. 'Exactly, and that's why I want to reallocate her: *enhancement, significance* and *form*! I think she'll work extremely well in tandem with Professor McWhelk.'

Moxey shook her head. Her face expressed incomprehension, the vehemence of which was only constrained by politeness.

'Look,' said Conquest, feeling kindly. 'I wanted to give you a heads-up, but I'll put it to Dr Shellbrooke myself. I'm sure I can persuade her it would be an all-round good move for her personally, and for her development.'

Moxey was still troubled. 'You do know, don't you,' she said, 'that she's seventy-two?'

News of Shellbrooke's age slightly dented Conquest's confidence. 'No, I didn't. Still, hale and hearty, I presume?'

'Very much so.'

'Well, well, we don't deny the possibility of career development at any age, do we, Linda?'

'No, I suppose not. And when will these changes occur?'

'Oh, I hope to have some new film studies modules available to the students before the beginning of the second semester.'

'Good Heavens, Cliff, that's almost tomorrow!'

'Seize the day, Linda, seize the day! As I've said, don't say anything to Dr Shellbrooke yet. I'll speak to her myself… when the time is right.'

As their meeting came to an end, Moxey regarded Conquest with a slightly wounded look and said, 'she is a singular voice, you know.'

'Linda, we love singular voices. It's our mission to foster them, but they must pay their way!'

Once alone, Conquest was possessed by a sense of tranquillity, thinking that another piece in the creation of the film school was as good as in place. He sat gazing at the view out of the picture window.

Inspired by Cornelius Pye, I've found an aim that gives me instant gratification – something that's small, specific and realised in short order! A model I can apply to the university at large! Utility! Real-world experience! Social engagement! Up-skilling! An exemplar of meaningful reform!

Conquest enjoyed his reveries for several minutes and felt emboldened to call in Eunice to quiz her about the peach.

'It's instead of the biscuit,' she explained.

He regarded it darkly. 'But why... *a peach?*'

'It's better for you than a biscuit. I mean, it's *fruit!*'

He was exasperated. 'But Eunice, I don't particularly like peaches. And I'm perfectly happy with the biscuit.'

'It could be passion fruit then.' She said it with a straight face, but suddenly she put her hand to her mouth and, so he thought, smothered a smirk... or a giggle or a snigger, even.

Conquest shook his head and sighed. 'Eunice, please go and get on, *we have a lot to do!*'

Once Eunice had closed the door, he dismissed thoughts of her strange aberrations and sat down in front of his computer. He had more ideas he wished to commit to paper. He reckoned he could write another five hundred words before he finished for the day, *perhaps more!*

TWENTY-EIGHT

It was not even a week since Graduation Day and again the members of University London Central's senate had assembled, this time in the university's council chamber for their first meeting of the new academic year. Perk had decreed the meeting was to go ahead despite Conquest's suggestion it shouldn't. The anodyne nature of the agenda was plain and the several apologies for absence vindicated the latter's view. Needless to say, the proponents of the Rising Left and the vulgarians of the Right were *all* in attendance, guarding against the possibility that their vice-chancellor might try to slip something through the meeting of which they disapproved. Since Conquest had no such intention, and the agenda items were entirely devoid of controversy, the meeting ran its course with not a ripple of dissent, scarcely a querulous note of enquiry. That is, until AOB: *any other business*. Those three letters at the end of the agenda have, as any experienced chair will attest, the capacity to put a sting in the tail of even the most benign of meetings.

In this case, it all began with the seemingly innocuous matter of the expression 'journeyman craftsman'. The phrase had appeared in a module descriptor of the MA in Ecology and Spirituality. When the students had pointed out to the course leader that this broke the university's Gender Neutrality Directive, he had changed the phrase to 'journeyman craftsperson'. Now, one of the two student representatives on senate used the opportunity of AOB to complain that the course leader's regrettable blindness to the gender specific designation in 'journeyman' meant the phrase was still in breach of the directive. This had brought out the worst in Sir Norman Fleet, who had gone on at length, using the phrase 'blushing violet', not about the complainant *exactly*, although Perk, in response, had insinuated that he thought the implication was there. As a consequence of further intemperate words, Perk had felt moved to remind members they should address their remarks through the chair. As if enough aspersions were not already in the air, Emma Stitch, Vicar-in-General of the Dockland Diocese – who prefaced her every statement by adding 'with the greatest respect' – had commended to senate what she had termed 'person sensitivities', twice mentioning the word 'bullying', although without in any way being particular about Sir Norman's intervention. By this time the atmosphere was explosive and Perk had tried to pour balm, even making a witticism about 'journeymum craftsmum'. Adroitly enough, he had referred the regrettable wording to the vice-chancellor for action. Satisfied that the moment of danger was past, he had moved to close the meeting. It was then that Sir Norman had stuck up his hand with the look of a man quietly infuriated.

'Chair, I too have an item to be taken under any other business,' he announced loudly.

Perk apologised for not having asked the meeting if there were any other AOB matters and simultaneously shot Sir Norman a look that had the equivalency of Mace. 'Sir Norman, of course, I'm happy to take whatever you wish to raise,' he lied.

'Chair, it's the issue of political balance in our choice of honorary doctorates. We seem to have slipped into the habit of only valorising the worthies on the political Left. Mr Farthing might have been everyman's choice, but so was Dame Peggy Mordent before him. And before her there was someone else – I forget his name – of similar persuasion, politically speaking. Meanwhile, the real heavy lifting of the last umpteen governments has been done by the Right side of the Chamber. This smacks of bias! I propose that next year, in order to restore some semblance of political neutrality, we have a shortlist drawn up solely from the political Right.'

'Unless, chair,' added Nancy Spurling, who was in rumbustious mood, 'we intend to honour a footballer, in which case it would be unfair to expect his political affiliation to stretch any further than his current club.'

There was a low murmur of outrage from the meeting.

'Chair, we cannot have a shortlist that excludes candidates based on their political affiliation,' Fred Crannick, the local MP, said indignantly. 'Nor should we be implying that footballers are incapable of thinking any further than their current employer!'

'I'm saying – *not implying* – that footballers can be on the list without having to consider their political affiliations!' retorted Nancy Spurling waspishly. 'For the purposes of our present discussion that includes them in, not includes them out! Hardly negative discrimination, *is it?*'

'Chair, this is a backdoor way of saying that some people are willing to sell their political affiliation!' To the utter amazement of everyone, Crannick, stirred by the boisterous atmosphere, banged the table with his fist. 'It's tantamount to undermining confidence in universal suffrage!'

'Members of senate, I would like to say, from the chair, that no good –'

'Chair, I must protest at any attempt to close down this discussion.'

'Chair, with the greatest resp –'

'Universities are inclined to the left for the very good reason that they are islands of right thinking in a sea of the worst kind of commercial expediency,' declaimed Alistair Vox in the needling style of an Oxbridge debate, 'the kind of expediency that undermines the living standards of hard-working families. We cannot be surprised, therefore, if universities want to honour their own!'

'Chair, with the greatest –'

'Neither the fight for individual rights, nor the illuminations of education are the inheritance of the Left,' retorted Nancy furiously. 'To the contrary, we see its authoritarian bent, if unchecked, putting people and free thought in chains everywhere!'

'Universities are becoming the lapdogs of newspeak, donkeys led by carrots!'

'That is *outrageous*!'

'With the greatest respect, chair, I –'

'If I may, I would –'

'None of this addresses my point, chair. Would you please –'

'Order! Order!'

A sudden silence descended upon the council chamber. It was as if everybody had simultaneous come to their senses and were mortified by their collective behaviour. But before Perk could redirect the business of the meeting, Alistair Vox broke the silence, his voice at its most assertive. He was more than ready to bang the table should histrionics require. 'Chair, senate should make it plain that it will not entertain the introduction of any private culture initiatives at this university, nor into the planning of this university behind senate's back!'

Conquest went rigid. He had been at pains to ensure he was a bystander of the verbal tumult, enjoying every moment of it, but now he saw that, in certain quarters, the accusation of him having truck with private culture – whatever that might be, he had no idea – had taken root. All eyes were turned on him.

'Chair, if I may?'

Perk, his face puckered like a pink, day-old balloon, assented with a nod.

'Let me be clear,' said Conquest in the most mellifluous tones, 'that no ideological baggage will play a part in this university's planning *while I am vice-chancellor*!' He flicked his left hand as if despatching ideological baggage. 'As to the issue of honorary degrees, it seems to me we're getting hot under the collar because there is no formal procedure for the selection of recipients. If I may, chair, I suggest we forego further discussion on this matter, and come back to it as a formal agenda item at the next meeting of senate and discuss how recipients for honorary degrees should be selected.' He observed that Vox, having let the private culture demon loose, was studying his papers with singular concentration.

Now Sir Norman had his hand up. Perk recognised him unenthusiastically.

'*I say, chair,* we have a *special* meeting of senate to discuss honorary degrees *as a matter of some urgency.*' It was Sir Norman turn to look ready to bang the table. 'Universities are supposed to be places of free speech, not the home of satraps preaching ideological conformity.'

A groan arose, which he batted down vigorously. In the general hubbub there was the suggestion of a muttered 'tommyrot'.

'*The matter of whom we're seen to honour,*' Sir Norman continued with great deliberation, 'is clearly a contentious issue *and it needs airing*! If I might put it like this, the longer the advanced notice the more likely we are to land someone of stature for such an honour. *Recipients of our honours reflect our status!*'

There was a clamour from all parts of the room and all parts of the political spectrum until Perk held up his hand for silence.

'Very well!' Perk looked around the room frostily, without fixing his eye on anyone in particular. 'If the opinion of the meeting is that this is something to be debated *calmly* at a special meeting, then we will have one ASAP. Vice-Chancellor, could you suggest a convenient date?'

Conquest was already leafing through his diary. 'Chair, in not less than two weeks' time, not more than three, given the academic year will soon be upon us.'

So it was that a date was fixed for the Wednesday of freshers' week. All parties to the ballyhoo trooped out of the meeting in high dudgeon, already preparing their battle plans for the fight to come. As the council chamber emptied and the members of senate made their way to the senior common room, where afternoon tea was awaiting them, Conquest turned to Perk. 'Should we discuss this special meeting before we join the others?'

Perk was flapping about with his papers. 'I thought it was too good to last,' he muttered discomposedly. 'We had better get across there before it's *daggers drawn.*'

But before we do…?'

'Senate is not supposed to be a bar brawl!' Perk said it – not accusingly *exactly* – but implying that Conquest was somehow not without blame.

Conquest pulled a face of gentle sorrow. 'I'm sorry? Should I have jumped in? I thought you handled it perfectly well. But look, I'll circulate a paper suggesting a way forward on the issue of honorary doctorates. Perhaps we won't need a special meeting once people have seen my suggestions.'

Perk havered. 'You'd better tell me what you have in mind.'

'Yes, fine. Perhaps *you* could tell me about this private culture business? You used that expression the other day; in today's meeting Alistair Vox accused me of fostering it. He's your man, Perk, and I have no idea...?' Conquest raised his eyebrows in an expression of one seeking enlightenment.

'Oh, you know how it is, Cliff: as the political debate moves on, new social phenomena emerge requiring new terminology. Alistair's made InProFESPol the most progressive think tank on the Left. They have a handle on these things, and the full confidence of the Camlington faction.

'So...?'

'Well, as I understand it, the private culture impulse can be identified in the various ways cultural material is withdrawn from the public sphere. It's an idea whose time seems to have come: the unconscious desire to take culture private.'

'Meaning?'

'The urge to deprive the wider community of culture's benefits; privatising the meta-narrative, as it were.'

'If it's unconscious, one doesn't know one's doing it. Is that correct?'

'Well, yes,' Perk looked uncomfortable. 'I suppose you could say private culture's the consequence of a form of social agoraphobia. What bitcoin is to central banks, private culture is to community, in the cultural domain. Same impulse, from what I can gather. But, Cliff, *I'm no expert*! I asked you because I thought it was something you were thinking about, not necessarily in an active way, but you do sometimes seem rather impatient with mediocrity.'

'So, this is an idea Alistair Vox and his institute are peddling, is it?'

'Well, I wouldn't put it like that! It's rather that he has his ear to the ground.'

'*Ah, I see!* It's impossibly hazy, to my way of thinking. I don't know, perhaps it's one of those sealed-box ideologies. So, *who is* propounding this concept?'

Perk hands went out in the gesture of one who was being berated for trying to be helpful. 'I understand where you're coming from, Cliff, but I asked the other day because I thought it might have some bearing on your ideas; not because I'm an expert; *far from it*! But being in the air, one does pick up on it when there's a suspicion it's informing someone's actions.'

'Oh, yes,' said Conquest, rather acidly, 'especially when one doesn't know one's doing it... *or properly understand what it is*!'

'Well, there it is,' said Perk stiffly. 'Naturally, I absolutely understand your concern that it should be bandied about. Not rigorous intellectual practice, I know. Now, as you suggested, I think we'd better join the others before there's another shouting match. It's not how I like my committees to conduct themselves!'

Even as the two of them were making their way across the quadrangle towards the Pearson Building, Nancy Spurling and Sir Norman were retiring to the most distant corner of the senior common. They had spent the last ten minutes exchanging polite nothings with their rivals of the Rising Left in an excruciating display designed to show, on all sides, that their disagreements were civilized.

Sir Norman was indignant. 'What the hell is this private culture thing they made Conquest disown?'

Nancy shook her head in bafflement. 'It wouldn't surprise me if that twerp Vox and his think tank were promoting stuff like that to the Camlington faction.'

'Typical manoeuvre to bring Conquest over to their side, trying to make him recant in public like that. Private culture is typical closed-shop university jargon, I'll be bound!'

Sir Norman felt moved to do a little philosophising. 'I know we have our political differences, Nancy, but there's the Left and there's the Left, if you follow my meaning. We have to be sure that when the Right's done its worst, the right Left is in a position to step in. This is what's meant by long-term planning; it's essential if we're going to keep up with the Chinese. Conquest is part of the future, and in the meantime we have to keep him out of the clutches of the likes of Piers Hazlett and that viper Vox. The glamour boys of the Rising Left will lead the party into perdition if we don't curb their influence.'

TWENTY-NINE

It was some time before Poppy Trench realised that for research students the library of University London Central was open twenty-four hours a day. Such was Graham Lester's growing devotion to the recreation of *Candide In Tinseltown* that occasionally he stayed there all night, refining the latest plot ideas suggested by the scraps of dialogue they had found during the day, typing up the fragments, trying to fit them together, expanding the scenes already established, turning them into a coherent narrative of sorts. She would come in the following day and find a neat pile of revisions on the table. Most of them Poppy would refuse to countenance, but even so the screenplay gradually grew in length and narrative complexity. The fact was, Graham Lester had become firmly possessed by the idea that what they were trying to do was reconstruct a ghost story. The tropes of ghostliness interested him. He realised in a moment of lucidity that he was engaged in their possibilities in a way he was not with his research topic. For her part, Poppy could see he was enjoying himself. Whether she thought they were remaining faithful to Goldman's screenplay is a moot point, but she wasn't going to discourage his efforts because she could see that, in a general sense, he was being productive. It was hard being a truth-seeker when rank speculation was the order of the day.

The most pressing question they faced was what happened as a result of Lionel Armstrong's complaint that his house was haunted. Then Graham Lester found the following fragment of text amongst a fresh batch of loose sheets he'd just taken from one of the last document boxes. He handed it over to her with an enthusiastic grin.

Coral Strick, Van Holt's Principal PA, brings him news.

'Lionel Armstrong can't stand that ghost catcher we've sent up to his house. He says she's had plastic surgery and he can't look at her. He's kicked her out.'

Van Holt is inclined to give Armstrong's ghost saga short shrift. 'Oh God! Can we send somebody else?' He looks around the office speculatively. 'Send that new girl; she's been up there. Armstrong seems to like her; maybe she'll sort it out.'

'*She'll sort it out*,' quoted Graham Lester to Poppy. 'It must be Candide they're sending.'

'So, what happens next?' she wondered.

'I suppose Candide says something like: *I sure would like to believe in angels, Mr Van Holt, but in general I'm no great believer in the supernatural. Catching ghosts would definitely be up there with turning water into wine. It isn't on my CV, but I'll give it a try if you want me to. I'm sure I'll succeed if I go with your blessing.* Wouldn't it be better if I typed it up, do you think?'

Poppy could see the sense in what he was proposing.

Graham Lester found his immersion in Poppy's project to reconstruct *Candide In Tinseltown* much more fun than mapping out how *cinema concrete* fulfilled the expectations of recent French philosophical enquiry into the nature of praxis under politico-linguistic duress. The fact was the joys of narrativity were destroying an allegiance to *cinema concrete* that only months before had seemed absolute. Prudence and perspective were vanquished now something as lovely as Poppy Trench and the glamorous imponderables of her task had entered his life.

THIRTY

Conquest had stressed the need for urgency to Bert Pocock and it was only a matter of days before he witnessed the effects of his instructions. It was late in the afternoon when Eunice came in to see him in a state of scandalised excitement. 'Vice-Chancellor,' she said, 'there's a delegation here from the Department of Media and Communications.'

Conquest had been working on his book for several hours and resented the intrusion. '*Delegation*, Eunice?'

'Yes.'

'Do I meet with delegations, Eunice?'

'No, you *do not*!' She looked appalled at the idea. 'You only meet with heads of departments and higher.'

'Thank you, Eunice. Quite right! So, who's in this delegation?'

'Professors.'

'*Professors!* And do they have names?'

'Shunk, Cloak and Partington.'

Conquest pondered for a moment. They were the Department of Media and Communications' professors, other than McWhelk, and he guessed they had come to see him about his directive to their department concerning film studies. What was in the offing, he suspected, was a minor insurrection and he sensed a show of democratic consultation was needed to break it up.

I'll meet them with benign malevolence, polite scorn, indifferent interest, charming rudeness and a sense of accommodating refusal.

'Ask them in, Eunice. *Flexibility!* One has to show it!'

The three professors trooped in. Conquest rather wished he had whoopee cushions to sit them on. He motioned for them to take a seat on his sofa, in a row like three monkeys.

He feigned some business with the papers lying on his desk

so that he could keep them waiting. A slight tremor afflicted his bowels.

Not only am I an impostor, wherever I go I spawn Frankenstein monsters!

'Gentlemen!' he said, seating himself opposite them in the steel and leather chair of American design.

'It seems appropriate, Vice-Chancellor,' said Professor Cloak gravely, 'we should express our concern... Bert Pocock is rather overreaching in response to your recent request concerning film studies.'

'In what way *overreaching*?' wondered Conquest, his voice modulated between bland niceness and kindly enquiry.

Professor Shunk intervened. 'The point is,' he said, rather too brusquely for Conquest's liking, 'that Bert has put together this list of film study options that includes Editing as Narration, Documentary Film Making, er... Writing for Long-form Drama, Sci-fi on a Shoestring, Authenticity and Historical Drama, and so forth. It's all quite impractical.'

'But Bert Pocock is your head of department,' responded Conquest, with an air of quizzical concern. 'Surely he knows better than anyone what film study topics your department can support?'

'Bert seems to think the department can find state-of-the-art support for any old topics he dreams up! He's not being realistic. Nor are some of our junior members of staff who find it *refreshing*! Our students would smell a rat if we led on most of these topics.'

'Let's be clear, this is my idea,' said Conquest with sudden menace. 'I can promise you that where necessary this initiative will be properly supported by additional resources. Be assured, arrangements are underway! There seems to be some aversion to narrativity in your department.'

'I am *not* averse to narrativity,' declared Professor Shunk indignantly.

'*Nor I!*' said Professor Cloak, going very red in the face.

As we see it, Vice-Chancellor,' said Professor Partington in a voice of impeccable, unimpeachable reasonableness, 'what is also at stake here, is academic freedom. We support Professor

McWhelk's espousal of *cinema concrete*. It may not be a popular position, *vis-à-vis* the current politics of cinema, but universities have to be safe spaces where the expression of unpopular causes and ideas is sanctioned!'

Conquest nodded, a study in sagacity. 'I agree... *absolutely*! I would not allow this university to impede, in any way, Professor McWhelk's pursuit of his personal research interests. What I want him to do, as a senior member of the academic staff, is to contribute to the creation of a film school in which a diversity of practical and theoretical outcomes is encouraged!'

'You mean "all styles served here",' said Professor Partington with lofty disdain.

Despite fearing he was about to fall into an artfully laid intellectual trap, Conquest was adamant. 'Yes, I believe I do.'

The look on Partington's face suggested he shared Conquest's thought. 'Surely that means the students will simply end up enacting within existing conventions?' Although phrased as a question, it was said as though an utter certainty.

For a moment Conquest felt that to contradict him would expose him to ridicule. But no, he was familiar with such attempts at intellectual intimidation and mustered his powers of dissent.

'*No, it does not!*'

'I see,' said Partington weakly, not expecting such an uncompromising riposte. 'I would argue –'

'This is an ideological matter best kept for your seminars,' said Conquest tartly.

Professor Shunk, who had been silent for a while, now took a new tack. 'We would not want issues of an academic nature, Vice-Chancellor, to be muddied by claims of constructive dismissal.'

'Heaven forbid! Who is claiming that?'

'Professor McWhelk.'

'I see.' This was a definite setback. 'Gentlemen, let me say, loud and clear, *I would not wish any such interpretation to get abroad*!' Conquest was losing his patience with the three obdurate faces before him and was already plotting his way out of the meeting. 'I see the possibility of a sizable endowment coming to your department for precisely the purpose of creating a film school.

With that in mind, we have to demonstrate that our offering in film studies has relevance to larger notions of contemporary cultural practice! Obscurantism, I fear, will not carry the day! I am sure academic board will be more than ready to approve whatever Bert puts forward.'

Mention of endowment gave them pause for thought. Conquest detected a certain wilting in their powers of rebellion. 'Look, I appreciate you coming to see me and sharing your thoughts. I can see there is need for further consultation… *further assurances*! If you will leave this with me, I will take up the practicalities again with Professor McWhelk and Dr Pocock.' He stood up, indicating the meeting was over. 'I can assure you that expanding our portfolio of courses and specialisms *will not* be bought at the expense of anybody's academic freedom, nor will constructive dismissal occur on my watch!'

When they had gone, Conquest paced before the picture window, a picture himself; a picture of a man who thought himself skilled at thinking through his options, where he commanded many and was opposed by a few. He did, indeed, have an insurrection on his hands and he guessed Professor Shunk, who was plainly the ringleader, would not be content unless he dropped his film school plan, and that he was not about to do. What was required was to indulge the others sufficiently to mollify their concerns. That suspicions of constructive dismissal were abroad was a sure sign McWhelk was determined to be a martyr for *cinema concrete*. The secret of a successful constructive dismissal was to avoid giving the target the grounds for claiming constructive dismissal.

So be it!

He was still considering the way forward when his landline sounded, indicating Eunice had a call for him.

'Yes, Eunice?'

'It's Olaf Gundersson from the Arts Council. Do you want to take his call?'

Conquest made it a rule to be always available to members of senate. Something told him that a call from Arts Council Olaf so soon after his meeting with the three professors was likely to share its purpose.

'Olaf, how are you? Nice to hear from you.'

'Very well, thank you, Clifford. I am very glad to speak to you. Are you well?'

'Yes, fine.'

'And the family? And everything at work?'

'Yes, can't complain.'

'No... It does no good, does it?'

'It hasn't recently, Olaf. What can I do for you?'

'Ah, Cliff, a sensitive matter. I wanted to exchange thoughts with you before anybody else does.'

'Oh?'

'Yes, indeed! I have a colleague; works for UNESCO in Paris. He has a colleague who's an arts officer in one of the South American field offices. There's a bit of a fuss being kicked up down there about a threat to an arts initiative hosted by your university.'

'Yes, Olaf? *Initiative?*' Conquest smiled grimly, gratified that his suspicion of more canvassing on behalf of Professor McWhelk's academic freedom was about to be proven right.

'It's seen as supporting progressive cultural attainment in Latin America. My colleague's colleague thinks it's of seminal importance.'

'*Really?* Did you say *seminal*, Olaf?'

'Yes, it's your *cinema concrete* website. In Latin America, apparently, it's the foremost showcase for *cinema concrete* practitioners. And, as I said, *supporting progressive cultural attainment!* I've had a look myself. It is very, very comprehensive, bilingual, offers extensive support and feedback to practitioners. According to Pierre, it's particularly active and supportive in geographies where UNESCO is interested in developing civil society through cultural activities, particularly those activities, like film-making, that embrace new media. The field office in question covers Bolivia, Columbia, Ecuador and Venezuela.'

It was obvious to Conquest that Olaf had prepared for his call with some care. 'I see,' he said. It was news to him that *cinema concrete* had a website.

'It seems *cinema concrete* is big in Caracas, Cliff.'

'*Good Lord!*'

'Not with the regime,' added Olaf, lowering his voice as though they were in danger of being overheard by agencies of the Venezuelan state, 'but in the circles that count for the future.'

Conquest was uncertain how he should respond. 'To tell you the truth, Olaf, I wasn't aware we went in for supporting websites, other than our own.'

'I'm on it now, Cliff. I see your logo is very prominent. I'm told it started as an off-shoot of the *International Journal of Cinema Concrete*. The Spanish version of the journal is very popular too. Apparently, it's political in a way that escapes normal authoritarian repression. It's subversive in the way UNESCO likes its subversion.'

'I see.'

'In fact, if you drop it, it could become political hot potatoes.'

'Potato, singular, Olaf. It's *hot potato*.'

'Yes? Well, apparently there is talk of the university withdrawing support.'

'This is a misunderstanding, Olaf. We don't do that sort of thing. We're committed to widening participation, even in Caracas. More to the point, we want to widen the types of study we offer in film, not close one of them down. I think you should assure your colleague in Paris that *cinema concrete* is safe with us.'

And so, with several social niceties, Conquest brought their exchange to a close. He sat for a while reflecting on the amount of support there seemed to be for *cinema concrete*. He had wanted to ask Olaf who had put him up to calling, but he had refrained because experience had taught him that to do so was likely to be construed as preparation for later retribution. He doubted a colleague at UNESCO was the chief proponent; more likely it was McWhelk, but such speculation was, at the moment, useless. More to the point, he decided, was to inspect *cinema concrete's* online presence.

Conquest was disconcerted by how easily he found the *cinema concrete* website, and how different the home page was to the journal Professor Cronker had shown him! It was slick and not the least bit hobbyist. He scanned the several links at the top of the home page. One was 'shop', another 'study *cinema concrete*'. The presence of a commercial dimension made him click on the 'shop' link. He found a considerable catalogue of *cinema concrete* downloads were for sale, and a black *cinema concrete* tee-shirt. He returned to the home page and clicked on the 'study *cinema concrete*' link and found himself transported to the Department of Media and Communications' home page on the university's website. He had to agree with Olaf's estimation that the website was very comprehensive, alarmingly so. Back at its home page, he scrolled down. It was then that he saw something that made his blood run cold: a link proclaimed by the headline 'Candyfloss Cinema: A Denunciation'. It came to him instantly: *Candyfloss cinema was an expression used by both McWhelk and Cornelius Pye!*

With trepidation, he clicked on the link and was transported to what looked like a page of scholarly text, but the title was not in the least bit scholarly: 'Candyfloss: The Cinema of Cornelius Pye Exposed. Professor McWhelk takes the axe to cinematic recidivist'. He read the first sentence and uttered a low growl of disapproval: *'Nothing exemplifies the saccharine nature of contemporary cinema so much as the output of supposed auteur, C.R. Pye, and never was the term "auteur" so badly used.'*

It did not take him long to see that what he had lighted upon was a demolition of Cornelius Pye's filmic career crafted as a rallying cry for *cinema concrete*. It used, in expanded form, many of the terms Conquest was familiar with from his encounter with McWhelk. The language was over-ripe; a sentence that ran, 'Candyfloss cinema takes a sledgehammer to crack a nut', particularly revolted him. So, was this the source, the wellspring, of the talk of candyfloss cinema that had blighted Pye's enjoyment of his new release? The more Conquest read, the more likely it seemed. The tempo of his groans increased with every paragraph, and there were many paragraphs to accompany. What Conquest was inclined to think of as a sophisticated way of creating light entertainment was, in the McWhelkian worldview, an ideological battleground, and McWhelk waged the war of words with ghastly vigour!

Finally, Conquest could read no more. There was, after all, free speech, and then there was *free speech*, and this was of the kind that would not go down well with an autocratic filmmaker!

He cursed McWhelk. What of his plans might this undo if ever Pye learnt his university harboured the viperous swine? He saw the fruits of a Pye's endowment burning on a large celluloid pyre. It did not bear thinking about. The one thing Conquest was absolutely certain of was that he could not take the *cinema concrete* website off-line. Such an act would be tantamount to an admission of constructive dismissal.

He rose from his desk and began to pace agitatedly. It now struck him that although he thought he knew that Professor Woolworth, in his capacity of dean of academic affairs, was responsible for the contents of the university's website, he had no idea how it, or any other of the university's websites, were produced or policed. He fetched his wiring diagram out of the umbrella stand and reminded himself that four boxes below the heading of *Chief Operating Officer & General Counsel,* sandwiched between *Library and Learning Services* and *Marketing and Communications,* there was one labelled *Information Technology Services.*

This descending ladder of services was currently the responsibility of the university's secretary! *Miriam Micklethwaite!* He might have guessed.

That's perfect, he thought, *an archipelago of imbeciles!*

In a moment he was on the phone to her.

'Miriam, Clifford here. How are you?'

'Oh, good to middling, Vice-Chancellor. What can I do you for? Developments in the crocodile business?'

'No,' said Conquest coldly, her jocular facetiousness striking quite the wrong note. 'I'm wondering if you can tell me who's in charge of website design? I seem to think it lies within your bailiwick.'

'Well, IT services are nominally responsible for all digital fulfilment, but originally the university's website was the responsibility of the public relations office and they still oversee the web design unit. It's run by Ted Monkton, but I expect there's some overlap with IT services.'

'Isn't having an overlap rather confusing?'

'It's a legacy issue, Vice-Chancellor. The web design team were the university's experts, but it's not beyond the bounds of possibility that IT services now support website design. It's a question I've never had reason to ask. The important distinction is, surely, between technical support and editorial content? My people are not permitted to devise or have any opinion about editorial content. I've warned them to do so would be ill-advised, from a legal standpoint. Content is always an academic matter. That's certainly *not* in my bailiwick. Isn't Professor Woolworth responsible for our prospectus, and hence, by extension, all information published online?'

'Quite possibly,' said Conquest with guarded truculence.

'Departments have online course information for students, but that's all password protected. Then there are research units with external funding... You'd have to speak to Professor Woolworth. We haven't received any complaints, as far as I know.'

'So, I gather there are all manner of websites out there originated here, in the university, linked to the university website... *or not*! Websites we know nothing about! For instance, I am on one at the moment for something called *cinema concrete*; a major online presence. I take it you are unaware of any such thing?'

She laughed. '*Indeed, I am!* I would regard such free expression inadvisable at any time.'

'Yes, thanks for that. So, who knows how many websites the web design unit provides technical support for?'

'You'd have to ask Ted Monkton. Or his line manager, Sandra Torpington, in public relations. She might have a tally.' She paused to think. 'Oh no, they're both on holiday. They're married, you see.'

Conquest groaned quite audibly, sufficient for Miriam Micklethwaite to hear him.

'Are you all right, Vice-Chancellor?'

'So, let me recap: you're Sandra's line manager and she's her husband's line manager? Is that correct?'

'Except for content. That's a matter for Professor Woolworth.'

'Thank you, Miriam.' He slammed down the receiver and reeled over to the steel and leather chair of American design. Here were the administrative boondocks of the university at their very finest! And behind it all lurked menaces like McWhelk!

Shortly, Eunice came in with a cup of tea. He had been staring morosely out of the picture window and, stirred to some kind of response, he offered her his view that it was remarkable how the yearly rebirth of a new academic year was in vivid contrast to the first signs, evident everywhere, of nature hunkering down for winter.

'Look,' he said, 'the sycamore trees over there are already flecked with the golds and yellows of autumn!'

'Oh yes!' she enthused, teetering up to the picture window to peer at the line of trees as though they were some strange specimens in a zoo. 'I've never noticed them before.' She peered again, with greater intensity. 'Oh, how sweet!' she exclaimed, 'that one looks like a Scottie dog!'

Conquest stared at her, fascinated, as she continued to marvel at the canine resemblance she had found in the sycamore foliage. So mesmeric was her doltish, juvenile absorption that he found it an immense effort to return to business. The management of web publishing was an issue in need of clarification. He suspected Miriam Micklethwaite was right in pointing the finger at Professor Woolworth. It was a delegation of responsibility that called for an urgent meeting with him. He looked at his watch and saw it was near the end of the day.

'Eunice, unless he's in Tuscany, I want to speak to Professor Woolworth first thing tomorrow morning. Can you contact him immediately and ask him to strain every sinew to be here by nine? And call Howard Huddle in Human Resources and ask him to come over right away.'

'Now?'

'*Yes, now!*'

Conquest's cry denoted extreme urgency and Eunice responded in kind. She reeled out of his office and had the head of Human Resources, Howard Huddle, practically bounding up the stairs to his office within ten minutes.

'How can I help, Vice-Chancellor?' said the slightly craven figure of the head of HR.

'I need you to brief me, Howard,' said Conquest, pointing to the sofa. 'Take a seat.'

'Thank you, Vice-Chancellor.'

If there was one person whom Conquest thought it right and proper that he should use his official title it was Howard Huddle and he had never tried to break him of the habit.

'Now Howard, what about Professor McWhelk? I've had a delegation from the Department of Media and Communications. Do we have an HR problem?'

'Ah, yes, McWhelk! We've been in discussion with him.'

'Who's that, besides you?'

'Well, Sheila, my deputy. We don't think we have a problem, Vice-Chancellor, so much as an opportunity.'

'I see, *an opportunity*! Am I to understand we're talking about the same thing: a claim for constructive dismissal?'

'Yes, Vice-Chancellor, an opportunity.'

'That's extremely helpful: *positive thinking, Howard*! And how is McWhelk's situation an opportunity?'

'An opportunity for the university to re-assess the value of his enthusiasm. I am not an academic –'

'No, you're not, indeed, thank goodness! I take it that by *enthusiasm* you refer to his research, to *cinema concrete*?'

'Yes, Vice-Chancellor. It seems Professor McWhelk feels he has become somewhat superfluous and therefore suitable as a fill-in wherever one is needed as the university develops and changes.'

'I see! So, you suggest what?'

'Empowerment! I suggest we give *cinema concrete* more prominence as one of the great and exciting things that are unique about University London Central. Turn him into a standard-bearer! I'm certain that Professor McWhelk would respond positively if we showed him how much we value his contribution.'

Conquest looked duly thoughtful. 'That's certainly something worth considering! We don't want him to feel left out, do we? I admire positive thinking, Howard. Have you or Sheila put this to Professor McWhelk?'

'No, but I see he's due an appraisal, and I think it would be a gesture in the right direction if you conducted it in person. It would be natural during such an event to express your gratitude to him for his performance over the years and let him see that even greater things lie ahead.'

'Howard, I thank you for that.' Conquest heaved himself to his feet. 'Most constructive, as usual. I will give the utmost consideration to your suggestion. How are you settling in over at the old boiler house building? Everything fine?'

'Fine, thank you, Vice-Chancellor,' said Huddle. He regarded the room with eyes of basset hound sadness. 'This was my office, if you remember. I was very happy here. Fourteen years.'

'Ah, well, we all have to make sacrifices just now. Things will undoubtedly return to normal in the long-term, don't you think?'

THIRTY-ONE

Conquest had the habit of browsing the newspapers over coffee first thing in the morning. Eunice, who always arrived before he did, was at pains to ensure they were laid out on his desk in a serried rank in descending order of importance, the *Guardian* uppermost. Conquest's fifteen minutes spent looking for any news or comment relating to Higher Education was a moment of tranquillity before the bustle of the day began.

That Thursday morning, as he idly turned the pages, he was more acutely aware of his enjoyment than normal since he knew full well that in a short time he was due to meet professor Woolworth and confront the problem of McWhelk, *cinema concrete* and its website. He had hardly settled into the peaceful interlude before a headline in the *Guardian,* towards the bottom of a page in the home news section, caught his eye: *Veteran Poet Honoured*. Arts correspondent, Winsome Blunt, reported as follows: 'In a surprise move that is delighting her fans, Alice Shellbrooke, poet of what she describes as 'the kwerks and kwaintness of language', is to be appointed poet laureate by Her Majesty the Queen.'

Conquest stopped, blinked and went back to the beginning.

'In a surprise move that is delighting her fans, *Alice Shellbrooke…*!'

He lowered the paper and stared into space, digesting what he'd just read. Slowly the feeling of utter, dumbfounding disorientation passed. He knew trouble when he saw it, *and this was it*! He forced himself to continue reading:

Always willing to laugh at herself, and what she thinks of as her 'craft', Shellbrooke's poem *High Street* begins:

The ghastly blue of Barclay's bank,

Disappearing from the High Street as we speak!

Come high, come low, it always stank.

Now a lively septuagenarian, it was her epic poem *Midden* that first brought her to the attention of poetry-loving circles. More recently, her poem *Commonplace*, the opening lines of which were used by London Transport for its 'Poetry on the Underground' campaign, was widely misunderstood, although one commuter pressure group said it opened their eyes to the beauty of everyday language:

So, from the get-go he is the go-to person, but don't go there,
He's out of his comfort zone, climbing a wall of worry.
He needs to man-up, then he's good to go.
The good news is it's a win-win situation.
Blue sky thinking, out of the box.
It's a learning curve that comes with the territory.
Do the maths, it's a no-brainer,
Weaponised, on an industrial scale!
Having said that, *they're* all on the same page,
Running on empty.
But *he's* in a good place, pushing at an open door.
It's a level playing field that does what it says on the tin.
That curved ball from left field was a real game changer.
He smashed it out of the park, twenty-four seven.
It's a work-in-progress, but what's not to like?
It is what it is: *job done*!

She has long laboured away at her modest, unassuming and yet breath-taking poems in the sheltered groves of academe. Whilst teaching English at University London Central, she has developed into one of Britain's most meditative poets, joyously dwelling on the microscopic detail of ordinariness, the humdrum and drab.

What Shellbrooke calls 'my little snatches of the everyday' were once thought to be a little too prosaic, an exercise in what her academic colleagues have termed *post-everything foraging*, but popular opinion seems to have caught up with her! Ms Shellbrooke was not available to comment on whether or not, in her new role, she would be addressing, in her own inimitable style, the great occasions of state.

Conquest sat back. He tossed aside the newspaper as if to be rid of the thing. Here was an undoubted setback! *No, here is a great big fuck-up!* He still hadn't found time to meet Alice Shellbrooke, even though he had promised her head of department he would. The staffing arrangements for his film school were looking more absurd by the minute. Had his intention to move Shellbrooke to the Department of Media and Communications already been made public he would now be facing a tremendous outcry! One didn't dismantle a creative writing unit headed by a poet laureate! To do so would be to look a complete idiot!

He was still transfixed, staring into space, marvelling at his lucky escape, when Eunice appeared at his door, a look of extreme displeasure on her face.

'Professor Woolworth wants to see you. Shall I let him in, or not?' She asked the question in a tone of voice that left him in no doubt she thought not.

Conquest stirred himself. 'Eunice, yesterday I asked you to make sure he was here this morning at nine! Don't you remember?'

She looked at him blankly until he gestured vigorously that she should go and admit him.

When Woolworth entered the room, his tread was uncharacteristically buoyant. '*The most extraordinary thing, Vice-Chancellor!*' he gushed. There were no preliminaries; his face was a picture of innocent delight. He wielded his copy of the *Guardian* in a manner expressive of great tidings.

Conquest brought him to a halt with a limp hand, indicating his own copy of the newspaper with the other. Woolworth's enthusiasm was not dampened by the apparent lack of the same in Conquest's demeanour.

'Isn't it marvellous? I've already booked the senior common room for an impromptu celebration at lunchtime.' He came to a halt before Conquest's desk as if he expected to be commended for the speed and manner of his response to the news.

Conquest had the self-control to know he was in imminent danger of striking the wrong note. He cleared his throat laboriously. 'Good. I was thinking along similar lines. She is here, I suppose?'

'Oh, I expect so,' said Woolworth, beaming. 'She's always in the library when not teaching. She likes to compose in the music section. She says she feels the sympathetic vibrations emanating from the scores.'

'Well, well!' Conquest managed a gloomy smile. 'I'm guessing you're an Alice Shellbrooke enthusiast.'

'Alice is such a jolly person. Been with us for absolutely ever. Singular honour! No doubt she will do an excellent job and bring plaudits to the university! Will you say a few words? It would be much appreciated, I'm sure.'

Conquest appeared to consider Woolworth's question. The only personal things he knew about Woolworth were that he lived out in Essex and grew specimen dahlias. He was thinking that the specimen before him exuding gladness was destined to be, should his wiring diagram come to pass, *Provost and Pro-Vice-Chancellor (Quality Assurance & Advancement)*.

Another grand title for an idiot! When I thought up these titles I was thinking of an ideal, like a fourth century BC Greek sculptor. Ah me, how far short individual humans do fall!

'Of course; delighted to say a few words! You must introduce us; I haven't had the pleasure. And how are you, Murray?'

'Very fair, Cliff. And you?'

'Ah, well, weighed down by the cares of office.'

Woolworth's face fell. 'Oh, I am sorry. Have you sought help?'

'Yes, but they tell me it's in the nature of things. How are the dahlias?'

'They're in the fullness of their blooming. Thank you for asking, Cliff.'

'And have you been in touch with the Stagg family, by any chance?'

'Ah, yes, a bit of a hiccup there.' Woolworth's face fell. 'Their solicitor is a very unpleasant chap and they're still abroad.'

'So, nothing's happened?'

'I do believe the crocodiles still rankle. I have apologised on more than one occasion... for the university, you know? I hope to do so in person to the Staggs very soon. They'll be back in a matter of days and I shall do my best to see them then.'

'I see. Well, let's hope they're no longer in a litigious mood when they arrive. Where are they at the moment?'

'Tuscany, I believe.'

'Goodness, half the university's there!' Conquest grew noticeably agitated. 'Had I known, I would have instructed some of our colleagues to visit on bended knees. Well, let's put the crocodiles aside for a moment, shall we?' He proffered the sofa to Woolworth as a place to park himself. He took surprisingly little pleasure in the thought that he was about to ruin Woolworth's ebullient mood. '*Websites!*'

Woolworth looked expectant, but as no further explanation accompanied that single word, he began to look a little worried. 'Yes, Cliff, websites. What of them?'

'For instance, have we any idea what websites, representing aspects of our work here at the university, are online, readily available for anyone to access?'

'Well, there's a university's main portal, and *My University London Central* is password protected and only for the students.' He held out his hands for a moment as if he wasn't quite sure what Conquest was driving at.

'There's no oversight, is there? I mean, if a member of staff has a burning issue to share with the world, he – or she – can do so online without let or hindrance. Isn't that correct?'

Woolworth looked at him glassy-eyed. 'I can assure you we comply with all privacy protocols –'

'Yes, all very well, but what of the I'm-sharing-my-thoughts-with-the-world business? What then?'

'Discretion is an important –'

'Excellent! We're about to build a digital hub and we don't have a website oversight policy! Isn't that rather odd?'

'I'm not sure it's been felt necessary. There hasn't been an eventuality that required such a thing.'

'Well, Murray, I want all websites we host other than the university's taken off-line until we know what they're about. We could have a member of staff selling students on the dark web for all we know!' Conquest said this with an air of bitter dissatisfaction. 'I'd like you to investigate immediately.'

At that moment Eunice stole into the room with papers that Conquest had told her to bring in the moment she'd made duplicates.

Conquest appraised them briefly. Finally, he spoke.

'These, Murray, are the new film studies modules drafted by Dr Pocock for the Department of Media and Communications.' The top one was entitled *Tropes of Suspense in Post-Hitchcockian Narrativity*. Glancing at it further, it struck him as a bit overwrought, but he comforted himself with the thought that it wasn't his business to criticise the specifics. 'They're to go to the next academic board for approval. Can you select the readers with care to ensure they receive a sympathetic reading? And make sure the readers' reports are circulated as soon as possible. I'm sure Dr Pocock will confirm that the department has the resources to teach what he's proposing, should any reader wish to enquire.'

Woolworth took the papers Conquest was proffering with slight puzzlement. 'I don't recall new modules being mentioned in the department's strategic plan.'

'We're going to start a film school, Murray. And when it's big and feisty – all grown up! – it's going to gobble up the Department of Media and Communications. What do you think of that?'

Woolworth could see that now was not the time to make difficulties. 'Excellent, Cliff. I'm sure it will be marvellous.'

'Good, I'll see you later at the Alice Shellbrooke reception. And, Murray, an exception: for the time being you'd better leave the *cinema concrete* website online; it seems it's big in Caracas. And let's check the blogs and social media accounts out there as well, shall we?'

As soon as the door had closed behind Woolworth he took to his pacing. What was needed now was for the *cinema concrete* website to be taken off-line in a way that allowed him to deny any responsibility for its fate.

THIRTY-TWO

Twelve-thirty and Conquest was surprised by how full the senior common room was. It seemed possible there were as many members of academic staff on campus as there were in Tuscany. He spotted the Department of Media and Communications Professors Shunk, Cloak and Partington conspiring in a far corner. Their scowls said it all. Next, he saw Alice Shellbrooke. He recognised her by the admiring academics that surrounded her. She was barely visible, a little mouse of a woman, a crocheted shawl of many colours draped around her shoulders. Her audience nodded as she spoke, beatific expressions on their faces. Professor Woolworth had been watching for Conquest's arrival, and he rushed over to perform his introduction. Alice's audience fell back as they approached.

Conquest glimpsed Professor Linda Moxey, head of the Department of English, lurking at the edge of the scum. He knew exactly what she was hoping for: a moment to publicly upbraid him for trying to remove a poet laureate from her proper place in her department as *'an ornament, in the true spirit of ornamentation'*. *He* was equally determined to evade her rebuke as long as possible, and certainly avoid it happening in a crowded senior common room with Alice Shellbrooke listening in.

No, that would not do!

'Ah, Alice,' began Woolworth, 'can I introduce you to Professor Conquest, our vice-chancellor?'

She was much taken by the idea of meeting the head of the university. No sooner had Woolworth finished his introduction than she launched into a barrage of queries about what it was that a vice-chancellor did. 'Are you very busy determining policy at this time of year? I hope you have a say about what they serve in the canteen. Somebody needs to! The flowerbeds have been positively sumptuous this summer...'

While she talked, Conquest observed that Dr Pocock, head of the Department of Media and Communications was as far away as it was possible to be from Professors Shunk, Cloak and Partington. He was in conversation with a vivacious young woman who bore a passing resemblance to Jacqueline Kennedy. The picture they made was unsettling. What struck him as sinister was Pocock's studied absorption in what his companion was saying; the ludicrous extent to which he was ignoring what was going on in the rest of the room. Conquest's antenna for trouble told him something devious was afoot. It crossed his mind that Pocock's film studies proposals were a subversive prank designed as revenge on his senior colleagues for past slights. *Does the man have the audacity to do such a thing?* The title of the module he had noted earlier when talking to Woolworth came back to him: *Tropes of Suspense in Post-Hitchcockian Narrativity.* Was that a joke? He was thinking he should investigate, perhaps have a word with Pocock, but Alice Shellbrooke's chatter was like a dense fog and, after all, his role was to provide broad outlines of policy and delegate detail to others.

If Pocock wants to terrorise his professors, it's no business of mine!

While it might amuse Alice Shellbrooke to attach any number of picaresque duties to Conquest's role as vice-chancellor, it was becoming clear that she wasn't interested in him telling her anything about what he actually did, nor was she particularly moved by her appointment as poet laureate. Mention of poetics led to her appraising him with her views on cinema, a development he found disconcerting.

'...I have a great fondness for children's films of yesteryear. I find some quite excellent at capturing the poetics of childhood. The Gothic can take over sometimes, and that I see as a grown-up intrusion, the wellspring of which I am not enough of a spiritual type to divine...'

Conquest had the uncanny feeling he must have already spoken to her about his film school plan and then forgotten he'd done so.

Things would get back on track, he felt, if he could squeeze in his formal words of congratulation. 'I wanted to congratulate you, you know, on your success. It will add immeasurably to the prestige to the university, and of course, your department.'

'I've never yet seen a perfect Alice,' she babbled on, hardly acknowledging his praise. 'I suppose I would be interested in that, wouldn't I, seeing as we share the same name? I've often wondered if I was named after her, but somehow I never got round to asking. Such a shame, *but too late now*! If I had a wish, it would be to be given the opportunity to find the perfect Alice. Where would I go, though?' She tittered at the hopelessness of the task she had given herself, a merry twinkle in her eyes. 'I suppose you think me rather silly?'

'Not a bit of it!' said Conquest hastily.

'The Vice-Chancellor wishes to say a few words in honour of your appointment,' Woolworth told her.

'Yes!' agreed Conquest. 'Your contribution to poetry has finally been given the recognition it deserves!' The falsity of his enthusiasm pained him, but duty required it.

'Overdue,' chimed in Woolworth.

'Indeed, it is!' Conquest was beginning to feel he might get forever stuck, competing with Woolworth to utter flattering inanities. 'Perhaps now would be a good moment.'

'*Right now?*' said Woolworth. 'There's still many to come.'

A quick glance to his left told Conquest that Professor Moxey was in the vicinity, waiting to have it out with him. 'But the room is already full,' he protested. 'Surely the time is right?'

'Well, let's not go on about poetry,' said Alice. 'And let's not be too long; I'm going to the cinema this afternoon. Special treat!' When she saw the look on Conquest's face she laughed. 'All right, you can talk a little bit about poetry.'

'I know nothing of poetry,' confessed Conquest, rather disarmed by this tiny, cheerful speck of a woman. 'Why don't we make our way to the top of the room? You can lap up the adulation from there.'

The three of them began to move towards their goal, Alice Shellbrooke in the lead. As the press of people parted to let her through, expressions of congratulation rained down on her. At every one she ducked her head as though they were brickbats.

'*Ladies and gentlemen!*' announced an incongruous, stentorian voice that halted their progress. 'We have to evacuate the senior common room.'

A murmur of disapproval swept the room.

'I'm sorry, everyone...'

The groans died away.

'We have a bomb-scare down the road and we have to evacuate. Could you please make your way to the muster point in front of the students' union?'

By this time, most of those present had identified the speaker as the superintendent of the portering staff. He was ex-military and rather imposing. A well-mannered movement began towards the doorway. At the far end, where the Department of Media and Communications professors were gathered, someone opened the emergency exit and off went an alarm. It was the sort of situation that put Conquest on his metal. He strode over to the superintendent. 'Jeff, are we under some kind of attack?'

'Sorry, sir, I would have informed you first if I'd seen you there,' said the superintendent, stiffening in a faint suggestion of coming to attention. 'A mechanical digger's dug up a Nazi bomb behind the Keynes Building.'

'I see! Is it serious?'

'It's a bomb, sir, size unknown, but we're evacuating most of the buildings at this end of the campus.'

'Have the emergency services arrived?'

'Not yet. They've been informed.'

'I think I'd better go and see for myself; take stock.'

Conquest made off in haste, his spirits lifted by the sense of emergency. He was outside the Pearson Building before he realised Alice Shellbrooke was still with him.

'I suppose this might be subject matter for one of your poems,' he said fatuously.

'*Nazi bomb* sounds terribly romantic,' she agreed in the spirit of an owlish schoolgirl. 'Intimations of the Blitz are heart-warming in a blood-curdling way. Mind you, as a poet I eschew the dramatic. It's been done, don't you see?' She blinked up at him, expecting a response as earnest as her question.

Conquest came to a halt, thinking he was in the unique situation of wanting to be rid of a poet laureate.

'Alice,' he said, 'I have a feeling we have much to say to one another on the matter of praxis... even, I dare say, on orthopraxy, but now is *not* the time! It would not look good if I allowed a poet laureate to be blown up. I think you should make your way to the students' union.'

It was as if understanding had come to her. '*Ah-ha!*' she exclaimed. 'These are the moments that being a vice-chancellor are all about! You're doing the last person into the lifeboat thing, aren't you? Sustaining the leadership myth!'

A frown creased Conquest's brow. He did not approve of her disparaging leadership as if it were a party trick she'd seen through. 'Nevertheless, you should join the others. No point in you endangering yourself. I, on the other hand....' His voice trailed away. He stood there, resolute, until she acknowledged that he was right and turned back with a wave of farewell.

I, on the other hand, he thought, *am entirely dispensable and nobody would miss me for more than five seconds if I were blown to smithereens.*

Once she was out of sight, he set off for the Keynes Building, thoroughly reinforced in his view that poetry was the preserve of frivolous minds.

Not only am I an impostor, wherever I go I spawn Frankenstein monsters!

THIRTY-THREE

One of the successes that had marked Conquest's previous year as vice-chancellor – his first – had been the securing of capital funding for the university's most important building project in several years: a digital hub, a new central resource for digital technologies. Sir Norman Fleet had been a great proponent and facilitator of the scheme. When, in open competition, his construction company, Wainwright, Carter & Expandite, had won the design and construction contract, a few eyebrows had been raised, but no one had been really surprised.

A lack of development land on the campus had resulted in the decision to build the hub on the site of Keynes House, the administrative centre of the university. The building's original occupants had, in the Pool of London's heyday, supervised its wharfs and crossings. The rooms of the honourable officers of this organisation had been on the first floor. These were commodious and rather grand. A vast, ornate, open staircase leading to these rooms filled much of the centre of the building, The remainder of the accommodation was a warren of passageways and dark, pokey offices; the whole judged quite unsuited to the needs of modern work practices. The redevelopment budget had been somewhat constrained by the cost of clearing the site, while retaining the original, Victorian façade, behind which the new building was to be constructed. Economies had been made; certain luxuries had been disposed of, the size of the foyer had shrunk.

Once planning consent had been obtained and the occupants of Keynes House, like the vice-chancellor, re-housed, preparations had been made to brace the building's façade with an exoskeleton of steelwork and the site had been surrounded by hoarding proclaiming that Wainwright, Carter & Expandite was a *considerate contractor*. The site foreman and the surveyor had moved into the mobile office parked in the service yard to the rear of the building.

On one side of this yard there was a range of single storey buildings projecting out backwards from the main bulk of Keynes House. Originally these buildings had been where the stables, servants' quarters and storerooms necessary for the comfort of the honourable officers had been located. At nine o'clock on that Thursday morning, as Conquest first learnt of Alice Shellbrooke's success, the demolition had begun of these buildings. By mid-morning rubble was being loaded onto a succession of trucks. Next, the excavator had broken up the foundation slab and removed the subsoil. After three truckloads of rubble had been driven away and loading had begun on the fourth, the operator of the JCB had glimpsed a section of corroded cylinder in the deepest part of the excavation. Long experienced in the dangers of digging into the many historical layers of London, he had stopped and consulted with the surveyor and foreman. Their considered opinion was that what they could see was a German bomb. Later investigation would suggest that the bomb – for so it was – had fallen into the yard close to the wall of the stable, penetrating the ground at a diagonal and ending up beneath the floor, some four metres below ground level, where it had lain dormant for eighty years.

All work had been halted and the site foreman had called for an immediate evacuation. He had rushed round to the front of Keynes House to ensure that those about to start work on disconnecting the building's services left immediately for the emergency muster point. He then began to think about creating an exclusion zone greater than the limits of the demolition site, inducing a fear in the mind of the truck driver that his vehicle, onto which the excavated rubble was being loaded, would soon be trapped. He had thereupon decided to leave while he still could. To leave the building site and join the main road fronting Keynes House, required him to turn right onto a short length of one of the campus's pedestrianised roadways. In his haste to be gone he had taken the turn too sharply. Eunice Truepenny, who had left the vice-chancellor's offices during her lunch break to go to a nearby supermarket, was walking back on the hoarding side of the roadway. She stepped back to allow the truck to pass as it swung into its turn. The further it went the smaller became the gap between the side of the cargo bed and the hoarding. Eunice found herself being gently pushed back into what was, fortunately for her, an irregularity in the construction of the hoarding that amounted to a small recess. Meanwhile several people further down the roadway, seeing what was happening, had gestured wildly for the driver to stop, which he did just as Eunice was pinned against the hoarding and only moments before she would, undoubtedly, have been horribly crushed. She was now trapped between the side of the stationary truck and the hoarding. Hastily, the driver had climbed out of his cab, a glance in his rear-view mirror having made him belatedly aware of Eunice's presence. Soon a considerable crowd of would-be rescuers had gathered, disputing whether or not it was safe to extract her by reversing the truck. The majority opinion was that before it could be moved even a centimetre, Eunice had to be extracted by some other means. Meanwhile, one of the more adventurous amongst the crowd had crawled under the lorry to assess whether or not she was injured.

'Hi there!' said her rescuer in a voice full of urgency. 'Don't worry, we'll get you out. Are you injured?

'Please... please...,' Eunice had uttered in a tiny voice, her nose pressed against the side of the truck.

Her interlocutor took heart from the fact that there was no evidence of blood. 'Can you move? Try and scrunch down here and crawl out.'

She made some feeble attempts at movement but the space she occupied was so tight it was impossible for her to flex her body in any direction whatsoever.

On the other side of the truck a heated discussion about how to extract her was still in progress.

'We should wait until the fire service gets here.'

'She may be hurt. We should try and get her out now.'

'Maybe we can lift her out, if she can't get underneath.' The proponent of this solution had then climbed up onto the half-filled cargo bed and made his way to the other side where he could peer down at the top of Eunice's head.

Back at the main confabulation, the surveyor had the most straightforward idea. 'All we have to do is knock off the support struts at the back of a couple of lengths of the hoarding and we should be able to pull them down into the yard, and her with them.'

He signalled to a group of the contractor's men to go with him into the yard, which they did, followed by several on-lookers. The men armed themselves with the tools of demolition and set to work. Crowbar and sledgehammer were employed with surgeon-like precision. Levering off the stanchions bracing the panels of the hoarding proved to be a surprisingly easy task. By this time two of the university's first-aiders had arrived, adding to the crowd to the rear of the hoarding.

'Right, you lot,' said the surveyor. 'Stand back! We're going to lever these panels backwards and they might fall suddenly.'

His men took up positions to either side of the double length of hoarding and inserted their crowbars into the gaps between the panels. A concerted jerk forced the boards loose and with majestic slowness they toppled into the yard sending up a dramatic cloud of dust. And in the centre of the cloud could be seen Eunice, toppled with them.

Those who had been concerned to see to her first aid needs rushed to her stricken form with expressions of concern. Her eyes were tight shut; she didn't move. The first-aiders leaned in closer. One concerned bystander had taken off his jacket and, making a pillow of it, placed it beneath her head.

On the verge of unconsciousness, Eunice struggled to utter a heartfelt appeal to those around her. 'Please... please,' she repeated in an urgent whisper, 'tell Professor Conquest how very much I loved him, the dear, dear...'

And with that she passed out.

One of those bent over her, who had heard her plea, was Professor Cronker. He was still there, pulling on his jacket, which he had retrieved from one of the paramedics, when the ambulance departed.

'My God,' he said to himself as he watched the ambulance disappear from sight, 'the lass thought she was going to die!'

It was at this moment that Conquest came striding down the incline from the direction of the Pearson Building having just rid himself of Alice Shellbrooke. He could see immediately that something other than a bomb scare was going on. 'What's happened, Alan?' he said at a rush.

'Ah, Cliff, there's been an accident. Your PA, Eunice. A lorry. Close run thing.'

Conquest looked at Cronker in a daze.

'I was with her until the ambulance turned up. I think it was the shock as much as anything. I'm sure she'll be all right.'

Before he could enquire further, a man in a hardhat, the site foreman, approached. 'There's a bomb been found, gentlemen. You have to move back.'

They allowed themselves to be herded up the slope.

'Has the demolition site been cleared?' Conquest asked the foreman.

'Yes. The emergency services are on their way.'

Conquest was still digesting Cronker's news. 'Eunice, you say? What happened?'

Several policemen in hi-vis waistcoats were coming up the roadway and the sirens of distant emergency vehicles were beginning to make themselves heard.

'Eunice was trapped by a lorry, I'm afraid,' said Cronker. 'They've taken her to A&E.' He wondered whether he should deliver her message, and decided not. 'As a precaution, you understand.'

For a moment Conquest's face was frozen with incredulity. Then, 'Good God!' he cried with heartfelt anguish. 'Am I expected to conduct the affairs of this university *without a PA?*' It was the innocent cry of a leader bereft, whose plans had recently suffered grievous setbacks. Cronker saw it differently: the inchoate outburst of a man shocked by terrible news concerning a passion born in deceit! He regarded the whole episode as disreputable; there was only one recourse: *a word to the person best able to restrain the man!*

THIRTY-FOUR

The Royal Logistic Corps Explosive Ordinance Disposal unit worked into the night to defuse the bomb behind the Keynes Building. It turned out to be quite big enough, had it gone off, to have levelled the building and much of the surrounding area. The bomb disposal experts soon determined, despite its corroded state, that a faulty fuse mechanism had prevented successful detonation. Once the fuse was removed it was decided that the bomb was safe enough to be driven away and induced to explode on a military range in Essex.

A bulletin detailing the successful resolution of the state of emergency was lying on Miriam Micklethwaite's desk when she arrived at work that Friday morning. She gave a sigh of relief, but very soon her telephone rang, bringing bad news. Further inspection of the excavation from which the bomb had been lifted had revealed that as it had tunnelled its way into the ground its nose had clipped the corner of what turned out to be the finest tessellated Roman pavement ever found in Britain, once part of what would later become known as the Stag Hunt Villa. 'A remarkable addition to the archaeological sites of Roman London,' according to the chief archaeologist sent by the London Museum.

The news that archaeologists were moving in as the army moved out sent Miriam Micklethwaite on a frantic search through the various legal instruments spelling out the terms of the construction of the digital hub. Sometime later, her assistant found her sitting quite rigid at her desk, unable to move, the contract open on the desk before her at page thirty-seven, clause twenty-nine, sub-section three. The next person on the scene was the local first aider, Len Hurry, the head of maintenance.

'It's a relapse,' said Miriam Micklethwaite out of the corner of her mouth as if her head was caught in a trap.

'Are you suffering? In pain?' shouted Len Hurry as he tried to decide on the first-aid procedures for the symptoms she displayed.

'No, quite numb. I must go and see what's going on behind Keynes House!'

'Good, confront your trauma!'

'But I can't...'

'You can. It just requires an act of will!' He spoke with the wisdom of the university's longest-serving first-aider.

In the end, a wheelchair was found and Len Hurry wheeled her out of her office and towards what had been a demolition site, and was now fast becoming an archaeological dig.

'It's no good,' said Miriam Micklethwaite when they were well on their way, 'I have to tell the vice-chancellor. He needs to know.'

Reluctantly, Len Hurry changed direction.

Alone in his office, dismayed by the accumulative effect of the events of the past few days, Conquest was feeling assailed by misfortune. Even Eunice was lost to him! He was prepared for further hammer blows to fall, being under no doubt that fall they would!

And fall they did! Miriam Micklethwaite was with him, looking very woebegone. Although struggling with her rigidity, she tried to choose her words with care.

'The thing is, Vice-Chancellor,' she began, 'Wainwright, Carter & Expandite have informed me that they are about to invoke a clause in our contract with them. It's an interruption clause: clause twenty-nine, subsection three. Basically, it says that we, the client, will indemnify the contractor if a cessation of work is occasioned by the discovery on the building site of any obstruction, hindrance, legal entitlement or other binding agreement not formally recognised in the schedule of works, assuming such was not identified by the surveyors and/or legal teams of either party to the agreement when the said schedule of works was agreed with the client.'

'Miriam,' said Conquest with all the coolness he could muster, 'I thought the bomb had been safely removed.'

That is so, Cliff, but where the bomb was there's a tessellated pavement. Third century AD. The archaeologist from the London

Museum's been to see it and she reckons it's the potential to be the finest tessellated pavement she's ever seen. There a clause in the planning consent –'

'*Don't tell me!*'

'If the archaeological remains are of sufficient significance, the local authority can trigger a clause in the planning consent that allows it to halt work while the archaeological find is excavated.' She paused for breath, 'Yes, and that triggers the clause in our contract with Wainwright, Carter & Expandite that says we, the client, will indemnify the contractor if a cessation of work is occasioned by the discovery on the building site of any obstruction, legal entitlement, or other let or hindrance not formally recognised in the schedule of works, consequential on such having not been identified by the surveyors and/or legal teams of either party prior to the said schedule of works having been agreed with the client.'

The litany of appalling mischief being done to his native tongue having finally ended, Conquest groaned. '*Meaning?*'

'Twenty-five thousand pounds a week, give or take.'

'*Oh, yes?*' Conquest hauled himself to his feet and paced with reckless abandon before the picture window.

I should have expected it! Another Miriam Micklethwaite mess! One hundred thousand pounds a month and the archaeologists here until Christmas! No, they could be here a year!

The choice was between strangling her or sending her to the medical centre. The better man triumphed, but with gritted teeth.

Once alone, his annoyance began to drain away and he was left with a feeling of bereavement. In only a few months, Eunice had taken command of his affairs to such an extent that he felt bereft without her presence in the adjacent office. Apparently unharmed but heavily sedated, she had gone to her mother's to recover from her ordeal, on indefinite sick leave. Little though he felt like it, there was nothing for it but to take matters into his own hands. First, he needed to persuade Sir Norman Fleet to mitigate the interruption clause in Wainwright, Carter & Expandite's contract with the university. As its CEO, and a beneficiary of a connection with an institution he apparently cherished, Sir Norman was surely in a position to influence the company's legal department.

He called in the secretariat's manager, Vernon Pinhorn. 'Vernon, do we have a copy of our contract with Wainwright, Carter & Expandite for the digital hub?'

'Yes, Vice-Chancellor, we keep duplicates of all legal contracts as a matter of course.'

'Good, can you look it out for me? A problem has arisen and I need to speak to Sir Norman.'

Vernon duly delivered the Wainwright, Carter & Expandite contract, a bulky, bound document of many pages and clauses. Conquest was horrified by the thought of having to study it in any detail. He turned to clause twenty-nine, sub-section three, and saw it was as Miriam Micklethwaite had said. He picked up his phone and found Sir Norman's office number. A loud, brassy voice assailed him.

'Sir Norman is out of his office today and he won't be back until Monday.'

Conquest tried Sir Norman's mobile. A robotic voice invited him to leave a message, an invitation he declined, but almost immediately he called back and spoke to the machinery.

'Sir Norman, could we please discuss Wainwright, Carter & Expandite's implementation of the –?' The mobile made an electronic whimpering noise and the line went dead.

This was the last straw. He tossed the contract onto his desk, and slumped into the steel and leather chair of American design. His plans had been utterly undone. The cumulative blows to his pilot scheme for the transformation of his university were bad enough, but the thought of Keynes House standing empty and forlorn for goodness knows how long while the university leaked money to Wainwright, Carter & Expandite was utterly discouraging. He felt like doing nothing but hiding where he was, in his office, as slowly, irrevocably, minute by minute, the time came when the campus would start to flood with students. The start of the new academic year was nearly upon him! It occurred to him – horror of horrors – that his only recourse was to go back to his wiring diagram!

No, never!

Much better to beat an orderly retreat to his home in Wolverhampton, to Marj, his wife, and nurse his wounds. The university could manage without him. The students' arrival was quite sufficient to kickstart the machinery of a new academic year. He would call in sick for a day or two and let them all get on with it. Why not?

Everyone else does!

The telephone rang. He raised the receiver to his ear thinking Sir Norman had had the goodness to call him back, but instead a cool, soft voice like a May breeze blowing in from the Azores rolled back his gloom.

'…so we are expecting you, and I thought I should just make sure you've remembered us, what with everything you have on your mind.'

My God! he thought. *It's Fawn Williams!*

'Hello?'

'Ah, there you are! I haven't been able to get through to your extension. What's happened?'

'Bomb scare… and I lost my PA. I suppose you could call it a *temporary dislocation.*'

'*Bomb scare?* You mean a terrorist outrage? Surely they're not attacking our universities now?'

'No, no, not terrorists; a Second World War thing. Didn't go off. Been defused and whatever.'

'Oh… *good*! Our music festival's tomorrow. You remember? I hope this doesn't mean you can't make it?'

'Er… no! Yes, I suppose I can.'

'Clifford, *you must*! Don't be late, the programme starts at twelve. It'll be a lovely opportunity to talk to Cornelius about your film school… and don't forget to bring your oboe with you!' At that she laughed her silvery, seductive laugh and rang off.

Conquest heaved himself to his feet and paced. He noticed he had developed a limp like a wounded animal. He tried to walk it off. The ferment that Fawn Williams always seemed to induce in him had again taken hold. The thought that he might see her tomorrow revived his spirits utterly. On the turn he tripped and almost fell. His only problem was that, instead of pursuing the possibility of an endowment, he would have to tell her he didn't have even the semblance of a film school to be endowed. Shellbrooke and McWhelk had, each in their own way, bested him by demonstrating they had more value to the world at large than they had within his university. He could see now that compared to the contributions they were making to their respective fields, his plan to use them to create a film school had been crassly expedient.

And this was supposed to be his showcase for how his university should be modernised! He had but one thought: *I am an impostor, wherever I go I spawn Frankenstein monsters*!

It was as though the pathway to the imagined place of success and adulation where, beckoning him at the threshold, stood Fawn Williams, was unreachable because he, in every way, fell short. Yes, abasement was the only answer! He threw back his shoulders and resolved he would drive to Thieves for their music festival. He would confess all; she would forgive him. The record would be put straight and he would begin again.

I may be down, he thought, *but don't count me out! I may be wounded but the wound is far from fatal! Even* in extremis *I am not without resource! And I shall not leave without striking a blow against those who have opposed me!*

Conquest took up the telephone and in a moment he was speaking to Tommy Ballantyne, the director of finance.

'Tommy, I've been giving thought to something we spoke of in passing a couple of weeks ago. *McWhelk!* You remember the name?'

'Yes, you had some plan for him concerning… er… was it film studies?'

'Spot on. Well, change of plan. Enhance the enhancement!'

'I'm sorry?'

'*Enhance the enhancement!* Didn't you say he'd been enquiring about enhanced voluntary redundancy? I think we should help him on his way.'

'Well… is that an executive order? There are guidelines, you know!'

'Exceptional service… re-jigging of academic priorities… grounds for exceeding the guidelines? I'd be grateful if you could find a way to get it done.'

'I'll look into it, Cliff.'

'Good. Let me know.'

THIRTY-FIVE

Later that same morning, at Professor Cronker's urging, Professor Perk Hingley met him for coffee at the forecourt café in front of the Royal Academy. Perk was travelling east, Cronker travelling west, making it a convenient place for a hasty exchange of sensitive information. Cronker was basking in the midday sunshine when Perk arrived. They shook hands.

'Thanks for agreeing to meet me here. I have to go to The Hague,' said Perk, fiddling with the contents of his briefcase, checking for the tenth time that morning that he hadn't forgotten his passport. 'Weekend conference concerning the War Crimes Tribunal. Re-match with the Serbs.'

'Aye, I expect so,' commented Cronker dryly, somewhat uneasy in Perk's company. He thought all internationalists had a capacity for incoherent thought, something he was rock-solid certain his own beliefs never betrayed. He looked about the courtyard. 'This is the sort of place where spies meet.'

'Ah!' Perk had suggested their meeting place and he too gazed about him, coming to no particular view about the character of their surroundings. 'Are you going to pass me a message to read, soak in my tea and swallow?' He gave a snuffle of mirth.

Cronker was in no mood to be amused. 'I came into some information yesterday afternoon I thought you should be made aware of.'

'Oh, yes?'

'It's Clifford. Did you know he's having an affair with his secretary?'

Perk sat up. 'You mean Eunice, the new one?'

'You have heard about the bomb, haven't you?'

'*No!* What bomb?'

Cronker explained about the discovery of the bomb and the subsequent events up to, and including, Eunice's close escape.

'*Good Lord, extraordinary!* And she really said that, did she?'

Cronker nodded. 'I was there. I think she thought she was going to die. It had the character of a deathbed confessional.'

'And the bomb?'

'Aye, well the army was there very promptly; disarmed it.'

'*Good Lord!*' He looked about him blankly while he gathered his thoughts. 'So, is Eunice all right?'

'A bit knocked up, y'know. They took her to hospital in an ambulance. All very dramatic. It's him I'm worried about.'

'She's only been working for him for a few weeks.'

'Clifford's a philanderer. He's trampling on academic freedoms. You need to have a word.'

Perk looked at his watch uneasily. 'I'm actually on my way to London City Airport. My flight's this afternoon.'

'He's driven a senior member of staff to claiming constructive dismissal. There could be a strike.'

'Oh dear, there's never a dull moment with Cliff!' Perk sighed. 'I suppose, in the nicest possible way, I'll have to read him the riot act. Who's claiming constructive dismissal?'

'Professor McWhelk.'

'Ah, *McWhelk*! That's different; he's important: an upholder of the right to think differently in South America! I've already intervened about this.'

Cronker was surprised. 'Really? With the vice-chancellor?'

'No, no! My influence has been applied very circuitously… Soft power, you know; behind the scenes.'

Cronker smelled something fishy. 'You haven't been influencing academic matters behind the vice-chancellor's back, have you?'

'Of course not! I asked an old chum from UNESCO to offer some support, that's all.'

Cronker was dubious. He didn't approve. 'I'm not sure that's politic… not in your position. You might be seen as having divided loyalties; playing both ends against the middle.'

'Nonsense,' said Perk, looking a little sheepish. 'In any case, Professor McWhelk's initiative is helping to sustain civil society in parts of South American where human rights are greatly in need of support.'

'Yes, but have you been in touch with McWhelk personally?'

'Quite so, I have.'

'I see,' Cronker didn't comment further, but he disdained any such clandestine actions. Highly irregular! He was ever willing to offer his support to a fellow Scot, but this was not the way one did things, not when one chaired the governing body. Some things one had to be above!

'Senate has its special meeting next Wednesday to discuss the vexed issue of honorary doctorates!' said Perk, still wondering how best to respond to Cronker's news. 'I'll be back on Sunday evening. It might be as well to take some precautions against any repetition of this sort of thing. When suspicions gather like clouds there can be a sudden downpour, if you know what I mean.' He then repeated one of his favourite mantras. 'I am the custodian of the university's values, long term,' he said. 'Can't compromise that.'

'I'll leave it with you, then,' decided Cronker, hoping Perk would be circumspect in acting on his information.

Perk prepared to depart, peering into his briefcase one last time. 'In any case, I imagine that you and I can keep my little intervention on behalf of Professor McWhelk to ourselves. After all, we're not here discussing the performance of a VC whose behaviour hasn't previously given us cause for concern, are we?'

'Constructive dismissal is an ugly thing!'

'When you have my kind of responsibilities, it's necessary to have key people prepared to take my advisements,' said Perk loftily. He rose to his feet. 'And even a vice-chancellor can be encouraged to do the right thing.'

THIRTY-SIX

Where Conquest had failed, Lord N'Gabi, being *Access All Areas*, succeeded. He was on the phone to Sir Norman Fleet.

'What's going on, Norman? That man of yours, Conquest, has turned down an invitation to serve on the committee advising the Shadow Secretary of State for Higher Education! D'you know the one I'm talking about? It's the influential one we're trying to keep out of the hands of the Rising Left?'

'Damn and blast, of course I remember! *Turned it down?*'

'Yes, turned it down! I've got the letter from him right here. Says he's too busy with that university of his. What's he up to? Why can't he delegate?'

'He's been nobbled, Frangi! This is something Perk Hingley and his gang have concocted. They're running around with the levers of power in their panties! They're perfectly capable of discouraging Conquest from accepting your invitation so the Rising Left can shoo-in one of their Camlington blighters without anyone realising. In short, they've got him under their collective thumb!'

'Well look here, Norman, right now the Centre Left needs all the help it can get, and the vice-chancellors out there in the rest of England won't like it if the future of socialism looks North London style, so he's *not turning it down*. It's not an option, so I suggest you have a word, *several in fact*!'

THIRTY-SEVEN

Cornelius Pye had decamped to the country. Since it was the eve of his annual music festival, his collaborators, colleagues and friends had followed, or were about to. Those not staying at Thieves – there was only room for his closest associates – were in the offing, lodged in inns and rural hotels across half of north Norfolk. Pye had enjoyed the fuss around the premiere of *Confess, Undercover Girl!* but his drive to move on meant he couldn't take his ease for long. Even now, at a time of day when the thoughts of everyone around him had turned to the pleasures of the evening, he was preoccupied with his plans for the future. He had been waiting awhile for Sophie Flambeau to join him, pacing the vast turning circle that fronted Thieves. Sophie had recently arrived from London and had had only had a few minutes to establish herself in one of the bedrooms on the first floor.

'Ah, Cornelius, lovely evening!' she said as finally she arrived, reaching for her cigarettes in the pocket of her voluminous mackintosh. 'Have I time for a fag?'

'Evening, Sweetie,' said Pye, kissing her quickly before the cigarette was in place. 'I thought we'd walk. Plenty of time to get your nicotine level up.'

The evening was mellow, the weather utterly quiescent. Sophie had spent the morning at a screening of a new film about August Rodin called *Clay, Bronze, Marble*. It had been something of a spying mission because the movie's director was once a *protégée* of Pye's and had used an actress for the part of Rodin's young assistant and sometime lover, Camille Claudel, that Pye had an interest in. Pye had seen some of the rushes in an editing suite in Soho some months before. Her performance had so struck him he had called her and promised her something important in his next movie. He had sent Sophie to see the finished film to confirm his hunch had been right.

'Here's the good news,' she said, 'Orpington Girl as Camille Claudel is mesmerising. She steals every scene!'

Pye gave a hollow laugh.

'Yes, she makes Oliver look a dullard.'

'Poor old Oliver!' Pye's commiseration was genuine. 'You have to convey something remarkable to transcend an age difference like that. Twenty-four years!'

Sophie exhaled a lungful of smoke. 'There's more to it than that. I'm thinking about something very subtle here, Connie, and it's nothing to do with realism. It's to do with projection. Orpington Girl projects something new, and that's like a new species has come into being.'

They had crossed the lawn and reached the old estate gate that led to a footpath descending the hill.

'You know how it is when you're casting a movie and you're trying to match actors with what the writer's conjured up? You have to pour living flesh into an imagined being and sometimes you can't find that match. It's near, or somebody comes along you think will grow into the role, but when you see the result, you realise the person you've cast doesn't come anywhere near. You've missed by a mile! Am I explaining myself?'

Pye, whose eyes were fixed on the path ahead, nodded.

'Have you thought what you're going to do about her? I mean, you're not going to let her go, are you? Once people see her Camille it'll be too late. She'll be snapped up.'

Pye gave Sophie an enigmatic smile. 'Sure, I've promised her something.'

They passed through some trees and skirted the yurts of the Young Persons' Chorus of Leipzig, Pye reflecting on what Sophie had said. She was a veteran of twenty years casting movies and had an encyclopaedic knowledge of acting talent. Like many who helped to contrive magic from flesh and bone, she was a scientist of the ineffable ability of a face to bring colour to the black-and-white of a script, to clothe the most wretched of cliché-ridden texts with human vitality and warmth. This was a great skill, and there are no acronyms one can acquire to place after one's name that can guarantee this skill. In short, she was the casting director every film director dreams of, but she was almost impossible to get hold of, even more difficult to recognise. In her homemade, knitted cardigans and tartan skirts she looked like nothing so much as an old-fashioned ledger keeper, peering out from behind specs forever in need of a polish. She thought Cornelius Pye a clever man, had followed his rise, and enjoyed working with him on the casting of several of his films. He, in turn, had great trust in her judgement and was gratified by her opinion of Ariel Gracechurch, AKA Orpington Girl.

Their ramble had taken them at a diagonal down the long, gentle slope that lay to the south of Thieves. They arrived at another estate gate and crossed a paddock where two ponies frisked a little at their intrusion but then decided they were of negligible interest. Beyond the paddock, down a short length of lane, lay *The Nelson*, the pubic house they were heading for. In the restaurant, Avril Morgan was already seated at their table.

'Where's Fawn?' he asked as they joined him.

Pye held out his hands helplessly. 'The girls won't let her go.'

Fawn's three daughters were a frequent reason for her absence and Morgan nodded sympathetically, as if for someone enduring a minor curse. He and Sophie Flambeau were old friends long absent from one another's lives, and it served Pye's purpose to bring them together on the eve of his music festival. Like all such informal get-togethers, information was traded and important ideas first mooted between bits of inconsequential gossip. The table was at the back of the restaurant and the conversation had turned to a discussion of a film project Angus Farthing was interested in developing: a long-form historical drama called *Darwins and Wedgewoods*. Pye had already given Avril Morgan his opinion about whether he should help Farthing find funding for the project and his attention wandered as Morgan filled in Sophie on the background.

At the next table there was a nondescript-looking man sitting with a much younger woman, quite beautiful in her own way. Pye could admire her out of the corner of his eye without seeming to stare. Rather indulging himself, he eavesdropped on their conversation. Maybe it was more of a monologue. The man seemed to be giving her, in big, expansive terms, his thoughts about the latest political and cultural developments. It caught Pye's attention when he thought he heard the man refer to private culture.

'Some of them are very involved,' the man was saying. 'I hear it's quite a hot number. The Camlington faction have been very against it from the start. They think the establishment doesn't get it. I mean, the insiders think it's going to be very successful, whatever they say.'

Morgan tried to draw Pye back into their discussion of Farthing's project.

'A family saga,' said Pye mechanically, his ears still tuned to the next table, 'full of charm, wit, tragedy, industrial innovation and scientific discovery.'

'*Meaning?*' prompted Sophie, laughing.

Reluctantly Pye reined in his interest in the couple at the next table sufficiently to expand, but delivered the words as though he'd leant them by rote. 'Charles Darwin marries Emma Wedgwood, joining two of the great names of the English nineteenth century. Unlike other dramatizations of Darwin's story, this one commences with the publication of *On the Origin of Species*. The over-arching storyline here is of its public reception and its consequences for science, religious belief and Victorian society.'

'The sort of thing the BBC used to do,' said Sophie.

'We observe its effects through the lens of Darwin's family life, following family members through three generations, spanning the best part of the century. Their lives and loves capture many of the significant themes of the changing times... Providing plenty of delightful eccentrics and non-conformists... Through them we experience the dilemmas and opportunities... The inexorable pace of progress... Aspiration, success, heart-rending bereavement, ceramic elegance, moral courage and conflict are woven into this family saga, all addressed at their most dramatic and heart-warming.'

'It sounds as if Farthing's gone soft in the head!' decided Sophie.

'It might go down well my side of the Atlantic,' said Morgan shrewdly.

'Fawn's going to star in Angus Farthing's off-Broadway production of *Lysistrata*. That's why we're going to New York next week.'

Sophie laughed mercilessly. 'Ah, wheels within wheels! *Lysistrata*! *Interesting!* Sounds more like Farthing's sort of thing than pottery and natural selection.'

'*Agreed!* His *Hamlet* was a great success there.' Pye gave her a wan smile. 'Rather awkward about the Darwin thing. I need to keep a low profile.'

The man at the next table looked like one of the boys from Hedge Fund Alley and Pye wondered whether he was one of a group interested in film financing. He was aware of such a thing. It had *cache* to divert a little of one's wealth in that direction and the tax breaks were kind to people with certain kinds of liabilities. When they rose to leave, he watched them go.

'You seemed very interested in them,' said Morgan.

Pye shook his head, puzzled. 'Well, it's rather odd. I thought I heard that man discussing *Private Culture*. *Yes*, those people at the next table... And he mentioned Camlington.'

'Ah!' Sophie looked suddenly knowing. '*Camlington!* That's a conflation of Camden and Islington: North London politicos. It's the Rising Left writ large.'

'*Really?* That's ever odder! What's the Rising Left?'

'The latest twist in Labour party factionalism. They're driving out the old-school technocrats to reinstate a meritocracy based on community activism. It's taking to the streets for the digital age.'

Her explanation only increased Pye's bafflement. 'Are you *serious?*'

'Not entirely, but the Rising Left does have a populist tinge about it that's sometimes a bit distasteful. They're young and full of enthusiasm for a new start. Private culture sounds like their kind of jargon. Do you want me to enquire? I could have a word.'

Pye was still troubled. 'I could have sworn they were talking about my movie. For a while there it sounded like they were treading on my toes! My Camlington's a picturesque village on the north slope of the South Downs.' If it was politics, he was not normally interested, but this was different and Sophie looked keen to enquire. 'Yes, ask about it by all means. It sounds kind of duff, but titles are everything and I wouldn't want to change mine now!'

'*Duff?*' said Morgan. 'What the heck?'

The other two laughed; the American looked humorously quizzical.

Later they stood in the car park, not quite ready to part company. Morgan was staying with an American couple not far away. He played with his electronic key until this car flashed at him.

'You know,' said Pye, breaking the silence, 'I've been thinking Orpington Girl would be perfect for Candide.'

For a moment Sophie's normally placid face took on a pained expression. 'Ah, *Candide*! You're still pursuing that idea, are you?'

'Yes, maybe after *Private Culture*,' ruminated Pye. 'You know Poppy Trench, don't you?'

Sophie nodded as she lit a cigarette.

'She's trying to resuscitate the *Candide In Tinseltown* screenplay.'

'How's she doing?'

'I don't know; haven't had time to catch up with her... and I won't before I go to New York. I was wondering whether you might take an interest. She's been mining the Goldman papers for drafts with some success, apparently. You worked on the casting originally, didn't you?'

Sophie groaned 'For that idiot who lost the screenplay? *Yes. I did!* Funnily enough, I thought Candide was impossible to cast but there wasn't any Orpington Girl then. *Well...* I suppose she was a fourteen-year-old at an Orpington grammar school. Maybe you're right; maybe the time is right.'

'You remember the story?'

'Of course. Goldman deluxe.'

'Good. Why don't you look at what Poppy's put together? She's bringing it with her when she comes tomorrow. If she's managed to unearth the spirit of the original, you can cast it for me. If we already have our Candide, everyone else might fall into place nicely.'

She laughed. 'Anything for you, Connie. Are you serious about making it though?' She glanced at him, thinking she might be the butt of one of his sly jokes.

Morgan had been an onlooker to the discussion for some time. Now he stirred ponderously, wanting to have his say for Sophie's benefit. 'Goldman's wife gave his archive to University London Central. The vice-chancellor, a guy called Clifford Conquest, has some idea about Connie funding a film school.'

'Sounds commendable,' said Sophie, 'Could earn you a knighthood.'

Morgan's voice grew sharper. 'What's not been so clear is that the university owns the copyright of everything in the Goldman archive not previously published, and that applies to *Candide In Tinseltown*. It's something Conquest's keeping very quiet about.'

'That's awkward,' decided Sophie.

He nodded in Pye's direction. 'He's got Connie over a barrel.'

Pye started to speak but Morgan overrode him. 'It seems to me Conquest's playing a very subtle hand and you're letting him run rings round you!' He said it reprovingly. 'It's like you've got Poppy Trench working for *him*, digging out this *Candide In Tinseltown* stuff! It's crazy!'

Pye sighed. 'Yes, all a bit complicated. If Poppy's been successful, I suppose I'll have to have it out with him.'

'No, no, if anyone's going to deal with him it's me!' said Morgan. 'He'll stretch it out and make you pay through the nose if you try.'

Pye gestured hopelessly. 'For some reason Fawn seems keen on helping him.'

Sophie scratched her nose and rubbed her chin. '*Very awkward.*'

'I'm feeling the pull of Hollywood. That makes *Candide In Tinseltown* perfect. Avril wants me to set up shop there more permanently, don't you, Avril?'

'It's your future, Connie!'

Sophie gave Pye a look of mock disapproval. 'Ah, the man no longer wants to do the cute English stuff! Thinks it might be more strategic to make an endowment to CalArts... *or some such*!'

THIRTY-EIGHT

It was still quite early on Saturday morning and Conquest was driving along one of the many straight, minor roads that crisscross north Norfolk. His side window was down and he could smell newly-mown grass. It was a delight to be away from University London Central. Even though the countryside looked wonderful in the sparkling sunshine he renewed his vow that however great the attractions of the music festival at Thieves, he would be in Wolverhampton with Marj that evening. All he was going to do was call by, drop in and confess all. It was then that he noticed the sign. The sign said *Private Culture* and there was an arrow pointing down the road in the direction he was going. On the rest of his journey, across half the county, he saw two more of the signs, both attached to telegraph poles, both pointing to a destination he didn't pass before he arrived at Thieves Cross. He came round a bend, squeezed through a narrowing of the road where a hump-backed bridge crossed a stream and almost ran into the back of a stationary Waitrose van. There was a village green and a duck pond shaded by enormous beech trees. Beyond stood a pub called *The Nelson* where several Range Rovers were parked. Next came a cluster of quaint flint cottages and houses nestling in gardens overflowing with curated vegetation Then, on a corner, there was a ribbon of gravel drive seen through a huge, crenulated gateway, gates wide open, suggesting the highway's proper function was not to continue on, but to become the drive. A sign announced, 'Thieves. Private'. Beyond the cattle grid shaggy longhorns grazed in a meadow of lush grass on one side, on the other, horse chestnut trees dotted parkland that ran down towards a lake or river, Conquest couldn't tell which. The drive wended gradually uphill, this way and that through several distinct scenes replete with bucolic incident until, at the hill's crest, promising far-flung views on every side, appeared a grand, foursquare Palladian house. Some distance from the house, across an extensive plateau of lawn, stood a marquee festooned with bunting. As he drew to a halt in front of the house, he was aware that the view beyond the crest of the hill looked out over a gentle descent of a mile or so until the land ended at the North Sea in a distant blur of muddy blue. Not another building was to be seen in that placid vista of prime agricultural real estate.

Conquest climbed out of his car. The house was bright in the morning sun. It seemed completely new and fantastical, scarcely rooted to the ground. There were only a few cars parked on the turning circle, but when he looked around he realised there were many more parked in the shade of some cedars a little distance away. No one appeared to greet him and he began to wonder if he had correctly understood what Fawn Williams had told him. He couldn't see – or hear – any indication of a music festival and it occurred to him that the *Private Culture* signs he'd seen pointing in the direction of Thieves might indicate that a conclave of the Rising Left was in session somewhere nearby, theorising the threat of private culture. For a moment he couldn't decide between the marquee and the house. In the end the marquee seemed a more likely place to find whatever activity was going on and he headed in that direction.

He was midway across the expanse of lawn when he heard his name called. He looked round and saw Fawn Williams standing at the corner of the house, her hand raised to shade her eyes, as though she wasn't entirely sure she knew who he was. She looked immensely posed, like something from a *Fête Belle Époque* illustration.

'Is that you, Clifford?'

'I'm sorry,' he shouted back. 'Am I early?'

She seemed to chuckle to herself as she made her way towards him. 'Yes, you are, *rather*,' she said as she drew near. 'If you've come from London, you must have made a *very* early start!'

He looked at his watch and saw it was barely half past ten. He had set out on his journey not long after seven. 'Yes, I suppose I was eager to get away,' he said apologetically.

She appraised him up and down. 'We have a no-tie policy during the day,' she said, with a slight air of mockery.

Hastily he loosened his tie and thrust it in his jacket pocket.

She laughed. 'Let me show you round,' she said, impulsively taking him by the arm. She propelled him in the direction of the marquee.

'I'm afraid the house is full,' she added, 'but we've made a reservation for you at *The Nelson*. Did you pass it on the way here?'

'I wasn't thinking of staying overnight. I ought –'

'Don't be ridiculous; you have to stay. There's a whole orchestra coming from Norwich this evening.'

They inspected the marquee, which was set out with rows of upright gilt chairs facing a raised stage. Conquest's will to insist he was on his way to Wolverhampton was already wilting before her gentle charm.

'I did see it in the village.'

'It's very comfortable. *Mein host* had a spell as *sous chef* with Ferran.' Fawn pointed to the Steinway currently standing centre-stage. 'Valerie Givings will be playing Ravel at noon.'

They rounded the marquee on the side furthest from the house. Conquest was possessed of a growing feeling that he was an interloper who had stumbled into something strange and exotic. When he thought of a music festival, what he had in mind was something muddy and high-pitched, like a mini-Glastonbury, but what he could see ahead of them were decorous young women with violins sauntering beneath the cedars. It hadn't occurred to him that Pye had a taste for classical music. He felt adrift and tried to anchor himself by admiring the view. His first impression had been that the lawn blended indiscernibly into parkland but now he could see, as they approached its limits, that it was bounded by the retaining wall of a ha-ha, the lower level of the parkland being accessible by a short flight of stone steps. Their elevated position opened up an expansive vista before them. Some way down the hillside there was a hollow, a natural amphitheatre, dotted with buttercups. A film crew was at work.

'What are they doing there?' asked Conquest.

'Oh, they're filming my husband. Some network obliged him to honour a promise to give an interview, so he made them come here.' She laughed at the folly of chasing after her husband.

Conquest stared. At the centre of the activity there were two seated men. One was Cornelius Pye, the other, he was almost certain, was... *Piers Hazlett*!

'Good God,' he exclaimed involuntarily.

She looked at him enquiringly. 'Do you know that man?'

He hesitated. 'I believe I do. Is that something to do with private culture?'

'Oh, yes, I expect so. *Private Culture* is Connie's latest thing, you know. He's being constantly pursued about it.'

'It's a real thing, then!'

'Oh yes, very much so! It was frightfully hush-hush, of course; the details, I mean. Connie loves to surprise, but he's been found out.'

'I see.' said Conquest, his suspicion that he had wandered into a gathering of the Rising Left given substance by the sight of Hazlett. 'I came for the music, you know.'

'*The music?* Of course you did!' She gestured dismissively to the activity below them. 'That's just a sideshow! Let's go and find the others.'

They wandered further round the perimeter of the lawn and as they did so another view opened up before them. They were now beyond the marquee. Here the ground dropped away more steeply and they were looking down upon a well-ordered encampment of yurts set out in a circle with a large bell tent at its centre. A dozen or more young people were playing a ball game, and further away still others were coming up the hill in swimming costumes.

'That's the Young Persons' Chorus of Leipzig. They come to camp here every summer.'

'Marvellous!' he said numbly. 'And the audience?'

'Ah, too early yet. There are refreshments in the rose garden on the other side of the house, *but*,' she confessed, 'I wanted to get you by yourself.'

The suggestion of intimacy further unsettled him and he felt that now was the time to confess. 'I have to tell you –' he blurted out.

She had raised her index finger to her lips to stop him. 'Whatever it is,' she said, 'I don't want to know.' She turned away with a seraphic smile. 'You're used to speaking in public, aren't you?'

'I suppose...'

'Connie was wondering whether you might read one of Alice Shellbrooke's poems before Valerie Givings plays. She is yours, after all, so he thinks it would be most fitting.'

The voice in his head telling him that now was the time to confess about the film school was quite stilled by his surprise at her request.

'Connie's only just learnt what an extraordinary little gem you have,' she chided as though he had been keeping something from them. 'From what we understand, your university's been supporting her for ages.'

'I'm not sure...' The way Fawn had put it – as if University London Central had been sponsoring Alice Shellbrooke as a sort of poet-in-residence – caused him such a tangle of emotions that he was quite lost for words. Not very long ago, Alice Shellbrooke had been an obscure member of his university's academic staff with very few students, now she was a national treasure people seemed to think his university had been nurturing for years! He wasn't sure he shouldn't disperse the air of intimacy by disclaiming all responsibility for her.

'He wants you to recite her poem that begins, "So long as men can breathe, or eyes can see, so long lives this, and this gives life to thee".'

For several moments Conquest didn't know what to say. Had he been asked beforehand, he would have been confident it was impossible for her to intensify his sense of discomfort, but intensify it she had! Finally, he said, 'you do know that's Shakespeare, don't you?'

'Ah yes, but for Shakespeare it's an ending, for Shellbrooke it's just a beginning! Everything else being pure her.' She smiled winningly, innocent of all guile.

He, in response, laughed as pleasantly as possible. 'Why does your husband think it's an appropriate way to start things off?'

'Oh, he's had this extraordinary revelation about her... and the poem's a perfect paradox, isn't it? It's like blessing a vessel before it leaves port. Connie is keen on that sort of thing. It's a lovely poem anyway... so starry, and so fortunate you're here.'

'Well. I'm not sure I'm the person —'

'*Oh, you must!*'

'But I don't really know her work, and I'm certainly not familiar with the poem you're thinking of.'

'You have time to familiarise yourself with it thoroughly.' She pointed towards the house, the flank of which they were now facing. 'You see the French windows? That's the library. There's an Alice Shellbrooke anthology on the table. Page 64.'

At this point it was fortunate — it saved Conquest's standing as someone with a calm and commanding nature — that their conversation was interrupted by a call on his mobile. He put it unwilling to his ear, almost a reflex.

'Clifford, it's Norman!'

For a moment Conquest was baffled, and then: 'Oh, yes, I'm sorry, *of course*, *Sir Norman*! I've been trying to reach you, Sir Norman.' He held out the mobile in Fawn's direction with a look of apology. 'Would you mind if I took this? It's Sir Norman... *Fleet.*'

Obligingly, with a wave, she sauntered off.

Conquest couldn't believe his luck. He plunged in. 'Our contract with Wainwright, Carter & Expandite, Sir Norman! The interruption clause —'

'Where are you, man? I can hear a bird!'

'I'm in Norfolk.'

'Norfolk? Shooting duck?'

'No, attending a music festival.'

'Ah, open-air opera and so on! Fine thing: music! Listen, this committee you've declined to join. It can't be.'

'I'm sorry, what committee?'

'The Higher Education rabble advising the leader of the opposition. The future of Higher Education is too important to fall into certain hands. The universities are in a mess as it is, and the powers that be don't want the North Londonites digging their trenches all over this committee. They're bent on turning universities into political indoctrination camps, so it's up to you to stop them!'

'I'm sorry...?'

'It's the Camlington blighters, Clifford! They're on the march, leading the party into the stink bog of political oblivion.'

'I'm not aware I've been —'

'Look, never mind about all that. This is here and now, and when you get back to London. have that lassie of yours give Lord N'Garbi's office a call and get the date of the next meeting in your diary.'

'Sir Norman, I've been wanting to speak to you about the Wainwright, Carter & Expandite interruption clause. Surely there's a way —'

'*Clifford*, it's *Saturday* and you're *talking business*! I have a golden rule: *no business at the weekend*! We'd all be driven mad if we did business all the time. I'm going to go and throw my weight about on a golf course. I suggest you do the same... when the music's over.'

He rang off. Conquest grimaced and thought about calling him back, but better counsels prevailed. His several attempts to reach him the previous day had left him with little doubt that Sir Norman was trying to avoid him. Now, an opportunity to speak to him, instead of resulting in a mitigation of the interruption clause, had landed him with another task, a task he had no idea what to make of. There was clearly a failure of communication somewhere and it didn't take long for the suspicion to form that Eunice might be responsible for him not knowing what Sir Norman was talking about. News of the Rising Left manoeuvring in the corridors of Westminster took him right back to his present predicament. He did not know what to make of the strange pastoral he had wandered into. Chief amongst his several imaginings was that somewhere nearby the Rising Left, led on by the odious Alistair Vox, was gathering to theorise the threat of private culture, with him standing accused of fostering it! He had no idea what he felt or what to say; even less how to behave.

Re-awakening to his immediate surroundings, he found himself again alone. Reluctantly, he decided he had better grant Pye his wish and read the poem. He could hardly refuse. His confession would have to wait. He had no doubt a little preparation would save him from something even more humiliating than his present predicament.

He made his way towards the house. The French windows were open and hesitantly he entered. The room was indeed a library, in the proper Country Life manner. It was brown and vellum beige, and stocked with the accoutrements of weekend reading from ancient tome to Ian Fleming. A long table was burdened with neat piles of the sort of books where glossy illustrative matter was the point, and guides to azaleas and making cocktails were almost certainly to be discovered. He quickly found the anthology of Alice Shellbrooke's poems. It was titled *Concocted*. When he picked it up, he saw that beneath it lay a copy of *The Times* folded open at a full-page profile headlined, *Alice Shellbrooke: Perseverance Rewarded*. The following caught his eye because it had been highlighted with a florescent marker:

> *It is a little-known fact that in her youth, Shellbrooke – then called by her maiden name, Alice Mountjoy – was the rebellious femme fatal at the heart of the Camlington set, named after the village beneath the South Downs where, in the early seventies, their activities were centred. Their social experiment is now largely forgotten, long dismissed as an idealistic but misconceived programme of utopian mutuality. In its day, its members were thought mad, bad and dangerous to know. If anything, the Camlington set is now remembered for the outré music festival it hosted for several years. Shellbrooke went on to re-invent herself, teaching English for several years in Zambia before studying for her PhD at Warwick University. She buried her past, dismissing the other members of the set as 'a bunch of toffee-nosed anarchists and Right-wing windbags'. The Camlington set's scandalous derring-does were celebrated, thinly-veiled, in the minor classic, Consent Withheld, written in blank verse by seventies chronicler, R.S. Watkins.*

> *The latest rumour from the camp of celebrated film-maker Cornelius Pye is that he is currently preparing to film Consent Withheld, re-titled Private Culture, the term the Camlington set adopted for their particular brand of ruralist, collectivist artistic and social endeavour. It is believed that star-in-the-making, Ariel Gracechurch, known as Orpington Girl because of her South London roots, is slated to feature as the young Alice Shellbrooke. The hot news from the sneak previews of Ariel Gracechurch's latest outing, Clay, Bronze, Marble – streaming on channel 982 from October 28th – is that she is sensational as August Rodin's young assistant and lover, Camille Claudel, in Massimo Fullerton's re-telling of Rodin's tragic, École de Paris love triangle.*

As he took in what he was reading, a slight noise from the direction of the French windows disturbed him. He turned and saw that Fawn was standing there, watching him.

'I don't understand,' he said, gesturing with the newspaper. 'There are *two* private cultures, and *two* Camlington sets?'

'Well,' she said, with a laugh, 'strictly speaking one is Camlington *set*, the other Camlington *faction*, if that makes any difference.'

'But are there different notions of private culture too?'

'Who knows. Connie thinks it's irrelevant. It's the human story that interests him. Nobody seems to have realised that Shellbrooke and Mountjoy are the same person, you know? He relies on his researchers, but he didn't ask them the right question… so he says. I suppose he thought Camlington was all a lovely fiction. Anyway, now you know why he wants you to read her poem. He's having to recalibrate!'

Conquest was in a daze. 'I suppose so. And this –' he held up *Concocted* – 'is the poem he wants me to read?'

'Page 64.'

'Perhaps I should rehearse.'

'Yes, bring the book, and come and have a cup of coffee.'

To the rear of the house there was another, small marquee pitched on a broad stretch of lawn between two magnificent borders of roses. As Fawn and Conquest walked towards it, they heard a shout from behind them and turned to see, spilling out of the house, three girls, each an enlargement of the first, all unmistakably versions of their mother.

'Girls,' said Fawn as her breathless daughters joined them, 'I want you to meet Professor Conquest. He runs University London Central, so you must show him the *greatest* respect.'

The three girls, now clustered round their mother, squinted at him critically.

'Rachel, Mona and my youngest, Gabriella.'

'Hello, you three,' said Conquest, feeling a little uneasy beneath their withering scrutiny.

'Hello,' they chanted with stubborn malevolence. It occurred to Conquest that they had no intention of sharing their mother with anyone, especially him.

They made their way towards the tent where a group of teenagers were managing the refreshments, fussing about behind several urns and a tabletop array of bottles, glasses and coffee cups. They made a pretty picture but seemed hardly to know how to transfer coffee from the largest of the urns to a cup. Two of the teenagers eventually managed to serve them, but not without several false starts. It struck Conquest, not for the first time, that what he was seeing was window dressing, and some hidden agency must be at work behind the scenes making sure everything ran smoothly.

'Did the Young Persons' Chorus of Leipzig do *all this*?' he asked fatuously.

'No, we all lent a hand,' replied Fawn, seeming to imply it was her hand that in some mysterious way was largely responsible for the effortless effect of marquees, campsites and manicured lawn.

The coffee was surprisingly potent and delicious. Looking about him, it was obvious to Conquest that only the early arrivals were yet present. Seated on a bench gossiping were what looked like the membership of the local flower-arranging society. The other side of the marquee was rolled up and a dozen or so other people were talking in groups on a further stretch of lawn. Everyone looked relaxed and out to enjoy themselves, making him aware of how tight was his grip on *Concocted*. He couldn't help but feel there was something seriously neurotic about his watchfulness.

Fawn had asked for glasses of milk and straws for her three daughters, and now the littlest said, 'Mummy, there's a beetle in my milk. Can I have a Coke instead?'

Conquest could see that a beetle of a shockingly iridescent green was paddling about in her milk. He said, 'Page 64,' to himself.

'*You* put that there,' said the oldest sister, '*now drink it!*'

'I don't think that would be a very good idea,' said Conquest. He instantly regretted intervening. Rachel's baleful stare made it obvious that he was not entitled to interfere and nothing he could say would divert her from her purpose of making Gabriella drink the milk.

Fawn, whose attention had momentarily been elsewhere, now saw the beetle. 'Gabriella, do you have an inexhaustible supply of those green things?'

'It'll give you Ebola,' said the middle sister.

'It's all because she has an eating disorder,' said Rachel in the same placid voice as her mother.

'It's disgusting, mummy, and I do so want a Coke,' pleaded Gabriella.

Conquest looked from one to the other, thinking the thread of alikeness that ran through them was uncanny. He had previously noticed that one of the people on the further side of the marquee was Poppy Trench. Now he decided he should go and speak to her. It was a decision that brought a certain amount of relief; four Fawns at once were definitely more than he could cope with, especially when the smallest was proclaiming, 'life is a cruel mockery'.

'Will you excuse me, Fawn? I must say hello to Poppy. She's been working in our library. I'm curious to know how she's getting on.'

'Ah, yes, *Candide In Tinseltown*!' she murmured. 'Come back when you've read that poem and tell us what it means.'

The prospect of Poppy's company was a relief. After all, she had been his guide at the tumultuous experience of the premiere of *Confess Undercover Girl!* Here, he felt, was someone he could rely on for information delivered clearly and concisely!

'Professor Conquest!' said Poppy rather formally as he approached.

'Hello, Poppy. To be frank, I'm rather surprised to find myself here…' He looked around guardedly '…in this truly wonderful place. Are you here for the music too?'

'I suppose so, although I'm having my homework marked.'

'Homework?'

'The screenplay I've been researching.'

'Of course, the Goldman papers! How's that going?'

'I can't say. The Goldman papers were – still are – an impenetrable mess. If I'm honest, there's still a lot of guessing going on, so it's difficult to tell. One of Connie's associates is looking at what I've been doing as we speak. She's intimidating, so I'm rather on tenterhooks.'

'I'm sure you've nothing to worry about.'

Poppy uttered an ironic laugh. 'Oh, no? She knows her Goldman and she's very sharp!'

'I see. Well, I'm on tenterhooks myself. Fawn wants me to open proceedings by reading one of these poems.' He showed her the copy of *Concocted*. He felt the need to confess and his next sentence came out in a rush. 'I need to clarify that we don't yet have a film school. Do you know what's going on here, because I'm not really sure I do?'

'Well, there's *always* an *awful lot* going on around Fawn and Connie. Is that what you mean?'

'Yes, I suppose I do. I mean, this private culture business. There seem to be two versions circulating in different places, at the same time.'

Poppy was about to reply when a loud halloo announced the arrival of Cornelius Pye in the company of Piers Hazlett. Having finished recording his interview, Pye had brought him up the hill for refreshments. He made straight for them, throwing wide his arms in a gesture of welcome, while Hazlett went to the counter.

'Ah, here we are! Very glad to see you both! We've a splendid day for it! Last year it rained all afternoon; we had to go indoors. Have you got what you need? Those girls are willing, but slow!'

'This place; quite extraordinary,' said Conquest by way of a greeting. 'Everything with such an air of perfection!'

'Very perceptive; it's all down to Freddie! We come and go, but he's always here, tending the place with his fantastic eye for detail.' Pye laughed as though Freddie's attention to detail was an unfathomable miracle. 'You should see his composting: a biochemical wonder! *Yes, good,* I see you have Alice Shellbrooke's book! Well done! We need something memorable to start us off! What marvels your university harbours!'

Conquest was acutely aware that one of the marvels it harboured was the chief exponent of *cinema concrete*. Mercifully, it appeared, Pye still hadn't learnt the source of the 'candyfloss cinema' jibe. 'I'm really rather baffled by this private culture business,' he confessed, Pye's every exclamation threatening what remained of his sense of equilibrium.

Pye looked ruefully amused. 'Yes, I had *no idea* the two Alices – yours and mine – were one and the same! What an *extraordinary* life!' Pye's exclamations gave the moment an immense sense of superficiality and Conquest felt an overwhelming desire to admit there was no film school.

'I should have told you... I mean, about the film school,' he began.

Pye held up his hand to stop him. He turned to Poppy. 'Have you seen Sophie?'

Poppy assured him she had already given Sophie Flambeau her text.

'*Good!*' Pye turned to Conquest. 'If you and I have something to discuss, we can do it later. You know Piers, I understand? Hotfoot from Sandringham, or some such place. I'll leave you to your coffee; I have a call to make. Poppy, why not come with me?' And with that he led Poppy off towards the house, wielding his mobile. As he disappeared from sight, Conquest was joined by Hazlett, carrying two cups of coffee.

'He's gone,' said Conquest.

Simultaneously, they both recalled that Conquest had said the same thing about Pye at the graduation ceremony.

'At least I now have the interview,' said Hazlett with a grim smile, 'so I can relax.' He immediately cast his eyes about the tent as if looking for whom he might buttonhole next – influencer, activist or celebrity, of whatever stripe.

'So, did you get to the bottom of the private culture thing?' asked Conquest pointedly. 'I seem to think there's some confusion going on. I don't wish to sound resentful, but your friend Vox accused me of fostering it, Perk seemed to think it was a credible claim. Now I discover Cornelius Pye's making a film called *Private Culture*, which seems to be about something entirely different.'

'Yes, private culture is a work-in-progress,' said Hazlett with a hint of an apology in his voice. 'You have to see Alistair as the dynamic nodal point in a force-field of discursive impulses.'

Conquest laughed scornfully. 'I hear you've been to Sandringham.'

'Near-Sandringham.' There was a hint of embarrassment in the way he said it, as if he was finding it difficult to sustain the image of a man who both consorted with royalty and supported the Rising Left.

'Do you realise,' said Conquest dryly, 'that around here the electorate will vote for a pig with a blue rosette if it swears it's Tory?'

Hazlett nodded meaningfully at the group of flower-arranging ladies. 'This is where the private culture impulse has its roots.'

Conquest laughed, suddenly sure he'd never get to the bottom of the private culture thing. It had discursive impulse written all over it. 'So,' he said, weary of the subject, 'you're taking cinema under your wing? Interviewing Cornelius Pye must be quite a scoop.'

'Between you and me, a bit of a damp squib. He plays his cards very close to his chest. On that subject –' He had become suddenly confidential – 'I hear you have plans for a film school. I was thinking I might take up some academic work again. A bit of economic stability wouldn't go amiss.'

'*What*, you really want to go back to working in a university?' Given the circumstances, Conquest thought Hazlett's candour inopportune, but the idea amused him. 'I would have imagined you were far too well paid to contemplate such a thing!'

'Well, actually, TV work is all very well, but it can be a bit slow coming. Then there's always a production company trying to muscle in on one's expertise. On top of that you've got podcasts and YouTube to contend with. Do you know how much a good researcher costs to hire? To be frank, I've been running to stand still of late *and* I'm somewhat over-borrowed.'

'I see.' It was only minutes since Conquest was at the point of capitulation, now he realised Hazlett was teetering towards capitulation! The man was at his mercy.

'I mean,' continued Hazlett, beginning to ramble, 'I'd bring a bit of real-world actuality to the subject, wouldn't I? I have a wealth of contacts in the movie world. All-in-all, for three days a week you'd be getting some pretty terrific input.'

What was, as far as Conquest was concerned, on the brink of becoming an unwelcome heart-to-heart was suddenly interrupted by a loud musical discord. A contingent of the Young Persons' Chorus of Leipzig was heading in their direction armed with wind instruments and percussion.

'*Aha!*' somebody nearby cried appreciatively. '*A Soweto lullaby!*'

The Young Persons seemed intent on some form of beating of the bounds because they marched past at full volume, following the perimeter of the garden. A few steps behind them came the littlest Fawn – Gabriella – impudently holding out a half-empty bottle of Coke in the manner of one displaying the regimental colours.

Fawn re-appeared at Conquest's elbow. 'That's the half an hour signal,' she said softly. 'Thirty minutes until Valerie Givings will be enthralling us with her Ravel. Have you familiarised yourself with the poem?' She smiled winningly, innocent of all subterfuge.

And all cultural baggage, thought Conquest uncharitably. *She speaks with the guileless deliberation of a child! By what kind of creature am I bewitched?*

The sense of false innocence was intensified by the presence of her daughters. Seemingly, they were all of a piece, but he knew he must be deceived. No grown woman could have retained a child's innocence through the travails of adulthood. It was a deception, a sophisticated fraud, *a front*!

Ah...! It came to him. *She's a consummate actress. This is acting! This has all been acting!*

At that moment he would not have been surprised had he walked round that foursquare mansion across the way and discovered it was nothing more than a cunning assemblage of painted canvas flats, scenery for an impossible countryside idyll.

'I'm just about to read through it,' he stammered. He made a vague gesture of apology to Hazlett with *Concocted*. 'You'll have to excuse me…' He pulled a face of despair and made off to discover what he'd been persuaded to read.

He stopped under one of the cedar trees. The Young Persons' Soweto band were now at the furthest reach of its elliptical circuit and its tattarrattating was no longer ear-splitting. He opened *Concocted* at page 64.

EXULTATION

> So long as men can breathe, or eyes can see,
> So long lives his, and this gives life to thee.
> Mellifluous notes wing the welkin
> And with fragrant fanfare,
> Assail the harmoniphile.
> Angel fingers atwang upon a lute of gold –
> How sweet,
> How sweet.
> Oh, that such phonetic beauty should emit
> From so invidious an instrument,
> By the hand of so mean a maestro!
> Ah, the delight that came to my ears…
> Ah-h-h the bitterness that twitted my eyes
> Oh, the sweet sourness of it all.
> So low a life,
> So exalted a gift.
> Ah, me!'

Conquest groaned, unable to believe what he was reading. Not only were the first two lines stolen from Shakespeare, the rest was the first poem by Shellbrooke he had ever seen, which, apparently, she had re-used here, slapping it onto the tail end of the Shakespeare!

He seemed to remember her head of department telling him its origin was something she had appropriated from elsewhere. It was, he thought, a total, brazen cheek and enough to make copyright owners weep! He snapped the book shut in an instant of resolve. He would go back to the refreshments tent and have it out with Fawn. Just then the Young Persons' Soweto band came marching by and he found himself trailing after Gabriella, still parading her trophy Coke, as the procession made its noisy way towards the refreshments tent for a second time.

The piano recital was close to starting and a good-humoured crowd dressed as though for an Edwardian boating trip at Henley now filled the tent. He couldn't see Fawn, but Hazlett saw him and gave him an enquiring look.

'*Piers!*' Conquest cried, his voice coloured with urgency. 'Look, if you want to help further film studies at University London Central why don't you speak to me about it next week? Let's talk it over. In the meantime, do me a favour: read this to the audience before the recital.' He pressed the copy of *Concocted* into his hands. 'It's your kind of thing and I think Fawn would want it. Page 64.'

'What would I want?' said a cool, gently modulated voice in his ear.

He turned and saw that Fawn had again appeared out of nowhere and was standing right behind him.

'I was thinking... You know, I'm not sure... Couldn't it be seen as rather derogatory about...?' It was as if his thought processes had all frozen.

She came very close to him and searched his eyes – their eyes were very close to being at the same level – as if looking for some affliction deep inside him that made him doubt himself.

'I know you will make a great success of it. Everyone here –' briefly she turned to embrace with her eyes the crowd now overflowing from the refreshment tent – 'is wanting you to be a great success; delivering a keynote moment everyone will long remember.'

Conquest felt his will to do anything other than what she wished, buckle. It was, he realised, another capitulation before her Chernobyl-like irradiancy.

THIRTY-NINE

Conquest's performance of *Exaltation* was a tremendous success. He injected just the right amount of ironic dismay into his reading. The adult members of the audience, bar the flower-arranging ladies, exchanged amused glances as they applauded, congratulating themselves that intertextuality was their thing. The three junior Fawns thought it was a lark, although not quite up to the standard of their favourite nonsense poems.

A handsome buffet lunch was followed by a string quartet and then a programme of exuberant *a cappella* singing by the Young Persons' Chorus of Leipzig. After that it was time for tea and cakes. Then tea and cakes became champagne. A bus arrived carrying the orchestra from Norwich. People slipped away to change into eveningwear wherever they could, some behind car doors and others in the shrubbery on the northern slope away from Thieves.

Hazlett was in his element. Was this not the *schmoozefest* of *schmoozefests*? And was he not the *schmoozemeister*? He did the rounds with accelerating *bonhomie* in pursuit of the answer to an urgent thought: '*Is Ariel Gracechurch coming?*' In his interview, Pye had been extremely guarded about her, but the news had reached Hazlett that she was hot property and slated to play the young Alice Shellbrooke.

This was probably the moment he incurred disfavour. The transformation of Ariel Gracechurch, AKA Orpington Girl, into a future star of unlimited potential was complete. She had been declared private property, not to be exposed to random media attention. *Definitely not!* It wasn't as if Hazlett's enquiries annoyed Pye. As Pye always maintained, nothing ever really annoyed him! But Hazlett was taken aside by Avril Morgan.

'Your camera crew; it's time our guests were left alone, I guess.

Could you collect them up and get them to remove their equipment? If it wasn't made clear, it should have been: this evening's event isn't available as background material for your interview. I'm sorry if there's been a misunderstanding. I'm afraid those who are yet to come will not be happy at the sight of anything that even remotely suggests recordings are being made. We have to respect folk's wish for privacy.'

The deeper meaning was clear enough, and something of a humiliation. Hazlett wasn't quite being shown the door, but even someone as thick-skinned as he knew that, despite his best efforts, he was classified as being part of the film crew and had out-stayed his welcome. Of course, it wasn't fair. The ladies of the local flower-arranging society were welcome because they didn't leak to the press or write diaries that might turn up serialised in Sunday papers. Nor would they use their mobiles if someone who shouldn't made an alcohol-fuelled spectacle of himself. And they wouldn't carry tales to rival production companies or inadvertently aid the theft of intellectual property. To be short, *he* was potentially capable of all of these things; *they* were an unreconstructed representation of wholesome village life.

On his way to round up the members of his film crew, he came upon Conquest sitting with his legs dangling over the edge of the ha-ha, a glass beside him in the grass.

'I suppose you're staying,' he said moodily.

Conquest held up a hand in a gesture of complacent indecision. 'I suppose...' He suddenly realised that Hazlett was about to depart and he scrambled to his feet and held out a hand, the gesture revealing, in some subtle way, how very much Hazlett had been reduced by his moment of confession. 'We are but cut flowers in a vase, Piers. We bloom for a brief moment and are gone!' He shook the other's hand with great formality. 'I meant what I said about film studies. Come and talk to me about it.'

Hazlett glanced at him guardedly as one does a madman, said he would and made off down the hillside.

FORTY

As late afternoon turned into evening, informality began to change into something resembling a charity gala. In the billiard room, Pye's meeting over dinner of the previous evening was reconvened. He wanted an answer to the question that had been much on his mind during the afternoon's events.

'How much of *Candide In Tinseltown* do we have?'

Sophie Flambeau was sitting at an open window, smoking. She took a last drag and flipped the butt into the dark. 'It's not *Candide In Tinseltown*,' she said as one says who has long mulled her opinion, 'but whoever wrote it has pulled off a masterstroke.'

Pye looked at her, his face a mask of stillness. 'Meaning?'

'I clearly recall the beginning of *Candide In Tinseltown*. This is undoubtedly similar. The beginning was always a rewrite of *Night Train To Fear*; the budget for that movie sold Goldman's idea very short. The point is, this has morphed into something completely different from either. In essence, this isn't Goldman, not even a study in Goldmanesque. It's novel.'

'But how can that be?'

Sophie shrugged. 'You say Poppy did it, so maybe we should get her in and ask her,' she suggested.

Avril Morgan gave a grunt and went to fetch her. He found her sitting in the kitchen with Fawn and her daughters.

'Poppy,' said Pye, 'according to Sophie this isn't *Candide In Tinseltown*. What happened?'

'Well... we tried.'

'It seems you embroidered.'

'Well, yes, all right, we embroidered... in part. But there were always gaps and we didn't really know which bits of text belonged.'

She remembered something Graham Lester had said on her first visit to University London Central's library: *Isn't that what writers do: string together clichés in the hope the story isn't one big fat cliché?* Now she repeated it, word for word. 'Maybe we were a bit over-enthusiastic and he led me astray!'

'What *we*? Who's *he*?'

'Graham Lester. You're paying him to help me. I did arrange it with your office.' She looked contrite. 'He's a research student doing a thesis on *cinema concrete*.'

'*Ah*,' said Pye, 'in the film school!'

Poppy shrugged. '*Film school?* There isn't a film school, just a few research students, like him.'

Avril Morgan gave a grunt of indignation. '*That* explains why I couldn't find any mention of a film school! It's just a pretext to ask for money!'

Sophie stood up as though suddenly restless. 'Well,' she said, 'I'm saying it's brilliant!'

Pye was lost in thought. 'Maybe it is, maybe it isn't.' He looked up from the floor and gazed speculatively at Poppy. 'I guess congratulations are in order, you certainly seem to have produce *something*. I'll take it to New York with me to read, and see what I think. I guess you should carry on doing whatever it is that you've been doing... if you can... and if you feel like it. *Can you?*'

'Yes, I can, I suppose. Of course.'

Morgan reached out for the screenplay and examined it, leafing through as though he could assess its worth from a cursory glance at each page. He had a thought for Pye. 'If what Sophie says is right, this guy Conquest and his university don't own the copyright.'

Sophie shrugged as though there was little room for doubt. 'It isn't *Candide In Tinseltown* and it isn't Goldman.'

'Awkward,' said Pye.

'I saw him hanging about earlier. Did you speak to him?' wondered Morgan.

Pye shook his head. 'Not since he read the Shellbrooke poem. I thought he did it rather well, but I wasn't near enough to congratulate him.'

'Whatever you two are up to,' decided Sophie, 'it needs an ending.'

'That's it then,' said Pye, suddenly animated. 'Poppy, if that's what it needs, while I'm away, *write an ending!*'

FORTY-ONE

Later that evening, the final encore played, the orchestra departed on its bus. The last of the guests still dotted the expanse of lawn in groups of twos and threes, murmuring under the stars. Conquest had scarcely moved a muscle during the performance, happy to let the music wash over him. Now he had gone back to his perch on the edge of the lawn. The velvet darkness, enlivened by the soft sounds of laughter, immersed him. He was content to sit there, utterly inert, even as his mind raced! He conceived of a muddy torrent sweeping through an endless logjam of cars in a short-term airport car park. Cars were bobbing about in the flood. As he watched, the driver of one, skis attached to the roof rack, mouthed at him silently as he passed: *'I am as the bitter sloe of the tree of worms!'*

Such were the imaginings he entertained at the moment Cornelius Pye happened upon him.

'I've been looking for you,' said Pye, having almost tripped over him in the dark.

'Yes,' said Conquest uneasily. 'And I you!'

'I suppose you want to buttonhole me about this film school business.'

'Well, actually, there is no film school, I'm sorry to say. Not only am I an impostor, wherever I go I spawn –'

'*No, no!* It really doesn't matter. We must look to the future.'

Conquest laughed. 'Yes, well, I'm not very hopeful when I do that.'

Pye gazed about him. Even in the moonless gloaming, Conquest could read something in his demeanour that said he was unusually preoccupied.

'*Imponderables!*' said Pye eventually, as though weighing

innumerable of them. 'Sometimes one has to make big decisions one wishes one didn't.'

Conquest wondered if what lay between them was *existential uncertainty*. It seemed far too cosy to be so, but to give it a name had the virtue of removing from them both the responsibility for informed decision-making. 'I suppose things have reached a crossroads of sorts,' he decided, enjoying the luxury of resignation.

'Monday evening I'm flying to New York. They're starting to build Camlington down there next week.' Pye gestured vaguely down the hill. 'For exteriors... for when I come back.'

Conquest was startled. 'You're filming *Private Culture* here?'

'Some, not all. Didn't you see the location signs on the way here? The real Camlington isn't as it was in the seventies.' There was a long pause. 'I'll have Avril contact you when I've decided what to do... about your film school, you know, and everything else. Difficult decisions...'

'I wonder how you achieve so much... It's impressive.'

'Ah... direct action. That's what it is: *direct action*! You must do what you must for your students. It's a sacred compact you have to honour.'

'Yes,' agreed Conquest.

There was an air of deep abstraction about the two of them. Perhaps it would have become embarrassing, as it does when two people who hardly know one another find they have nothing to say, but before that could happen, if indeed it would have, Pye wandered off, slipping away into the night in much the same way as he had come.

Conquest shivered; a heavy dew was beginning to settle. It might be time to make some decisions, but he felt curiously motiveless as though this summer night was perfectly suited for languishing.

FORTY-TWO

Conquest arrived back at University London Central just before nine on Tuesday morning. He parked his car under the wall of the old boiler house building in an area once occupied by mounds of furnace coke. He marvelled that it was only seventy-two hours since he had left that very spot. It seemed like an eternity. He sat behind the wheel, staring at the wall, wishing he could meditate like a Buddhist monk. Instead, he found himself reviewing the more significant events of the week ahead. Most notable was the special meeting of senate on Wednesday, called to discuss the procedure for the selection of recipients of honorary degrees. His extended weekend meant that the meeting was tomorrow! After reflecting for a while on the likely course of the meeting, he took his mobile from his pocket and found Professor Woolworth's number.

'Murray, could you join me in my car? I'm in the vice-chancellor's parking bay at the back of Human Resources.'

A few minutes later there was a tentative rap on the side window. Woolworth was peering in at him. Conquest gestured for him to get in.

'Good morning, Cliff. Are we going somewhere?'

'Murray, I have been sitting here thinking, and I didn't want to lose the thread of my thoughts by getting out and encountering distractions.'

Woolworth's laugh suggested he had described something familiar, but to have mentioned it was rather unbecoming.

'I'm starting to think I've been doing things all wrong,' continued Conquest. 'I've never been without a PA and I now realise the extent to which this convenience has isolated me from the rest of the university. This weekend has been an extraordinary journey. At the end of last week I was at a loss. Today I am certain that direct action is the order of the day; that I should go and find those I wish to speak to instead of having them come to me.' He chuckled, almost carefree. 'I think I'm in revolt! Don't you think that what I'm proposing would be, *in itself*, a novelty in university management?'

To Woolworth this all seemed disturbingly unconventional. 'But Cliff, your role is to be aloof! You might choose to be the hail-fellow-well-met sort when you talk to the press or chat with other vice-chancellors, but here, *in the university*, it's imperative you have the mystique of the court of last resort.'

'No, Murray, doing it that way is like swimming in treacle. We're going on walkabout. *Yes*, and you're going to accompany me!' He got out of the car and stretched awkwardly, leaving Woolworth sitting in the car.

Woolworth remained where he was until he realised Conquest was adamant. He climbed out of the car and hurried after him as he strode towards the nearest doorway. 'Fine, Cliff. I see your mind's made up. We'll do it your way.'

'Yes, and you will take notes,' said Conquest, 'and those notes will be written up as instructions, and the instructions will become missives to and from the establishment.'

'*To and from?* Won't that be rather confusing?'

Conquest stopped and stared into space, as though to give the question his full consideration.

Woolworth tried one more warning. 'The Vice-Chancellor's Strategic Secretariat is a bulwark, Cliff, and I've already instructed Human Resources to ask the recruitment agency to send you a replacement for Eunice.'

'Replacement?'

'On a temporary basis.'

'Ah, yes, *of course*! Well, let's visit my office *first*!'

They made their way towards the offices of the Vice-Chancellor's Strategic Secretariat. There was evidence everywhere that a new academic year was underway. Not teaching, or anything remotely like pedagogy, but the induction into student life that was freshers' week had definitely begun. The downstairs corridor was newly adorned with posters for every imaginable recreational sport, society, protest meeting and disco rave. Conquest thought he detected the low hum students produced, akin to the sound of ten thousand bees exchanging hive news. He found the new atmosphere bracing.

When they reached the corridor of the Vice-Chancellor's Strategic Secretariat there was the usual noise of Vernon photocopying. Conquest had the distinct impression that nobody had noticed his absence on the previous day. If they had, it had not concerned them in the least; it had been business as usual. His first stop was Eunice's office where, unceremoniously, he rifled her 'recent correspondence' tray. Woolworth watched with barely-disguised concern as he threw it into complete disarray. Eventually Conquest halted, a letter from the office of the Shadow Secretary of State clutched in his hand. Eunice's exemplary filing meant her reply was stapled to it.

'Ah-ha!' he cried, hastily scanning the letters. 'This is completely unacceptable, Murray! Once again, she's been answering my mail without informing me! This could have ditched my political career! Get on to HR and find out about that replacement.'

Woolworth took out his mobile and got through to Howard Huddle, head of Human Resources. 'Howard, Professor Conquest's arrived. Any news on his temporary PA?'

'There's an agency replacement coming to see him at eleven this morning.'

'Do we have a name?'

'Er... let's see. Could it be...? Yes, I believe his name is Brendan Musselburgh.'

'Excellent, *a he*!' He gave Conquest an enquiring look. 'Will he be coming to Cliff's office?'

'Yes, but via HR. Do you want somebody from HR in the interview?'

Woolworth cupped his hand over the mouthpiece. 'Do you want someone from HR in the interview?'

Conquest indicated he wanted to take the phone. 'Hello, Howard. Yes, I think that would be best, don't you? Why don't *you* bring him over? We can interview him together. I'm on walkabout, so call Murray on his mobile when he arrives.'

That settled, Conquest was eager to move on. 'Right, Murray, we need to go and inspect the archaeological dig behind Keynes House. Let's go.'

Down the stairs and out of the building they went. Woolworth found himself trotting to catch up. 'Cliff,' he began, coming up to his shoulder, 'I've been looking into that issue you were worried about last week.'

'You mean our oversight of websites?'

'It seems, one way and another, we have an extensive ecology of online information sources.'

Conquest came to an abrupt halt and looked askance at Woolworth. He knew that kind of terminology for what it was. It was diplomatic speak for untold sources of legal jeopardy. '*Do tell me more,* Murray!'

Woolworth cleared his throat, as someone does who brings ill tidings. 'As you so rightly pointed out, there is, perhaps, a growing need for regulation. All manner of semi-private, online enterprises seem to have sprung up. I gather you spoke to Miriam Micklethwaite about this last week. She's saying there's pornographic material on the *cinema concrete* website; they're selling porn downloads.'

'*Porn downloads?*'

'It seems she's rather got the bit between her teeth about it.'

Conquest was momentarily unsettled by the thought of Miriam Micklethwaite with the bit between her teeth in proximity to porn downloads. 'Have you viewed them?'

'Well, no. I only saw her email earlier today.'

They had stopped in a courtyard between registry and a wing of the geography department. Conquest eyed the passing students warily. 'And Miriam? Has she seen pornographic videos? Or is this hearsay?'

'Apparently she's watched a video called *Playing Don-the-Stud*. She says she was shocked.'

'Any idea of its content?'

'No.' Woolworth was consulting a message on his mobile. 'She claims there's another entitled *Double Chiasmic Invagination*.'

Conquest looked speculatively at Woolworth. Much though it gladdened his heart to think that McWhelk was selling porn online, he thought it unlikely it lurked behind such a recondite-sounding title. He was also mindful that Woolworth was a medieval scholar and Miriam Micklethwaite definitely not to be relied upon. Most likely, he decided, he was witnessing a epistemological misalignment reflecting the two cultures – scholarly and administrative – that he ruled over. Much though he would have wished it, he was sceptical he was being presented with the opportunity to boot McWhelk's behind as he departed from the university with his enhanced voluntary redundancy package.

'*Double invag* – *Oh dear,* that really doesn't sound good!'

'Miriam is consulting the university's solicitors as we speak.'

'Isn't that a bit precipitous? Freedom of thought… *self-expression*! *Murray!*'

'I know, but Miriam isn't very keen on any form of self-expression, Cliff. Her view is that, legally speaking, it's ill advised. I told her this was the one website you had made an exception for, but she says it will take hundreds of hours to view all the videos, and in meantime she strongly recommends you shut it down.'

Conquest couldn't believe his ears. For once Miriam Micklethwaite was behaving as though she were on the same team as he! For a moment he was dizzy with gratitude.

'Professor McWhelk seems bent on testing the limits of our tolerance, Murray. Perhaps, if Miriam's on the warpath, his head of department should be consulted.'

'Ah, yes, Dr Pocock. Perfectly nice man.'

'*Indeed!* But as its leader, does he, as we expect, have a comprehensive oversight of activities in his department? Let's find out.'

'*What, now?*'

'Murray, haven't I already said: *this morning we're engaging in direct action*!'

They doubled back, making for Rahmallah Green and the Department of Media and Communications. They surprised Bert Pocock standing in front of a large notice board in the ground floor corridor.

'*Vice-Chancellor!*' The papers Pocock was carrying dropped from limp fingers, the unexpected arrival of the vice-chancellor, in the company of another senior officer of the university, being enough to unnerve the most experienced head of department.

'We thought we should come and seek you out!' said Conquest. He glanced down. Gratifyingly, one of Pocock's papers had come to rest on the toe of his shoe.

'I was putting up the first semester course options,' mumbled Pocock as he retrieved the papers.

'I wanted to thank you for the effort you and your team put into writing those new film studies modules. Murray has put them out to readers and is already hearing positive things, aren't you, Murray?'

'Ah-hem, well early days to be sure, but yes, positive things.'

'If you can spare it,' continued Conquest agreeably, 'we'd like five minutes of your time… in your office.'

Pocock nodded. They went a little way along the corridor and Pocock pushed open a slightly undersized door with a frosted glass upper half. The office was little more than a stationary cupboard.

Conquest looked about with a frown. 'Isn't this rather small?'

With the three of them standing there was about enough room, but barely so when they sat down on the room's stacking chairs with worn canvas seats.

'Ah, well, our professors have all the best offices, don't they?'

'But you're the head of department!'

Pocock gave a humourless laugh.

'Well, look, we're seeking advice about the *cinema concrete* website.'

'Professor McWhelk isn't in today,' said Pocock, suddenly cautious.

'Are *you* familiar with it?'

'Reasonably.'

'It is being claimed that pornographic videos are being sold on it. The university's secretary has already seen fit to seek legal advice. Universities are spaces of free-thinking – *we all know that!* – but the presence of this website online while Professor McWhelk is deciding his future could be seen as something of a provocation.'

'*Deciding his future?*'

'Yes, he's applied for voluntary redundancy, which seems likely to go through.'

Pocock's face brightened at the news. 'Oh, well, then certainly it can come offline... *today!*'

'Do you happen to have seen a video called *Playing Don-the-Stud?*'

'Is that the one with a young woman in her undies with a strap-on dildo boning a blow-up sex doll?'

Conquest raised his eyebrows in the kind of disapproving look adults give naughty children.

'Is that pornographic enough?' said Pocock hopefully.

'I don't know. The question is: is it *cinema concrete?*'

'*Cinema concrete* is much more elusive than any explanation. Think of a revelation of all that is hidden in the filmic trope. Think of an undoing of its illusion, a movement that constitutes and deconstitutes the border, the limits of a closure!'

'How about a video entitled *Double Chiasmic Invagination?*'

Pocock laughed. 'Who knows what's meant by that!'

'Any ideas?'

'So, Vice-Chancellor, imagine a Möbius strip. An apparently complex, 3-D figure, yet it only has one edge and one surface! With that in mind, turn to invagination. It's the inverted reapplication of the outer edge of a planar form to its inside such that the outer region creates a receptacle-like form. As a result, the edge of the form turns out to be a fold within the form. Now, double chiasmic in–'

Conquest held up his hand. '*Stop!*' He had heard enough. 'Spare me the rest! I take it it's not pornographic?'

'Could be,' said Pocock blithely, 'I haven't seen it, so I couldn't say.'

'Well, if you're minded to act, there are those who advise that the website should be taken offline while its contents are verified.'

'Yes, I understand. This is not, I take it, a directive from you, or your office?'

'I'd regard institutional coercion as a little heavy-handed, wouldn't you? In the end, ownership's a matter for you.'

'I'll see to it,' said Pocock cheerfully. 'Given the circumstances, the department's espousal of the disinterested dissemination of news without causing offence is everything!'

Conquest looked him squarely in the face, searching for the slightest trace of irony... and found none. It occurred to him that either Pocock's professors had driven him to the point of insanity, or his encounter had been with a donkey suffering from advanced institutional idiocy.

FORTY-THREE

Conquest and Woolworth now hastened across the campus from north to south, making their way to the pedestrianised roadway where Eunice had found herself within an ace of being crushed. The gap where the hoarding had been pulled down to free her was still there, allowing them to view the activity in the yard. In the pit where once had stood the buildings to the rear of Keynes House, a team of bent backs was reverentially clearing soil and rubble. As they watched, one of the team – a sturdy and purposeful young woman – climbed out of the hole and came in their direction. She stood in their line of sight, lost in contemplation, her back to them. The longer she stood there the more evident it was that she had some responsibility for the management of the dig. Conquest was drawn to speak to her.

'Hello,' he said, 'I'm Vice-Chancellor Clifford Conquest. And this is Professor Woolworth. Have you any idea about what manner of thing you have here?'

'Jill Armstrong, Department of Archaeology, Museum of London.' She smiled in a business-like way and then turned back to gaze at her area of operations. 'I suppose you're wondering how disruptive this is going to be?'

Conquest laughed. 'Yes, you could say that!'

'Well, we don't know. Won't for some time. It's a fine thing and it's possible there's a great deal more. It's also possible we might want to leave it *in situ*, in which case we'll expect its preservation to be incorporated into your rebuilding plans. It'd be a shame to take up the floor if there's the remains of a whole villa, or complex of buildings in the yard here.'

'I see,' said Conquest. '*Awkward!*'

'Yes, indeed, but we'll try and minimize the fuss. Frankly, I wouldn't worry too much for the next week or so. By then we'll be in a position to give you more of a considered opinion.'

The three of them negotiated the piles of rubble and soil until they came to the brink of the pit. The tessellated pavement could plainly be seen emerging from the layers of earth. They stood mutely for a while, watching the diggers go about their painstaking work.

'Glad to meet you, anyway,' said Jill Armstrong finally. 'I must get on.' With that, she bustled off into the pit.

The other two retraced their steps to the edge of the site. Conquest gazed up at the rear of Keynes House, imagining the digital hub in its place. 'I'm beginning to think,' he said, articulating a line of thought that had been troubling him, mischievously, for some time, 'that centralised digital fulfilment has its dangers.' In place of Keynes House his imagination had materialised a palace of technocrats controlling access to the web for their own ends. Could a techno-autocracy holding sway over all the other branches of the university's administration be the inevitable consequence of a digital hub? The idea suddenly alarmed him... *and he was about to build it!*

'Perhaps, Murray, *hub* is the wrong term. Perhaps more dispersal would be beneficial; departments concentrating on doing their thing without communicating too much with the outside world.'

'Yes! And one another!'

'Steady, Murray, that's perhaps a step too far.' Yet was it perhaps an omen, Conquest wondered, that unearthing the bomb had stopped work on Keynes House as the life-blood of its services was about to be disconnected? He felt in the grip of a sudden perception. *'My God!'* he exclaimed. 'I'm beginning to understand: it's an *existential threat*!'

His outcry took Woolworth by surprise and he gazed at his vice-chancellor in meek enquiry.

'I can see what this archaeology business means, Murray. It means we're unlikely to see Keynes House demolished in the foreseeable future. Perhaps we should consider moving ahead on some other footing. Where else did we think might be a site for estate renewal?'

'Well, there was a time when the old boiler house building was a candidate, but that was dismissed as being too small.'

Conquest happily seized on that. 'Perhaps a leaner hub with more devolvement might work. You never know. One shouldn't be too hasty. But this delay is *force majeure*, as far as I'm concerned. We must think afresh!'

Just then a man in a hardhat and wearing a hi-vis jacket came by, intent on some errand. He examined Conquest and Woolworth, and decided they were a possible source of information. 'Are those museum Charlies setting up camp for the long haul?' he wondered. '*Never* seen such a mess made of a perfectly good demolition site!'

'It seems the archaeology is quite important,' responded Woolworth.

'*Oh, yeah?*' said the man as though the whole thing was a perverse folly. 'And how about that lass as was trapped by the truck when it all kicked off?'

'Quite unharmed.'

'*Really?* You do surprise me! She made a fuss like she was going to die.' He laughed, shaking his head at the thought. 'It was quite a circus, what with the bomb and all. And her broadcasting she was in love with her boss! I mean, what's the sense in *that* when all you've done is fall on your arse?'

'I'm sure it was simply an expression of extreme stress. Calm enough here now, anyway.'

'Aye, deadly dull, them scraping and scraping. We had a JCB they could have borrowed, but it's gone to another site now.'

The atmosphere had gone frigid from the moment the man had mentioned Eunice's declaration, not that he noticed. Woolworth was moved to actual asperity. 'Yes, well, I think they'll manage quite nicely without your JCB.'

'Suit yourself!' said the man cheerfully, and he moved off on his errand.

'Most extraordinary!' decided Woolworth once he was out of earshot. 'I can't think Eunice is having an affair with Vernon Pinhorn; her relationship with the other staff of the secretariat has always been rather strained.' He could feel Conquest's discomfort, but assumed that they had alighted on a bit of office scandal they'd both rather not know about. 'And I thought he was... *you know*!'

Conquest pulled himself together with an effort. He knew that Vernon Pinhorn, as head of the secretariat, was notionally Eunice's line manager, but he couldn't help wondering if *he* was the intended of her declaration. Her odd behaviour was something he was only too aware of, and he was beginning to think it amounted to a serious, even dangerous, problem. 'Frankly, I feel she's inclined to exaggeration,' he said evasively. 'She certainly over-does the protective bit. That letter she replied to on my behalf was unpardonable. I shall have to apologise to put *that* right!'

Woolworth was about to respond in kind when his mobile rang. He listened for a while and said, 'Thank you... Yes, he's here... I'll tell him.' He put the mobile back in his pocket and turned to Conquest. 'Well, your replacement PA's here. Howard's going to bring him across to your office in fifteen minutes. *Perhaps,*' he added meaningfully, 'it's an opportunity for a reassignment.'

They made their way back across the campus. There were students everywhere, going about their business, none of whom appreciated that the two most senior officers of the university were passing by. Walking amongst them as though he was invisible, Conquest felt like a ghost. It seemed the perfect moment to renew his mission to remake universities for their betterment. He did his best to stay fixed on the idea, but by the time they had reached the Vice-Chancellor's Strategic Secretariat building his thoughts had turned to a more immediate concern.

'With reference to crocodiles, Murray, is your apology to Matthew Stagg's parents imminent?'

'Yes, Cliff. They returned at the weekend. I have an appointment to see them tomorrow morning in Belgrave Square.'

'*Belgrave Square!* Unusual place for a meeting, isn't it?'

'Well, yes, but it's the address Marcia gave me, though I suppose I'd better check.'

'Excellent.'

'I shall do my bit, you can rely on it.'

'Good man. I'm sure you'll patch things up. They need to vent, but once that's done, they'll see we've behaved with total regard for all.'

They had now reached the corridor leading to Conquest's office and as he finished speaking, Howard Huddle stuck his head out of Eunice's office.

'Sorry to interrupt, Vice-Chancellor, but we're here.'

'Thank you, Howard,' said Conquest. 'Give me a moment before you come.' He turned to Woolworth and clapped him on the shoulder. 'Well, Murray, no need for note-taking after all!' He said this with great warmth as if it were crocodiles he was sending Woolworth to parley with rather than Matthew Stagg's parents. Having done his best to bolster his spirits, he pushed on to his office where, shortly, the head of HR joined him.

'Right,' he said once the door was closed, 'will you lead on this interview, Howard? I'm sure you're more adept at this than me.'

'I don't know about that, Vice-Chancellor.'

'Howard, for heaven's sake, you're the head of Human Resources!'

'Ah, yes, quite! I'll call him in, shall I?'

A spindly little man wearing a navy-blue suit that looked decidedly chalky at the cuffs was led in. Brendan Musselburgh did a fair bit of bowing and scraping before sitting down. Conquest eyed him dubiously. It wasn't as though PAs had to be female, but this specimen looked decidedly hidebound. He thought it was probably the suit that did it. It looked as though he'd put it on the moment he'd left school and never taken it off since then. It said *'life is office routine'* in a particularly gruesome way. The interview proceeded haltingly. Conquest couldn't understand what was going on. The man seemed to be sucking all the oxygen out of the room. His answers were impeccable, but it was as if he'd learn them by rote. When the interview was finally over and Brendan Musselburgh had left, Conquest found himself musing on what had just occurred. He wasn't sure it wasn't his own conduct that had made the interview seem so unsatisfactory.

'I don't know, Howard. It's a strange one. I can see he's competent and has lots of experience, but...'

'I assure you we could do no better, Vice-Chancellor. Not at short notice.'

Conquest wasn't convinced. He picked up Brendan Musselburgh's CV and studied it once more. 'Can you leave it with me, Howard? I want to think about it. I'm not sure he's for me.'

'Very well, Vice-Chancellor, I'll tell the agency you're –'

No, don't do anything for the time being. Let's just sit on it. Don't start any hares running just yet.'

After Howard Huddle had left, Conquest made himself a cup of tea in the galley kitchen next to Eunice's office. The fact was he didn't see himself replacing Eunice with Brendan Musselburgh. He took in the kitchen's orderly air, conscious that it was Eunice who was at pains to ensure it was so, and felt it would be a desecration to allow *that man*, as he imagined it, to come in and mess it up. No, it wouldn't do. He couldn't believe there wasn't something better out there. It was as if Howard Huddle had fluffed the whole thing in his usual manner. Maybe the criteria for the post were wrong. The only way to check was to ring the agency himself and see what somebody there had to say about finding someone better. He abandoned his half-drunk tea and went back into his office. The top sheet of Musselburgh's CV had a compliments slip stapled to it. He dialled the agency's number and asked to speak to Valerie Ogden, who had signed the slip.

'Hello. Valerie Ogden speaking.'

Conquest introduced himself and explained why he had called.

'Why, yes,' she said when he had finished, 'we do have other, equally qualified candidates, but Mr Huddle turned them all down. He was adamant that none of them were suitable. I did challenge him about it, but he denied it was anything discriminatory or post-specific.'

Conquest couldn't think what she meant for a moment. 'You mean the rest were *women*?'

'Yes.'

Conquest's mind was churning. Was Huddle determined he should have a male PA? It seemed odd; suspicion was in the air. Of course, he could ask Huddle directly why he had turned down all the female candidates, but something about Huddle's manner spoke against such a direct course of action. His intuition said that events around him were being manipulated.

'Well, Valerie, I would like a bit more choice and I don't think Mr Musselburgh will do. Can you bike over to me anything else you have?'

'Mr Huddle already has most of what I could send.'

'Yes, I'm afraid those copies aren't available,' he said, not wanting Huddle warned about what he was up to. 'Could you send duplicates directly to me?'

He rang off after the usual concluding pleasantries and sat for a while brooding. It struck him that Huddle might have tried to dump Musselburgh on him as petty revenge for dumping Human Resources in the old boiler house building. He remembered Huddle's melancholic simpering about being displaced from what formerly had been his office. By a strange twist of association, he suddenly felt an immense urge to be back in his old quarters on the first floor of Keynes House. The more he thought about it the more determined he was that if the archaeologists were moving in for the long-term, interminably delaying the demolition of Keynes House – *resulting in Wainwright, Carter and Expandite being paid for doing nothing!* – he would declare a *volte face*, reclaim his office and reformulate his plans for the digital hub. The fact was, he reluctantly acknowledged, that a year after falling for the idea, the words 'digital hub' had become odious to him.

FORTY-FOUR

The final arena for Conquest's application of direct action was the following day's special meeting of senate. The meeting was scheduled to start at two o'clock and Vernon Pinhorn, the secretariat's manager, had already arranged for a buffet lunch to be available from noon. Conquest hoped that, in the traditional manner of 'beer and sandwiches', substantial agreement on the business of the meeting could be achieved before it started. He reviewed Vernon's arrangements and decided to speak to the head of catering himself. A final decision on the menu having been agreed, the head of catering asked whether the lunch was to be held in the senior common room.

'I have in mind,' said Conquest musingly, as though experimenting with a form of words he hadn't used before, 'that given the circumstances, we need to bring Keynes House back into use. The senate should be aware of this, so what better way than to hold the lunch in my old office on the first floor? I'll speak to the head of the portering staff about moving some furniture back in.'

'Yes, that will be fine,' said the head of catering helpfully, unaware that he was the unwitting servant of high politics. 'We have some trestle tables you can use if you need them. Anything else?'

'Can you use larger glasses for the sherry? I seem to think the ones you normally provide are rather small.'

Satisfied with his improvements to the arrangements, Conquest decided to go and check on the photocopies Vernon Pinhorn was preparing for the meeting. As he reached the door his telephone called him back. It was Avril Morgan, Pye's American producer. Conquest could tell from the first that Morgan was determined to be brief.

'I'm sending over a sealed first and final offer by special delivery,' he growled.

Conquest, discomposed by the unexpected identity of the caller, wasn't sure he understood what he was saying. 'But I've already told Cornelius we don't really have a film school to endow!'

'No, no, it's not an endowment. It's a first and final offer for the use of material from the Goldman archive.'

'I see. Then I don't fully...' Conquest was further bewildered. The American's drawl meant he had to hang on to his every word to be sure he caught his meaning.

'Professor, you own the copyright of all material in the Goldman papers previously unpublished. Are you aware of this?'

'*Material?*'

'Correct.'

'No, I can't say I am. Haven't thought about it, even. I mean, is there anything unpublished of any real value? To a Goldman scholar perhaps, but only disinterested research, surely?'

'Cornelius Pye & Associates Incorporated is making an offer for certain material. That's all I can tell you.'

'You can't be more specific?'

'Professor, I'm not at liberty to discuss the offer, or in any way comment on it. You have forty-eight hours to respond, or the offer will be null and void. I am only able to advise you that a sealed bid will shortly be on its way to you by courier. Do you understand?'

'Yes, I suppose I do. Thank you, Mr Morgan, I –' He realise there was no point in finishing the sentence; the line had gone dead.

In the absence of Eunice, Conquest had decided that unless he was in conference, he would keep his office door ajar. This allowed him, when seated at his desk, a partial view of the corridor that ran the length of the floor occupied by his secretariat. It was a decision that made it easy for him to keep an impatient eye out for the arrival of Avril Morgan's mysterious 'sealed first and final offer'. It was not long before he heard someone come up the stairs shouting, *Hello! Delivery!* He leapt up and was in the corridor in a trice. Marcia, Woolworth's PA, had appeared from her office at the other end of the corridor. Conquest waved her away, met the courier at the head of the stairs and signed for the delivery. He took the package back to his office, tearing it open as he went. Much to his disappointment he realised the contents were not Morgan's first and final offer. They were the CVs sent by the recruitment agency of the candidates Howard Huddle had rejected. Scanning through them, he quickly concluded they were no less qualified than Brendan Musselburgh; something fishy was definitely going on. He put aside the CVs and thought again about what the workman had said about Eunice's dramatic declaration. The thought of what she was capable of made him suddenly feel hot with embarrassment. If Huddle's actions were a consequence of the belief that he was having an inappropriate relationship with her, he knew others must be behind his actions. He recalled arriving at the site of Eunice's accident just after the ambulance had taken her away. Professor Cronker had been there. Didn't he recall Cronker saying, *'I was with her until the ambulance turned up'*? If he was, wasn't it possible he'd heard Eunice's outburst? Had Cronker then talked to Huddle? That didn't seem quite right. Cronker didn't have enough institutional clout to launch Huddle on a moral crusade. There had to be a third party, somebody who had previously worked with Huddle on serious HR business, such as negotiating the departure of the chief officers of the university. Conquest had enough nous to work out there was only one candidate: Perk Hingley, chair of senate!

He was mulling over this idea when the telephone rang. It was Tommy Ballantyne, head of finance.

'I just finished negotiating with Professor McWhelk,' he said. 'We've agreed a voluntary redundancy package, suitably enhanced.' His voice became slightly scandalised. 'I hope you know what you're doing, Cliff, because he's jumping ship with a fine show of disdain.'

'Tommy, it's all a matter of the institutional agenda,' said Conquest without the least trace of irony. 'Our aims were misaligned.'

'He was telling me that he's going to an associate professorship at the University of Greater Gatwick.'

'I'm not surprised, in some academic settings *cinema concrete* could be seen as a valuable academic asset.'

'He was also going on about how the chair of senate backs him to the hilt.'

'Well, there we are! Perk is something of an influential voice at Greater Gatwick. I'm sure McWhelk will be an ornament there.'

Conquest sat back, a feeling of peace and goodwill stealing over him.

Life, he thought, *is a matter of perspective.*

'Thanks for letting me know, Tommy. Come across and have a nip before you leave. A little celebration's in order and there is much I want to share with you! At last I have a feeling... *things are on the move!*'

FORTY-FIVE

A sense of disquiet gripped Conquest when, first thing on Wednesday morning, he walked through the campus. By resorting to direct action the previous day, he felt he had, at the very least, stabilised matters in the face of fate's desire to disarray his mental faculties. But thoughts of the imminent arrival of the members of senate were enough to blight his day.

At least his contribution to the special meeting had already been circulated. It was a paper outlining his preferred process for the selection of recipients of honorary doctorates. His original hope had been that it would avert the necessity for the meeting. However, given the political dimension, he was not entirely surprised that members of senate still wanted to debate the matter. If his voting system was not particularly contentious, the stance of senate on the political complexion of those to whom the university awarded honorary doctorates certainly was. And on that matter, there were a few scores to be settled. Accordingly, it was with an uneasy sense of expecting the unexpected that he looked forward to the day's events.

Conquest's paper proposed that two nominations from members of senate were required for a candidate to be considered for an honorary doctorate. The candidates satisfying that condition were then subjected to a system of multiple-choice proportional representation over several rounds of voting. This was to encourage canvassing to occur between rounds in the hope that a consensus would gradually emerge on the preferred candidate, forestalling the need for a final vote. It was an intentionally complicated system guaranteed to keep senate tied up for hours. Conquest expected it to be adopted and, once its lack of utility was fully appreciated, speedily abandoned, allowing informal consensus building to pass to him.

He arrived in his office shortly after nine. There was no Eunice to lay out his newspapers and he had to fetch them from Vernon Pinhorn's office. After the drama of Avril Morgan's telephone call there had been no delivery of 'a sealed first and final offer'. Conquest was baffled by what in the Goldman bequest could be of meaningful value to Cornelius Pye & Associates Incorporated. He fully intended going over to the library later in the morning to see if Poppy Trench could enlighten him, but for the first hour of the day his mind was fully taken up with other business and the special delivery quite slipped his mind. Then he heard a clatter of footsteps from the stairwell and a motorcycle courier appeared at its head. His anticipation was such that he gave the courier a tip of ten pounds, but when it came to opening the letter, he did so with a sense of foreboding. This is what he read; it was brief and to the point.

'An offer of one hundred thousand US dollars to University London Central for the transfer of the copyright of the title, *Candide In Tinseltown*. The offer to expire at noon on Friday, September 28th. Signed, Avril Morgan, on behalf of Cornelius Pye & Associates Incorporated.'

He stood by his desk, rereading the letter, astonished and incredulous. One hundred thousand dollars for… *What did it mean?* The offer was on Cornelius Pye & Associates Incorporated notepaper and his first thought was to try the telephone number. The receptionist put him through to Avril Morgan without demur.

'I know you don't want to discuss this, Mr Morgan, but I'm not clear what this offer is for.'

'Professor, is the letter not clear?'

'It says one hundred thousand dollars for the title. It can't mean those three words, can it?'

'That's exactly what it does mean.'

'I see.' He was staggered. 'Does Cornelius Pye *really believe* they're worth such a *tremendous* amount of money? He *can't*, can he?'

'Mr Pye believes titles have the power to make or break a project, and once he's fixed on one, he'll brook no change, sir. There, I've already said more than I'm at liberty to say, so please convey to this office your acceptance, or not, in due course and no later than the time stated in the letter. Thank you, sir, and goodbye.'

Stunned, oblivious to everything but the letter in his hand, Conquest trod the length of his picture window wondering what the university should do with a hundred thousand dollars. It was a large sum of money, of course, but didn't constitute a significant contribution to the expenses of running a film school. Bargaining for an even greater sum was an option... or was it more strategic to refuse any money whatsoever? He had to think carefully. Whatever he decided, he would need to show Cornelius Pye gratitude for such fair dealing. And perhaps an endowment in addition was not out of the question!

He placed the offer on his desk and covered it with a folder so that no one entering his office could inadvertently catch sight of it. In a trance-like state of intoxication, he walked the length of the corridor to Vernon Pinhorn's office to pick up the photocopies required for the meeting of senate. He was standing in the corridor gazing sightlessly at one of the extra copies of his discussion paper, thinking about the one hundred thousand dollars, when he heard more footsteps from the direction of the stairs. He looked up to see Piers Hazlett emerge from the stairwell.

'*Piers!*' said Conquest with a start.

'Morning, Cliff,' said Hazlett as he approached.

'Let me hazard a guess,' said Conquest, overcome by a delicious sense of wry amusement. 'You've come in early to have a chat about helping us with our film school?'

'Well, you did say I –'

'Indeed, I did! *And* before things get busy! *Very thoughtful!* Yes, do come and have a chat.'

He led Hazlett back down the corridor to his office where he gestured to the sofa and sat opposite him in the steel and leather chair of American design. It struck him that Hazlett had taken more care with his appearance than he had for the Royal Personage on Graduation Day.

He's come dressed for an interview!

'So, Piers, a return to academic life! You still feel you have a contribution to make, then?'

'I think you know I do, Cliff. As I said at Thieves, if you want to expand your film studies offering, I'll bring a lot of credibility. I have the knowledge, academic experience *and the contacts*.'

'I don't doubt it. We academics always get drawn back! Actually, your interest is fortuitous. I think it would be an excellent thing if the university had access to your expertise. Let's cut the red tape, though. In the first instance I have it in mind to bring you in as an associate professor to avoid any equal opportunities issues. Would that be all right by you?'

'Pay scale negotiable?'

'Well... within the usual norms, yes. HR will handle that sort of thing. Have you met Bert Pocock, the head of department?'

'No.'

'Bit of an oddball, but perfectly nice man. Fancy going across and having a chat? I could telephone ahead and let him know. Perhaps I should come and introduce you. He's rather new to his job, so it might be for the best.'

He put a call through to Pocock and prepared to leave with Hazlett. They strolled up to Ramallah Green, discussing Pye's music festival in stilted terms as they went. Pocock, his face blank, was waiting for them at the entrance to the Department of Media and Communications building.

'...distinguished broadcaster who's going to help flesh out your film studies proposals,' said Conquest, introducing Hazlett. 'A chance to feel one another out!' He gestured genially in Pocock's direction. 'I'm going to requisition you a new office. And one for you too, Piers.' He nodded magisterially. 'Look, I have to go and see if the preparations for senate's meeting are underway at Keynes House. Meet me there, Piers, when you're done here.'

As Conquest approached the rear of Keynes House, he saw that the hoarding by the entrance to the yard was being repaired and new site safety notices had gone up alongside a Museum of London sign. A familiar figure was contemplating the signs: Professor Cronker.

Conquest hailed him cheerfully. 'Ah, good day to you, Alan! You've heard about the archaeologists taking up residence, I take it?'

'Indeed, Cliff! Makes things a bit difficult, doesn't it? I gather you've moved the meeting of senate to your old haunt. A statement of intent at all?' He looked mischievously quizzical.

'Yes, Alan, new contingencies!'

It was at this point that fair play moved Cronker to offer him a warning. 'You know, don't you, that our chair is taking an interest in Professor McWhelk's constructive dismissal issue?'

'*Is he!* Well, I gather Professor McWhelk's decided to move on; been offered a post at the University of Greater Gatwick.'

Cronker's face fell. 'Good Lord! That's news!'

'I'm sure he'll be a bracing presence there. Miriam Micklethwaite claims he's been selling pornography online. Not that that's necessarily a bad thing, but let's say there's a certain principled intransigence in his conduct, shall we? As far as Perk's concerned, I'm not sure it's ever wise for the chair of senate to take too detailed an interest in the university's internal affairs. Tell me, Alan, what did you say to him about Eunice and that incident with the truck?'

Cronker's granite features disguised his discomfort. 'I'm not sure I know what you mean.'

'Did you tell him what she said?'

'I don't recall her saying anything of note, Cliff.'

'I hear you were very solicitous of her wellbeing before the ambulance turned up. I'm told she was rather forthright.'

'As I say, Cliff, it's not –'

'Not what? Not the sort of thing you'd take up with Perk?'

Cronker looked like a man trapped. 'I may have expressed a certain… *apprehension*… but… I've always thought Eunice tended towards a rather… *giddy* view of the world.'

'I think that says it all, Alan. *Says it all!* Now, if you'll excuse me, I have to go and see if all's well in Keynes House. This afternoon I rely on you to ensure we reach agreement in an expeditious manner.'

'I'm sure that's right, Cliff,' said Cronker meekly. 'I wholly support your voting proposal.'

Conquest proceeded to Keynes House, entering the lobby through the swing doors. Stripped of its fittings, the building looked in a sad state, the posters were old and only one picture was left adorning the walls, but when he went through into the central stairwell where the stately staircase curved up to the floors above, his impression changed. The dust raised by the industrious, but ineffectual, contract cleaners made the shafts of sunlight striking down from the cupola skylights look like gorgeous gossamer contrails. Uplifted, he bound up the stairs. His old office, where several of the caterer's staff were still at work, was barely recognisable. It could have been the venue for a wedding reception. There was a scattering of small round tables for diners to sit at and the buffet at the far end of the room looked magnificent.

Well pleased, Conquest went to check the arrangements in the old boardroom where the meeting was to be held. He was there when Hazlett arrived from his meeting with Bert Pocock.

'A worthwhile exchange?'

'Yes, as you say, perfectly nice man.' Hazlett strained not to look shell-shocked. 'And I'm sure we'll get on perfectly nicely. He showed me some of his proposals for new modules. Did you know that for *Tropes of Suspense in Post-Hitchcockian Narrativity* he's devised ten assessment criteria, and each criterion has at least ten sub-sections?'

'Ah, yes, I believe Dr Pocock has a reputation for thoroughness.' Conquest drew him away from the door in a way that indicated he was about to impart a confidence. It was the action of a man who knew he was able to dispense with politeness, but who proceeded as though politeness was everything. 'He's an inexperienced HOD and I expect you to take him in hand. It's a marvellous opportunity! Look, Piers, there's a favour I want to ask. I've decided that Cornelius Pye should be the recipient of next year's honorary doctorate. I wonder if you would write the citation. Coming from you it would have the ring of authenticity.'

Hazlett looked bewildered. 'But Cliff, isn't that rather pre-empting this afternoon's deliberations by senate, never mind its final choice?'

'Well, yes and no. I see Pye as my candidate. I suppose there may be others, but as vice-chancellor...'

'Well, yes, I suppose...' Hazlett look uncomfortable but reluctantly compliant.

'There is another thing, Piers. I'm sorry to have to say this, but if you are to come in on an associate professor's ticket for this academic year, you'll have to forego membership of senate. As a member of academic staff, you're only eligible if you're one of the two elected representatives. I'm sure you understand; this year's were chosen before the summer break.'

Hazlett's deflation was complete. 'Yes, I see.'

'In the circumstances it might be best if you absented yourself from today's meeting. Best slip away, otherwise you might be seen as overstepping the mark. Not a good way to start, I'm sure. Meanwhile, I'll get HR up to speed with a suitable offer for you.'

Hazlett looked at him with thoughts of murderous mayhem, but knew his return to academic life was a Faustian pact, and he had been thoroughly put in his place. 'As my future vice-chancellor, I naturally take your advice on this sort of matter,' he drawled grimly. 'One wouldn't want to neglect the conventions, would one?'

'No, well, I'll give your apologies and so forth. I'm sure it's for the best.'

And with that Conquest awarded himself a gold star for having brought into line a second person that morning; Piers Hazlett was *de facto,* henceforth removed from senate. Conquest smiled a steely smile and wondered whether he could snag Perk on his interference in the internal affairs of the university.

FORTY-SIX

Strange as it might seem, the members of the Rising Left and their supporters on senate had not thought to gather somewhere as a preliminary to the meeting. Their confidence was high, their sense of the rightness of their cause deeply ingrained. It never occurred to them that they needed to strategize, that they couldn't take a majority of senate with them. The real issue of the meeting for them was not the matter of Conquest's system of voting; that was almost without controversy. What was to be established for all to understand was that universities were inalienably part of their political fiefdom and would be, if necessary, their last redoubt. It followed that the way Higher Education was personified by the luminaries it honoured was ideology in action. That University London Central might honour Tory bigwigs or the dubious intellectuals of the Right was anathema. It followed that Sir Norman Fleet's proposal that they should respect some notion of political neutrality was repellent, and a betrayal of their intellectual heartland.

Having despatched Piers Hazlett with kind words at the last, Conquest retired to his office and found plenty to occupy him until he calculated the moment was right to join the members of senate as they gathered for lunch. He checked his tie was not loose and the knot perfectly symmetrical with the wings of his collar. His suit had the anonymous perfection required of a public sector samurai. He regarded this, his official return to Keynes House, as a triumph of sorts. As he reached the first floor a throaty growl reached his ears and he turned to see Sir Norman Fleet, in the company of Nancy Spurling, approaching the foot of the stairs.

'Clifford, what the devil's happening?' Sir Norman exclaimed, gesticulating wildly. 'How come we're meeting in a demolition site?'

Conquest waited until they caught up with him before attempting a reply. 'Good day, Sir Norman, Nancy. I'm bringing Keynes House back into service. It's the interruption clause. I've been trying to talk to you about it.'

'I appreciate your concern, Clifford, but I'm hands-off in this matter. Can't interfere with the functions of head office.'

'I'm placed in an impossible situation unless something changes. Those archaeologists could be here for months.'

'Damn it, man, no activity here means Wainwright, Carter & Expandite have men and plant idle. After all, a contract is a contract!'

By now they had reached the doorway to Conquest's old office. Perk was standing just inside the door as if to greet arrivals. Some way beyond him Arts Council Olaf was in mid-exchange with Alistair Vox, ideological guru of think tank InProFESPol. Vox exploded with indignation when he saw Conquest.

'Vice-Chancellor, the closing down of the *cinema concrete* website is an intolerable example of institutional censorship at this university!'

'Alistair,' chided Nancy in her usual boisterous style, 'you're sporting your red tie again!'

'This is *exactly* the kind of thing that happens under the private culture impulse!'

'Oh, *really,* Alistair!' Nancy snorted. '*Private culture! Piffle!*'

'Alistair, this has been resolved,' said Conquest calmly. 'Your information's old.'

Nancy was still determined to get under Vox's skin. 'Let's not be so excitable, Alistair, until we've had a drink or two! The amount of tommyrot that think tank of yours produces you should get an award for creative fiction!'

Perk put out a hand as though to calm Vox and, plucking at Conquest's sleeve, he drew him aside. They found themselves in a corner, their backs to various members of the senate already gossiping over sherry. 'Is this true about Professor McWhelk?'

'His employment here is terminated by mutual agreement. Apparently, there's pornography on his website.'

Perk gawped. 'That must be the consequence of identity theft!'

'I couldn't say, my hands are tied. Confidentiality agreement. Don't you know: he's moving *cinema concrete* to your university?'

'*Really?*' Perk closed his eyes as if to erase what he had just heard. It took him a moment or two to recover his composure, but he had a more pressing concern than the fate of McWhelk and *cinema concrete*. 'I'm just back from The Hague. Rather bad news I'm afraid. I've been co-opted to work for the team prosecuting Serbian warlords. This is the second such trial. The last one took twelve years. How would you feel about the meetings of senate being scheduled for weekends? Saturday does have its attractions.'

In a true halleluiah moment Conquest gleamed. 'Perk, you haven't a leg to stand on!'

Perk looked at him askance. 'I'm sorry, I don't –'

At that moment a breathless figure thrust himself between them. It was Professor Woolworth.

'*Sorry, sorry, sorry!*' Woolworth spluttered, obviously beside himself. His face was pale and he was doing something Conquest had never seen him do before: *perspiring*! The gravity of his demeanour made it plain he'd come hotfoot from his meeting with the Stagg family in Belgrave Square. Conquest recoiled, no doubt about to hear a declaration of war in the matter of the crocodiles eating their son. He eased Woolworth away from Perk and towards the buffet where he thrust a glass of sherry into his unresisting hand.

'Tell me the worst,' said Conquest, grim-faced.

Woolworth rubbed his chin as if unsure how to start. 'It seems, Cliff, as though Matthew Stagg's mobile has been returned from Africa, along with his... er... *remains*. Yes, indeed! And the mobile has revealed further, shall we say, *correspondence...* between Stagg and his tutor. The Stagg parents were rather emotional about it, and wished us to know something of its tenor.'

Conquest felt himself shrinking with fear and apprehension.

Woolworth consulted his mobile. 'The last message he received from Frodo Figg reads: *Don't venture too far from the lodge, my darling. Africa is full of perils for the unwary. I trust we will travel there together once you're no longer a student, with me to protect you from its hidden dangers. Sleep tight, nighty, nighty.*' He looked up from his notebook, glassy-eyed.

'*Darling?*' said Conquest, dazed.

'It seems, Cliff, both were members of our LBGTQ+ community; and there was, let's say, a certain *Platonic* attachment.'

Conquest stared through Woolworth, not quite able to take in what he was hearing, such was the change of fortune it implied.

There's more,' added Woolworth, 'they want to make a donation.'

'What, to the university?' Conquest's brow furrowed with disbelief. He glanced up and saw that Perk had decided that Woolworth's interruption had gone on long enough and was about to intervene, an agitated expression on his face.

'I'm sorry, Clifford, but there's a rather important principle –'

'You're a lame duck, chair,' explained Conquest in the mildest of voices. 'You shouldn't stoop to conquer.'

Nancy, who had just finished exchanging insults with Vox, now intervened, determined to remonstrate with Perk. 'Couldn't you please get your attack dog back in its kennel?' she cried. 'Explain to him that this meeting's not to discuss –'

'Where the hell's Hazlett?' Alistair Vox was shouting. 'He may have a beautiful way with words, but he's never here when you want him!'

Professor Cronker, who had his back to Vox and was being informed about staffing matters by Tommy Ballantyne, turned and snapped: 'He's taken an academic post here. He's debarred himself from membership!'

Conquest tried to move away again, taking Woolworth with him, still agog at his news.

'Yes, Cliff,' said Woolworth, 'it appears there is something called the Lynda and Ralph Stagg Foundation. They're talking rather a lot of money to encourage Africa studies.'

Conquest put his hands to his head as if he feared it would explode. 'You mean *an endowment?*'

'I believe I do, Cliff. I was quite taken aback myself.'

Conquest still could quite take it in. 'Do you mean to say that Frodo Figg has come up trumps?'

'They seem willing to discount the lack of a risk assessment, Cliff. In fact, there was no talk *at all* about a risk assessment!'

'*Extraordinary!* And how much are they talking about?'

'A million, Cliff, a round million…"in the first instance".'

'*A million?*'

'Yes, that's what they said: "in the first instance".'

'Good grief, *that's extraordinary!*' For a moment Conquest stood transfixed, lost in thought. 'If this is true, Murray, I can only applaud!'

Murray did not look much cheered by his congratulations.

'Of course,' said Conquest, 'we'd have to re-jig the Department of Political Science. I gather Figg is a bit of a lone voice.'

'What million?' demanded Perk, having overheard Conquest's exclamation. 'I hope this is not something to do with Sir Norman.'

Sir Norman, who had had recourse to the salads, heard his name being mentioned. 'Eh?' He was about to join them, but Fred Crannick, the local MP, waylaid him.

'I vote Labour the Patsy Party,' said Crannick, daring him to disagree.

Conquest saw little need to humour Perk. 'I said, Perk, *you haven't got a leg to stand on!*'

'We could put it to the committee members; see what they think?'

'I don't think so, Perk. I'm afraid there's an incompatibility here that weekend working won't resolve. It's never advisable to miss the right moment to step down.'

In the background they could hear Vox declaiming: 'The wolf's at the door of European culture!'

'Aren't we getting rather ahead of ourselves?' said Perk, suddenly realising that events hostile to his interests had assumed an unstoppable momentum.

Conquest saw a sandwich skid across the floor not far from where he was standing. Briefly, he wondered who had thrown it, then thought better of the idea; members of senate didn't throw sandwiches. 'In the name of political even-handedness, I'm going to propose Lord N'Gabi as your replacement.'

'*My replacement!*' exclaimed Perk. He was about to demand a retraction when Sir Norman barged in.

'Lord N'Garbi did you say?'

Yes, I've just accepted Perk's resignation, haven't I Perk? War Crimes Tribunal in The Hague. I've always thought, Sir Norman, your suggestion of Lord N'Gabi as chair of senate was an excellent idea.'

Perk attempted a feeble interjection, but he had already been excluded from their exchange.

'But Clifford, you can't ride rough-shod over a contract!'

'No, no, Sir Norman, but this contract was written alternately by Tweedledum and Tweedledee, and double-checked this end by Miriam Micklethwaite. What about the late delivery clause – clause eighty-three, para B – which appears to be incompatible with the interruption clause?'

'Don't talk nonsense!'

'*No clause shall override the late delivery clause provided the client has made the site available to the developer by the agreed start date, beyond which the contractor shall be fully and solely responsible for the site.*'

'*Obviously*, it doesn't mean what it says!'

'In the circumstances, hadn't you and I best come to some sort of sensible agreement about how we get round this problem of the archaeologists? They're not going to go away anytime soon. I'm sure all these contingencies are sent to assist our endeavours, not to be fought against.'

Sir Norman, being a political animal, looked part indignant, part mollified. 'Are you trying to tell me that things are always for the best in the best of possible worlds, Clifford?'

'Yes, I think I am. *Id est quod id est.*'

'Blasted rubbish, Clifford. *Blasted rubbish!*'

FORTY-SEVEN

At Thieves the night was drawing in. On the southern slope, below the house, part of the village of Camlington had been built, as it was in the seventies. A week of shooting exteriors was about to begin, before the weather deteriorated. Looking up the hill, in the direction the cameras would be pointing, it was uncannily like the real thing as seen in the faded photographs in the village inn taken before commuters' residences were built on the green spaces between the cottages and farm buildings. Viewed from the other direction, from the edge of the lawn surrounding the house, it looked like a collection of half-finished billboards. Pye was standing there with Poppy Trench. She had recently delivered to him a new draft of *Candide In Tinseltown*. Pye had his hands in his pockets, thinking about how Ariel Gracechurch, AKA Orpington Girl, would bring the Camlington set to life with her stardust. Poppy looked at him, waiting for his verdict.

'I don't like the ending, Poppy,' he said finally. 'It's not the kind of ending I want. It doesn't suit what you've written. It's too neat a closure. Maybe I want to stop time and leave everyone as they are in that final moment. Maybe they should all stop in the midst of doing things, immortal beings. We hear a clock ticking, and the longer everything is frozen the louder the ticking becomes. Of course, it's going to be the kind of film where we want everyone to live happily ever after, but there must be a way to do it that's satisfying... but isn't so much like a closure.'

'You mean an eternal return?' she suggested.

'Yes, maybe go back to the beginning, to suggest it can start all over again. Not like a *Groundhog Day* exactly, because each time everything plays out slightly differently, but in the end it doesn't matter how things turn out, because it was all a lot of fuss about nothing. And what really went on was unspoken stuff that wasn't the point of what everyone was doing, or thought they were doing.'

There was a pause while he pondered what he was trying to say. 'I know,' he said finally. 'Come with me.'

They made their way across the lawn to the house and entered the library by the French windows. Somewhere in the house, quite distant, someone was playing a lilting, childish refrain on a xylophone. The refrain kept repeating with slight variations, and it was as though a second pair of hands were there too, playing alongside the first, echoing the refrain. Pye fetched down a book from one of the shelves. It was old and battered.

'This was my favourite book when I was young. It's called *Cornelia Underground*. She had a terrific adventure in the secret parts of the British Museum where the public never goes. I always loved the ending. Let me read it to you. I think it captures what I mean to say.' And so, he turned to the last chapter and read to her the book's closing paragraph.

OTHER TITLES BY GJ BABB

Of Art And Eros

When an inheritance means a family riven by disputes, who will heal the rifts? If the deceased is an artist of international repute, with an estate of almost incalculable worth, there will be advisors aplenty, but can they bring peace to the warring factions?

The renowned artist, Gustave Post, has been dead some four years. His estate is in the hands of the Collarii Foundation, which protects the integrity and value of his life's work. The heirs are fractious and unreliable. When an important but unknown Post appears at a New York auction house, it is strongly suspected that a family member is trying to sell it anonymously, in contravention of the family's obligation to the foundation. The foundation asks Professor Corey Templeton, expert in Post's work, to undertake a clandestine investigation to identify the owner of the painting. Templeton uses his assistant to get close to the more bloody-minded heirs, and soon finds himself entangled in her unscrupulous methods.

Damaging discoveries are made. The myth of the demonic artist-genius is any biographer's dream, not least the author of Post's! Can the Foundation keep control of Post's reputation, and maintain his blue-chip status? And can Templeton keep his equilibrium as emotions run high on all sides... and Eros comes to call?

ISBN 978 1800464 377

OF ART, BUT NOT FOR THE HARD OF HEART

OF
ART
FAMILY
AND
INHERITANCE
THE AFFLICTIONS OF LOVE
EROS

GJ BABB

AUTHOR OF NUDE, NOT NAKED

Nude, Not Naked

University London Central, a middling university, finds itself in a scandalous mess. The new vice-chancellor, Professor Clifford Conquest, is a seasoned public sector enforcer, a dedicated organisation man facing multiple challenges. As he sets about putting the university to rights he finds himself exposed to a terrible temptation. His conflicting desires – to succumb to temptation and to manage his university judiciously – put him in danger of becoming the target of the very machinery of academic disciplining he has set in motion. Schemes designed to rectify the ills of the university begin to crumble: inept academics defy his attempts to discredit them, an insurrection by Chinese students turns ugly and a symbolic dismemberment threatens all.

At the centre of this whirlwind is Professor Archie Pomfret, the unworldly head of the Department of Art. Is his department harbouring the vice-chancellor's nemesis? Can Conquest continue his rise to greater things? Or will the forces of disaffection biding their time in the darker corners of the senior common room bring him down? Surely, even a man driven by ambition, and a belief in his inevitable rise to the very top, cannot live by the righteous sword of administrative rectitude alone? There must be more, however great the risk!

ISBN 978 1838594 053

LARA BLISS LOVES ROSE MADDER GENUINE

The Emsbury locals call them 'grockles', summertime visitors that flock to the beautiful estuary of the river Em. The most famous grockle is Meade Daguerre, controversial artist with an international reputation to uphold. Lara Bliss, local artist and president of the Emsbury League of Artists, sees Daguerre as one of her own and takes him under her wing when she hears that journalist Jack Palanga, 'the Celebrities' Confidant', is in town after a story.

Palanga is playing his cards close to his chest, but gradually it transpires that he suspects the crew of Daguerre's racing yacht, which is berthed in Emsbury marina, are using it to smuggle something – possibly illegal immigrants – ashore.

Daguerre is beset by another distraction: nighthawks searching for a hoard of gold with metal detectors have plundered an archeological site on his estate. The archaeologists guarding the site are attacked at night in an apparent attempt to drive them off. Matters become more serious when Daguerre discovers a bloody chaos in the cabin of his racing yacht. The five members of the crew have disappeared and the suspicion grows that a murder has been committed.

As July unfolds the police, journalists and amateur sleuths – led by Lara Bliss – seek to solve the twin crimes. As Bliss navigates her own way to an understanding of who are behind them she begins to see that the clash of two communities – and two cultures – means that things are never quite what they seem.

ISBN 978 1838590 147

LARA BLISS LOVES ROSE MADDER GENUINE

A NOVEL

GJ BABB

This book is printed on paper from sustainable sources managed under the Forest Stewardship Council (FSC) scheme.

It has been printed in the UK to reduce transportation miles and their impact upon the environment.

For every new title that Matador publishes, we plant a tree to offset CO_2, partnering with the More Trees scheme.

For more about how Matador offsets its environmental impact, see www.troubador.co.uk/about/